PINK CARNATION

By
Casey Dorman

Avignon Press
Newport Beach, CA

© 2003 by Casey Dorman.

All rights reserved. No part of this book may be reproduced, stored in a retrieval system, or transmitted in any form or by any means without the prior written permission of the publishers, except by a reviewer who may quote brief passages in a review to be printed in a newspaper, magazine, or journal.

First Edition: Publish America, 2003

Second Edition: Avignon Press, 2019

ISBN: 9781082750014

Avignon Press
Newport Beach, CA

With love to Lai, Andrea, and Eric

In homage to Raymond Chandler, Dashiell Hammett, and Ross MacDonald

One

The white Cadillac convertible followed the narrow road between the endless rows of orange trees, trailing a fine dust that fell like mist upon the dark citrus leaves. The blonde ponytail of the driver flew from side to side as the car jounced along the uneven dirt track. The sounds of Marty Robbins' "White Sport Coat," drifted into the night. The furtive eyes of the girl's Mexican-American companion searched the shadows between the trees. The young woman switched off the engine and silence enveloped the car.

Black shadows and strands of pale moonlight spread an alternating pattern of light and dark across the widening in the road where the Cadillac had stopped. The blonde began to giggle, while the Mexican-American youth continued to search the night with his quick, shifting gaze. Without words, the young woman, who looked about seventeen or eighteen years old, slid across the seat and turned her companion's head toward hers. With trembling fingers she began unfastening the top of her taffeta evening gown, revealing small round breasts that showed pale and pink against the stark white of her bra in the moonlight. While she guided the young man's hands to her dress's metal snaps, she found the buttons on his shirt and eagerly began to unfasten them. Their hands undressed each other while their lips touched, at first just brushing then devouring each other hungrily. As their hands and mouths began a frenzied exploration, the girl's rapid breathing was punctuated by sighs and squeals of pleasure. The Mexican boy was more controlled, a fraction of his attention alert to the sounds of the night around them. But even that fraction gave way as the white dress of his young companion, with its pinned on pink carnation, fell the last few inches from her shoulders, revealing her slim, white arms and soft, narrow back. He fumbled with the clasp of her bra.

A metallic click interrupted the silence of the night. The boy turned his head in startled terror while the girl instinctively clutched her rumpled dress to her exposed breasts. She stared anxiously at her companion then watched in horror as his head snapped forward, his face exploding as the deafening sound of a gunshot shattered the stillness. She turned, still clutching her dress for protection; a terrified cry just reaching her lips as a second shot tore through her slim, soft neck, spewing bone, flesh, and blood across the dashboard and window of the car.

"CUT!" From the darkness surrounding the white Cadillac, a dozen blinding klieg lights switched on simultaneously, bathing the gory scene in stark white light.

"Jesus Christ that looked real." The film director's exclamation was the only sound from the shadowy figures of the crew who emerged from behind the lights. Thirty actors, cameramen, and assorted crewmembers edged toward the car, trading anxious glances. Their anxious looks remained as the first of them reached the car. A pink-cheeked, shaven-headed young man in a wrinkled UCLA football jersey reached out a tentative hand toward the Mexican boy slumped forward in the front seat.

" Oh shit!" the young man yelled, withdrawing a hand that was covered in bright wet blood. He turned to face the others, his face white with shock, his eyes wide in terror. "They're dead!" he screamed. " Holy shit, they're both dead!"

***

"And that's why this course represents one more misdirected step in the erosion of the quality of science this university offers to our students." George Baron's voice droned on as he sat stiffly upright, his half-glasses set severely on the end of his nose, giving the not completely inaccurate impression that he was permanently looking down at everyone else, his hands folded primly on the shiny surface of the mahogany table in front of him. My eyelids felt as if they had sandpaper glued to them but I couldn't stop them from slipping down over my eyes, which produced the dizzying sensation of my eyes rolling up and back into my head. George's monotone always had that effect on me. "You've been misinformed, George," I said while yawning. "Some of our efforts to erode science haven't been misdirected at all. I believe they hit their mark perfectly."

George's tone was acidic. "Why do you even bother to attend these meetings, Routledge? You don't seem to take anything at this university seriously."

I beamed at the senior professor. "That's why I'm here, George. It's good for my character. Maybe someday I'll grow up to be a serious professor like you."

Robinson, the representative from the English Department, snorted, as he tried to suppress a laugh. Norris, his look-alike match from Philosophy, kicked him under the table. Robinson elbowed him back. Baron looked even more sternly down his nose at the three of us.

I flipped through the Xeroxed pages of the agenda in front of me. It was difficult for me to achieve a comfortable position for my six-foot six-inch frame in the short-legged mahogany chairs that were a torturous fit for someone the height of an average NBA player. I wiggled and stretched, folded and unfolded my legs, and rued the fact that there were still four more courses for our curriculum committee to consider. And George was just getting warmed up. In vain, I let my eyes wander the walls of the faculty conference room with their dusky old pictures of former faculty senate presidents, each looking as imperious and solemn as George Baron. I took little comfort in knowing I wasn't the first person who'd fought to stay awake in that room.

I was rescued by the insistent buzz of my pager. Recognizing the number as that of the Student Counseling Center, I gave the three other committee members a helpless shrug. George glared at me, but Robinson and Norris watched with envious eyes as I unwound my legs from the contortionist position I'd finally achieved, pushed my chair back from the table, and stood. Whatever crisis had led to me being paged by the counseling center, it couldn't be any worse than the torture I would have had to endure if I'd had to listen to George Baron for even ten more minutes.

There was no need to ask what the problem was. Lucia Chavez, a dark haired freshman student, beautiful, brilliant, provocative, and habitually of a fiery temper, was pacing in front of the worn green velour couch, glaring like a caged lioness at the center's secretary and the three other students who sat in the waiting room. I ignored the distraught secretary and invited Lucia into my office.

Lucia sat poised on the edge of the chair opposite me, one slim leg crossed over the other, her short black skirt riding revealingly up her thigh as she angrily swung her leg to and fro. A lone tear slid from beneath the lash of one eye and formed a droplet that threatened to finish its trip down her cheek. She blinked the tear away in irritation but it was quickly replaced by another, larger one.

"Ramon is dead!" she said, raising red-rimmed eyes to look at me.

I stiffened in shock. Ramon was Lucia's older brother by two years. I had only met him twice, but I knew that he and Lucia were extremely close. No wonder she'd called me, even though we'd already terminated her weekly counseling sessions. I wasn't sure why I was hearing anger rather than grief, but I was sure that I was about to find out.

"I'm sorry, Lucia. How did it happen?"

She looked surprised. "You didn't read about it? He was killed while he was making a movie." She was trying to control her breathing, trying not to break down.

I remembered that Lucia had told me her brother was pursuing an acting career, but I hadn't made the connection when I'd seen the headline about the movie tragedy in Sunday's Orange County Register. I felt a hollow emptiness in my stomach when I thought of losing someone with such promise.

"I'm terribly sorry."

Her shoulders sagged as if they were burdened by a massive weight. Her tears now rolled untrammeled down her cheeks. "I'm sorry to come bursting in here like this," she said, her words punctuated by sobs." I don't know who else to turn to. They won't tell me anything." She looked up at me with large, sad eyes, her tears dotted with specks of mascara.

"Who won't tell you anything?" I asked, my voice sounding as if I had something stuck in my throat.

"The Sheriff's Department. The same assholes who arrested me when I was younger," she said, her anger flaring again.

"What are you talking about?"

"They told me to mind my own business."

What she was telling me didn't make sense. Jim Stapleton, my best friend since childhood, was Chief of Homicide in the Orange County Sheriff's Department's Criminal Investigations Division. Stapleton ran a tight ship when it came to protecting minority rights. Unfortunately, I couldn't say the same thing for the officers outside of Jim's division.

The department's anti-gang task force, dubbed SUAG, for "Special Unit Against Gangs," and pronounced "swag," was the unit that had most of the dealings with Latino youth. It was SUAG with whom Lucia had had her run-ins when she was younger. Some and maybe a whole lot of her anti-cop attitude was justified. But the investigation of a death on a movie set wouldn't have involved SUAG and there was no reason that Lucia should have gotten the cold shoulder from my friend's division.

"To whom did you talk?" I asked.

"Detective Torres."

"Torres is with SUAG," I said, remembering the tough, good-looking cop from my days working with the anti-gang force.

"Not any more. He's in charge of investigating the deaths of my brother and that girl."

"Girl?"

"She was in the movie scene with Ramon. They were playing a pair of teenagers who got killed. Somebody shot real bullets." She looked dazed. "That's all anyone will tell me."

I told her I had a friend in the Sheriff's department. I'd straighten everything out.

She looked up at me, her eyes dull, as though she was drugged. "Ramon was murdered," she said, her voice barely audible.

"Murdered?"

She cleared her throat. "My brother knew something he wasn't supposed to know."

I asked her what she thought her brother knew.

She gave me a helpless look as she slid down in the chair in a posture of defeat.

Accepting the tragedy of a senseless accident was always harder than accepting an act of villainy. That's why conspiracy theories popped up in cases of plane crashes, fires, and explosions. I wasn't going to tell her that, though. Not right now.

She straightened, uncrossed her legs and smoothed her skirt, trying to regain her composure although her lower lip continued to quiver. "I need your help, Dr. Routledge. I need to know what happened to my brother."

She needed to let her brother go, not look for a mysterious killer. I didn't say that. I told her I'd do what I could, and I wanted to see her again.

"Thank you." A spark of hope flashed in her eyes. "I knew I could come to you, Professor." She started to reach out to me, then caught herself.

I smiled and reached over and gave her hand a squeeze. She managed to return a weak smile and got up from her chair.

I watched Lucia leave the office, remembering when I'd first met her. Coming from nearby Santa Ana, the county's poorest community, she'd had an arrest record for vandalism and drug possession by the age of fourteen. Her next bust was for car theft, and with three arrests before her fifteenth birthday; her stay in juvenile hall was followed by referral to an experimental rehabilitation program sponsored by the county. The counselors and teachers in the program recognized that they had a diamond in the rough in Lucia. They threatened, cajoled, and pushed her to apply herself in school, stay off of drugs, and change her friends.

Pink Carnation

When she graduated with honors, her counselors wanted her to go to college and, because I occasionally did some consulting to their program, they approached me about getting Lucia into Chandler. I pulled a few strings with Minnie Washington, who ran our minority scholarship program, and Lucia was in—with one proviso—she had to attend counseling with me during her first year at Chandler.

Chandler University is a lot like other small, liberal arts colleges. We have a mostly affluent white student body, bright, but not brilliant; there are quite a few Asian students because of the large Asian community in Orange County, and a sprinkling of Latinos and African Americans—usually quite good students; like Lucia, who came to Chandler because of the generous minority scholarship program sponsored by Janet Erskine Jones, our school's principle benefactor and mine.

The magnanimous Mrs. Jones had recommended me for my teaching position following the amicable conclusion of a brief, but torrid affair between the two of us. That was five years ago-prior to my marriage and between Janet's third and fourth trips to the altar. Fortunately, marriage never was in the cards for Janet and me. I didn't need the money she'd inherited as an heir to the famous and vast Erskine Ranch landholdings, now transformed into the Erskine Company, the megacorporation that had developed all the land from Santa Ana down to Mission Viejo. I didn't need a job, either; but Janet had made it so easy, that I decided to try teaching.

To my astonishment, I enjoyed teaching and had even churned out enough research and writing to retain my job on my own merits after the expiration of my initial contract. With my degree in psychology, I'd specialized in delinquency, a topic familiar to me from personal experience.

Let me explain.

I'd been born with the proverbial silver spoon in my mouth, the only son of an old-moneyed family from Marblehead Massachusetts (it's actually Phineas Routledge, *the Third*). But as a spoiled and adventurous fourteen year old, I'd proceeded to steal the spoon as well as our neighbor's classic 1934 Rolls Royce in what I hoped would be an exhilarating joy-ride down the coast to Cape Cod. My trip was cut short less than a mile into it when I missed the narrow viaduct that crossed from Marblehead Neck onto the mainland, and the Rolls and I ended up in the harbor. I surfaced easily, which was more than I could say for the Rolls. The curmudgeon who owned the car insisted that my parents do something about me or he would file charges, so I was packed up and sent to Pickering Academy, a school for privileged misfits in the hills above Santa Barbara. It was at Pickering that I met my now closest friend, Jim Stapleton.

Jim was a Mutt to my Jeff and when he arrived at Pickering, he realized that being the smallest boy in a school full of delinquents was going to be a liability unless he teamed up with the largest boy, who was I. We were instant friends. I soon found out that Jimmy knew every ruse there was to avoid homework, extra duty assignments, and how to shift the blame for our myriad indiscretions to other students.

After graduation, Jimmy went to Cal State University Fullerton on a wrestling scholarship and studied criminology, having already learned the basics of the subject at Pickering. My parents had enough money that I didn't need a scholarship and my athletic interests were in martial arts, which was not yet a college sport. I went to the pricier Occidental College in Los Angeles and then, because my family donated a large sum of money to the scholarship fund, I moved onto graduate school at Stanford, where I managed to eke out a doctorate in psychology. I capitalized on my background by writing my doctoral thesis on the criminal mind. When I found myself in a teaching position at Chandler, Jim offered me some consulting with his department to strengthen my meager academic credentials. After a string of shocking gang murders, Jim let me interview the perpetrators and my series of articles in the *Journal of Delinquency* gained me some academic credibility.

As you may have surmised, I wasn't the type to be committed to a life in academia, but when I met my wife, a beautiful Vietnamese woman who believed in hard work and the principle that those who were

Pink Carnation

privileged to have been granted a higher degree from a prestigious university should do more with it than use it as the basis for a pickup line, I decided to continue on the faculty at Chandler. Besides, I felt guilty continuing to purchase my expensive clothes, vintage wines, and other accouterments of the good life if I wasn't adding something to the family coffers. So far, I hadn't regretted the decision. I enjoyed teaching and found that my additional duty of counseling the few, mostly minority, students, who needed help adjusting to their first year at a mostly white, middle class college, was fulfilling, and sometimes challenging. Which brings me back to Lucia Chavez.

***

"How's life with the Gestapo?" I greeted Jim Stapleton when he answered my phone call. I was back in my office, where I could slip off my Bruno Magli penny loafers and my Armani jacket and sit back and relax while I discharged my promise to Lucia to follow up on her inquiries with my closest friend, the Chief of Homicide in the County Sheriff's Department. I told him about Lucia's problem.

Stapleton didn't sound happy that I'd brought the subject up. In fact, his tone made it sound as if I'd jabbed him in a festering wound." Christ, Phin, there's nothing to tell the Chavez girl. It's a closed case."

"Two people were shot dead in the middle of a movie scene," I said. "What do you need to make it suspicious, a letter from a terrorist group claiming responsibility?"

"Thirty or forty people saw what happened," Jim said, his irritation starting to boil over into anger. "It was all out in the open. If Chavez's sister can't accept the fact that her brother died accidentally, then she needs to talk to somebody and get over it."

"She's talking to me. I told her that I'd get some answers for her. I didn't expect to get brushed off, especially not from you." I was starting to believe Lucia's story about getting the run around, but it wasn't coming only from Detective Torres.

"For Christ's sake, Phineas, don't get so hot about it," Stapleton said. "Nobody's brushing you off and nobody brushed the Chavez girl off. She talked to Torres. He's in charge of the case. He told her everything."

"He didn't tell her squat. She thinks Torres remembers her from SUAG and he's not telling her anything because of her record." I wasn't sure that that was why she was getting no information, but I was making a point.

I could virtually hear Stapleton bristle on the other end of the phone. "I'm sure that Torres told her everything he was allowed to tell her."

"Everything he was allowed to tell her?"

"Don't push this one, Phineas. The brass wants this put to rest as soon as possible. They're getting pressure from some of the county's heaviest hitters."

"Like who?"

Jim's voice was beleaguered." Don't even go there, Phin. You become a pain in the ass the way you usually do and it could backfire this time. You're not dealing with some university committee or the yacht club. These people play hardball."

"Don't worry. I never leave home without a baseball bat."

Stapleton's voice dropped into a confidential octave. "I'm not kidding around Phineas. Leave this one alone. You've got better things to do than mess with this case."

"Thanks for the warning," I told him. "I'll talk to Detective Torres and make up my own mind."

"You be careful, Phin. I mean it," he said.

Two

"I heard about you." Detective Ernie Torres lounged at his desk in the Orange County Sheriff's Department's Criminal Investigations Division. A partially peeled orange sat on a piece of Saran Wrap in front of him and a can of Classic Coke was wrapped in his fingers. Across his desk was Tom Desmond, a cop from the SUAG Force. A couple of years earlier I'd almost gotten Desmond busted by accusing him of planting drugs on a kid he'd arrested while I was on a ride-along for some research I was doing. For some reason he still held a grudge against me.

"I can see that you've got a completely unbiased source," I answered, nodding at Desmond. "Plant any drugs on anyone lately, Tom?"

Desmond, who was only a few inches shorter than I, came out of his chair like a rodeo bull let out of his pen. He started around Torres' desk. Torres stood and held out an arm. Desmond halted, but glared as hard as he could. "Still the wise-ass dick-head," he sneered.

"I'm impressed," I said. "Next week you can start learning five-letter words."

Desmond glowered at me even more darkly.

"Scram, Tom," Torres said. "The Professor's here to see me about a case." Desmond transferred his sour look to the other detective and then stood up and lumbered toward the door. As he passed by me, he shot out an elbow, aiming for my ribs. Fifteen years of Taekwondo, not to mention my deep--seated conviction that Tom Desmond was a jerk, helped me see the jab coming. I stepped aside and the SUAG officer had to catch himself on the edge of Torres' desk.

"First day with your new feet?" I asked.

Desmond glared back at me, then stumbled out of the room. "Some day I'll run into you on the street," he said.

Detective Torres wrapped the remainder of his orange in the Saran Wrap and placed it in the upper right hand drawer of his desk. He nodded toward the door where Desmond had exited. "He's not a good man to have as an enemy."

"He's probably not even a good man to have as a friend," I answered as I took the chair that Desmond had vacated. "What can you tell me about the two movie killings?"

Torres scowled. He was a young, good-looking Hispanic, but he'd been on the street long enough to have grown a chip on his shoulder. "Let's get something straight, professor. I don't give out information to whoever asks, especially not to somebody who takes pot shots at the men who do the real work on the streets."

"Thanks for the view from the blue-collar perspective, Detective, but you and I both know you didn't give any information to the deceased boy's sister, either. Lucia Chavez says she can't get any details about how her brother died from anyone in the department, especially you."

Torres leaned forward, both arms on the desk in front of him. He drummed the fingers of his right hand on the desktop. "That's just plain crap. I told her everything that I told the relatives of the girl who was killed. It was just a dumb accident."

"What kind of dumb accident was it?"

He gave a resigned sigh and leaned back in his chair. "Chavez and this actress were playing a couple of kids who got murdered back in the fifties. The movie crew was supposed to be using blanks in the gun. According to the witnesses, a bunch of the crew, including Chavez himself, were fooling around with the same gun a few hours earlier-using real bullets. Somebody screwed up and left the bullets in the gun." Torres frowned and shrugged, as if to say, "go figure."

"Somebody left the bullets in the gun?"

Torres resumed his finger tattoo on the desktop. "That's what I said."

Torres clearly subscribed to the theory that all Anglos, particularly the tall ones, were idiots. "Do you expect me to believe that?" I asked.

Torres ran his tongue around the inside of his mouth, giving me a long stare. "I really don't give a crap what you believe, Routledge."

"And how about the families of the victims? You're telling that canard to them?"

"That what?" He looked irritated.

Pink Carnation

"Falsehood, Torres." Someday I'll write the definitive *Gaining Social Power Through a Belter Vocabulary*. "Is that the falsehood you're telling the families?"

He shrugged again. "The families can take it or leave it. That's what happened."

"To put it in language you can understand, Detective Torres, that's bullshit."

He rolled his eyes toward the ceiling. "I heard you can be a pain in the ass, doc. I guess I heard right."

His voice sounded tired and angry. That usually meant I'd made my point. "You heard right, Detective. If that's the official story concerning these deaths, then I'm going to make myself a pain in the ass for sure."

He leaned forward again, all four legs of the chair on the floor and his elbows on the desk. He gave me a cool look. "It's your funeral, Doc — figuratively speaking of course."

"We'll see," I said, getting up to leave. I wasn't at all sure what I meant, but I could feel myself getting sucked into something that was far messier than I'd anticipated.

Three

From my large semi-oval office window I looked down and watched Lucia coming across the quad. She was headed toward the entrance to Macmillan Hall, directly below me. Her black hair glistened like smooth satin in the brittle morning light. She wore a black leather jacket, a holdover from her street days, and tight-fitting jeans that showed off her long slim legs.

When I opened my door, I saw that Lucia's large, dark eyes were red and swollen. Looking up at me, her lower lip began to quiver.

I fixed Lucia a cup of strong Kenyan coffee, giving her a few moments to compose herself. She'd removed her jacket, revealing a sleeveless maroon silk top, demurely buttoned high on her neck. We sat in silence sipping our coffee. She sat stiff and upright, her movements mechanical as she raised the cup to her lips. When she lowered her cup, she brushed her hair away from her face with a theatrical swipe, a gesture she probably carried out without thinking. She looked distractedly around my office, her gaze finally coming to rest on me.

"What did you find out? I'm sure that your friends at the Sheriff's Department treated you better than they treated me."

I told her she was wrong. Just as wrong as I'd been in my estimation of their helpfulness, especially Detective Torres.

"Torres is a pig!" she spat out in high dudgeon, raising her head imperiously. There were tiny lines around her mouth and eyes that I didn't remember from before. Beneath the theater, she was suffering.

"It must be terrible to have Ramon gone. Can we talk about it?"

"Don't patronize me, Professor!" she snapped." I'm not going to believe that my brother's death was an accident."

Thank goodness my mother raised a tolerant son.

"Why?" I asked. I still thought she was using her anger and her suspicions to avoid facing her grief, but I was willing to listen.

"I told you, he found out something...something about the movie or the people making it, that somebody wanted kept secret. The movie is

Pink Carnation

about this real murder that happened back in the fifties. Some white girl and a Chicano guy got killed. They arrested a bunch of Latino kids, thinking it was a gang murder, but they had to let them go when it turned out they didn't do it. Ramon was playing the part of the Chicano boyfriend who got killed."

I should have made the connection myself. In 1959, three members of a Mexican-American gang from Los Angeles were arrested for the murder of a Newport Beach high school debutante and her Mexican-American boyfriend. I'd never heard the crime referred to as the Pink Carnation Murders, the title of the movie, but that was probably something invented by Hollywood. After a flurry of public officials' and journalists' denunciations of the malevolent Chicano criminal element that had stretched its evil tentacles into even upper- class Newport Beach, it was discovered that the three suspects had been securely incarcerated in a Riverside drunk tank the very night the murder occurred.

"But if you don't know what kind of secret Ramon was hiding, what makes you think someone killed him?"

She narrowed her eyes as if gauging how much she should share, then she reached over to her jacket and unzipped a pocket, pulling out a piece of paper folded into a small square. She unfolded it, smoothing the paper on her leg like it was a sacred papyrus before thrusting it in my direction.

I reached over and took the paper. It was about three by six inches and looked as if it had been torn from a note pad. The writing was in Spanish. I studied it for a moment as if l could divine its meaning. "What does it say?" I finally asked.

"It says my brother's death was not an accident."

"Where did you get this?"

"It was folded and stuck under the wiper blade of my car. I found it after the funeral."

"May I show this to the police?"

She nodded.

I folded the note back into quarters and put it in my pocket. "So you think this means Ramon was murdered?" I asked.

"The girl who was killed with Ramon was dating a writer who worked for the studio. The writer was married."

"You think that was the secret your brother discovered?"

She gave me a defiant look. "Maybe."

I wanted her to know that I was treating her seriously, but I didn't want to lead her down a dead end street. "Men in the movie business have affairs with starlets all the time. They don't murder people to keep their affairs secret," I said. "Was there anything romantic between your brother and this girl?"

A dark flush spread across her slim features. She chose her words with care. "Ramon didn't date girls."

"Your brother was gay?" I asked with my usual tact.

"I guess so," she answered, avoiding my gaze. In six months of counseling she'd never mentioned that her brother was gay.

"Do you know the writer's name?" I asked.

"John Elmore."

"The novelist?"

Lucia raised her eyebrows. "You know him?"

"Only his work. I didn't know he did screenwriting. Remember *The LA Story*? That was his book. It was part of a quartet; four novels all about Los Angeles."

As far as I knew, Elmore was a weird, creepy guy.

"Ramon told me he was weird and creepy," she said.

Sometimes I amaze myself.

I scratched my head and thought. Then I said, "How about I talk to Elmore?

I'll give the note to my friend in the Sheriff's Department."

She looked at me warily. "And what do I do?"

"You go to class, study, think about the good times you had with your brother, and let me look into this further before you go off and do something we'll both regret."

Pink Carnation

I could tell that she was weighing how much to trust me. I was an Anglo and I was a friend of the cops, an inauspicious combination to a Latina. On the other hand, she'd shared her deepest fears and hopes with me over this last year and I hadn't violated her trust yet.

Lucia's shoulders sagged. "OK, Professor Routledge. You try things your way. But if you don't find out anything, then I'll have to do something." Her face hardened. "Either John Elmore or somebody else is going to pay for my brother's death. Believe me!"

I nodded and watched her get up and prepare to leave. I wasn't following any textbook model for counseling a grieving student that was for sure. On the other hand, I couldn't let her go off threatening a Hollywood writer. "I'll see you tomorrow at the same time," I said. It was probably the only thing I'd said that made me sound like a real psychologist.

… Casey Dorman

Four

A hot, dry Santa Ana wind tumbled candy wrappers and cigarette butts along the street gutters on Santa Ana Boulevard. A homeless man, his shopping cart piled high with clothing, flattened cardboard boxes, and flapping plastic bags, had taken off his shirt and lay across the steps of the Presbyterian Church, sunning himself. Across Sycamore Street, a crane with a thirty-foot long camera boom, mounted on the bed of a truck, had backed onto the sidewalk in front of the historic Old Orange County Courthouse.

I took off my sportcoat and slung it over my shoulder. The coat was hand-sewn of Chinese silk and was feather light, but with today's temperature I regretted not having left it in my car, which was parked in a two-dollar-a-day lot about three blocks away. I squinted up at the scorching sun and wondered how much of a mistake I was making just being here in the first place. Lucia Chavez was having a hysterical reaction to her brother's unfortunate death and here I was, knee-deep in the middle of her hysterical fantasy. I kicked myself in the mental rear-end and decided that I'd already waded far enough into the torrent that I might as well keep going.

Crossing Sycamore, I couldn't tell who was in charge of what looked to me like thoroughly disorganized activity across the street. I knew that John Elmore was one of the people in the crowd, because the studio secretary had told me he was here when I'd spoken to her earlier that morning. Elmore shouldn't be terribly occupied. What would a screenwriter be doing when they were actually filming a movie?

The crew was shooting scenes of the trial of the Mexican gang members. From what I remembered of the case, it had never come to trial, but I suppose literal truth doesn't make good drama. The Old Courthouse, which had been built in 1900 and restored in the late nineteen-eighties, was a good backdrop for a period film. The classic façade of the red Arizona sandstone building had been featured in scenes from over a dozen movies from such dramas as Henry Fonda's

Pink Carnation

Gideon's Trumpet to the recent farce, *Legally Blonde*. The building had also been the scene of a number of dramatic real-life trials, the most famous of which had been the 1947 case of the Newport Beach debutante, Beulah Louise Overell and her boyfriend, Bud Golum. The enterprising couple had been accused of blowing up Beulah's parents' yacht while it sat in Newport Harbor with the parents on it. Beulah inherited a fortune and she and her boyfriend got off Scot-free, much to the chagrin of the community, which had followed the trial with rapt attention for five exciting months. John Elmore had made a smart move by giving the Pink Carnation Murders a few trial scenes, whether they had really happened or not.

An old man, maybe seventy years or more, was leaning against the fat trunk of one of the huge palm trees that bordered the courthouse lawn. A cigarette hung lazily from the corner of his mouth, smoke curling from the cigarette's tip while the man watched the activity around him under half-closed lids. He looked comfortable enough to imply that he belonged on the set, so I decided he might be able to direct me to Elmore.

As I approached, the old man gave me an up from under look that took in all of my six foot six inches. His eyes were small and hard, like two dull rocks. He took his cigarette from his mouth and flicked it in the general direction of the sidewalk, staring at me with a flat, emotionless stare. He was about six feet tall, and the two hundred plus pounds that he weighed looked pretty solid for someone his age. He was wearing a pair of wrinkled slacks and an open-necked shirt beneath a sun-faded gray cotton sport coat, the collar and cuffs showing thin with years of wear. He must have been uncomfortably hot, but he didn't show it. He reminded me of an aged version of Nick Nolte in Mulholland Falls... minus the hat. He had cop written all over him.

"Who wants to know?" the old man responded to my question about Elmore.

"Dirk Nowitzki," I answered. "I'm hoping Elmore can write my life story."

He started to point in the direction of a small knot of men gathered around the back of the boom truck, and then he caught himself. "What did you say?"

I smiled. "Thanks."

He wheezed a little and I couldn't tell whether it was a derisive laugh or emphysema. "Asshole," I heard him mutter as I turned and walked away.

I hear that a lot.

I headed for the group standing at the rear of the boom truck. I was anxious to find Elmore before shooting started and someone ran me off the set. The old man kept a suspicious eye on me as I crossed the lawn. Four of the five men who were talking looked as if they were part of the crew; they were dressed in jeans or shorts, baggy shirts or no shirt at all, some with walkie-talkies hanging off their hips or in their hands. I approached the fifth man who was tall and was dressed in a wrinkled, white suit-like something out of a 50's movie in the tropics. He had a small Hitleresque mustache and thick, black-rimmed glasses. He was lounging against the side of the boom truck.

"John Elmore?" I asked, trying to act as if I belonged there. He stared at me. The thick lenses of his glasses magnified his eyes so I could see the red veins crisscrossing at the edges of the sclera. There were large, dark bags beneath both eyes.

"I'm a friend of Ramon Chavez' sister," I said.

"The spic who was killed," he answered, still staring.

"The Mexican-American actor who got shot, along with a young woman." I returned his gaze. "I understand you knew the woman."

He dug his hands deep into the pockets of his white jacket. "So?" he asked, narrowing his eyes.

This guy was a real charmer.

"So I'd like to talk to you about what happened," I answered.

Elmore maintained his hard look for a moment longer then gazed down at his feet. "She was an exceptional young lady. I don't know anything about your Mex kid, but losing Sally was a tragedy, a damned tragedy."

"Sally?" That wasn't the name I'd remembered from the newspaper account.

His face reddened. "I meant Lisa. Sally was the name of the girl she was playing in the movie."

I suppressed my urge to make "cuckoo" noises.

The four other men had moved off, and it looked as if something was about to happen on the set. Members of the crew were moving back from the entrance to the courthouse, making last minute checks to remove debris that had blown onto the set. A man wearing a T-shirt with cut-off sleeves, a pair of baggy shorts, and a pair of well-worn Birkenstocks, took a reading on the sunlight. On the concrete path leading from the parking lot to the building, three teenage Mexican-Americans in prison denim, wearing hand and ankle cuffs, stood sweating, waiting for their cues. Their dark hair was slicked back in the fashion of the fifties, using enough pomade that their heads reflected the sunlight. They were flanked by a pair of older actors dressed in old-fashioned Sheriff's uniforms with wide-brimmed, Smoky Bear hats. The actors were having a hard time keeping the hats on their heads in the stiff, hot breeze. A tall man with shoulder-length gray hair, wearing a faded purple sweatshirt with the sleeves cut off was giving them instructions. Beneath the oak tree, the heavyset old man was still giving me the eye.

Elmore followed my eyes to the man under the tree. When he looked back at me, his expression was more guarded. "Are you a private dick?"

"A what?" I asked.

"Are you a shamus?"

I nodded and gave him a steely-eyed stare. "Name's Doghouse Reilly," I said in my best Bogey imitation.

A thin smile played at the corner of his mouth but quickly gave up the game. "Very funny," he said.

"I'm a college professor—Phineas Routledge the Third —Ramon Chavez' sister is my student," I said.

"Phineas... the third?" He looked skeptical.

"Call me Doghouse, if you like that better."

Elmore continued to regard me with suspicion. "You're going out of your way for a professor, aren't you?"

I wasn't sure if I could explain my involvement in a way that would make sense to Elmore. It didn't entirely make sense to me. "I'm trying to help Chavez' sister get more information about her brother's death."

He stared at me as if he was waiting for more, then he glanced back toward the old man under the tree. The old man was no longer there but three muscular young men in narrow jeans and tight fitting T-shirts were headed our way, their eyes fastened on me. They looked like some kind of twinkle- toes security crew.

"Can we go somewhere and talk?" I asked.

Elmore glanced at the three men heading toward us. "There's a cafe across the street," he said.

"There's a bar around the corner," I countered.

He raised his eyebrows. "That sounds better, Professor."

"Call me Doghouse," I said.

The crewmembers had moved to the periphery of the shooting area and we had to thread our way through them to get to the street. The three security men stopped and watched us as we left the set and crossed Santa Ana Boulevard. They didn't look as if they were going to follow us. I headed up Broadway with Elmore in tow and crossed over to Fourth Avenue, where a string of cafes and bars served the employees and visitors to the new Federal Courthouse. The Courthouse Bistro was an open air eating establishment with sidewalk dining and a small, dark, air-conditioned bar in the back. Elmore and I headed for the back. We sat across from each other at a small table in the corner of the bar. Elmore sat stiffly, avoiding my eyes. His suit wasn't only wrinkled; the cuffs were gray and gritty, as if he'd been wearing it for days. When the waitress came over, Elmore ordered a gin and tonic and I asked for the same.

"What do you do on the movie set?" I asked.

Pink Carnation

He didn't look at me, but a smile flickered across his face. "Nothing really. I'm there for emergency first aid. For when Thornberg decides a scene needs to be re-written."

"Thornberg's the director, the guy in the purple sweatshirt? I thought he mostly did action movies."

"He does whatever keeps him in snort."

I ignored his reference to Thornberg's rumored cocaine use. "You rewrite on the spot?" I asked.

He nodded. "This is a picture. It's not Eugene O'Neil. Thornberg takes out half the dialogue anyway. He follows Raymond Chandler's admonition; 'When in doubt, have a man come through a door with a gun in his hand.' Then he has him shoot someone" Elmore tried to suppress a twitchy smile. "Not literally, of course."

"What did happen the other day when Chavez and Lisa Burke got killed?" The waitress brought our drinks. She was a petite blonde in her early thirties who gave my six foot six frame an appreciative look then stared at Elmore as If he was something I'd dragged in on the bottom of my shoe. He blinked back at her through his thick glasses.

"I think she likes you," I said, when the waitress left.

He frowned and glanced around the bar and then toward the small number of customers scattered among the tables on the sidewalk outside. His eyes darted back in my direction. "I'm just a writer." He waited a moment, still looking at me. "And you're just a professor. Some things shouldn't become our business."

"There's an old Vietnamese saying," I said. "The man who ignores what's in his own basement may find that he's raising cobras beneath his feet."

Elmore gave me a flat stare. "There aren't any cobras in Vietnam."

He was wrong, but I didn't tell him." That's what makes the saying enigmatic. Were you there when the shootings took place?"

"I was on the set."

23

"The Sheriff has already closed the case...ruled it an accident." I left the statement out on the table. Elmore blinked and looked back at me, saying nothing.

"Was it an accident?" I asked.

He turned back toward the window. The tables outside the restaurant were starting to fill. "Why are you asking me?"

"You were dating Lisa Burke, I thought you'd be more interested than most in finding out what happened."

"I was fucking her, not dating her. She knew the difference."

The eloquence of writers always amazes me.

"Was your affair with Lisa a secret?"

He smiled a little. "It never made the Inquirer, if that's what you mean, but things like that don't stay secret on a movie set."

"You don't care why she died?" I asked.

He frowned." I'm a writer not a cop. I don't investigate suspicious deaths." It was an unusual statement from a writer who'd built his career on writing about unsolved murders, including the two that were the subject of the Pink Carnation Murders.

"Nobody wants to look into these deaths ...not you, not the cops. What is it, studio pressure?"

He laughed a short, derisive snort. "Thornberg doesn't want anyone to look too far or they might find out he was diddling the homo spic. They were going at it in Thornberg's Beverly Hills fuck-pad the night before this happened."

"Thornberg was having an affair with Ramon Chavez?"

"Thornberg fucks anyone under 30, poofs and quiffs equally."

"How about Lisa Burke?"

Elmore's face reddened. He clenched his jaw. "Lisa wanted to become a star. Thornberg knew he could use her."

"How'd you feel about that?"

He looked past me and shrugged his shoulders. "I was using her, too." A thin smile edged onto his face." Maybe she was using both of us."

"Did Thornberg know about you and Lisa?"

Pink Carnation

"It was no secret. I'm sure the queer little spic told him. Probably pillow talk between them."

"So it's Thornberg or the studio who's squelching the investigation?"

He shook his head. "Thornberg hasn't got the clout to shut down a Sheriff's investigation. Neither does the studio."

"Who does?"

Elmore made a just perceptible movement in my direction, leaning his head forward. When he spoke, his voice was barely above a whisper. "If you want my advice, I'd say tell the spic's sister that you checked everything out and it's just the way the detectives said it was. Then go back to your teaching; it's safer." He wiped his mouth with a napkin and stood up, glancing nervously toward the street, as though he'd seen something that frightened him. "I'd better get back," he muttered, moving toward the door.

I didn't thank him.

Five

The heat hit me like a blast from an oven. I headed back toward the lot where I'd parked my car. The street leading away from the government buildings and the upscale cafes that surrounded them was dominated by small shops with their advertisements for flowers, bridal dresses, jewelry and travel, all in Spanish. The sounds of Mexican music came from open doorways. Vendors sold sodas and fresh fruit from sidewalk carts. Walking through old Santa Ana was like stepping across the border into Mexico. I'd heard they'd added an art center to the downtown area, so I kept an eye out for things artsy. I wasn't watching my back.

The first thing I felt was two sets of powerful hands grabbing me by the shoulders and pushing me toward a break between the buildings. The three thugs from the movie set must have followed me from the restaurant.

They weren't really thugs, and they weren't really trained in security either—probably muscle-bound actors hired to scare people off. I didn't scare easily. I swung my elbows into the rib cages of the two holding onto me and swept the feet from under the one on my right. He fell against the building, letting go of his grip on my shoulder. Using my free arm, I swung a fist around and caught the other young man squarely on the nose, which flattened across his face in an ugly spray of blood.

The third member of the trio hung behind the other two, but when he saw what had happened to his partners, he backpedaled as quickly as he could. The one who'd fallen against the wall rushed to the aid of his bleeding friend. I took two steps toward the injured pair, who huddled in front of me on the sidewalk. I kept my weight balanced by shifting it from one foot to the other, ready to land a finishing blow in case either of them made a move in my direction.

"Jesus, man, back off!" the one nearest me shouted, wincing in pain from his side, which probably contained a broken rib. His face was ashen.

Pink Carnation

I shook my head in dismay. "What was this little ballet supposed to be, girls?"

"Keep the hell away from Mr. Elmore," the one who'd lagged behind said, trying to sound tough but maintaining a safe distance. He wagged a finger toward me and postured as if he was playing a part in a bad movie.

"Whose message is that?"

"Mr. Thornberg's," the same young man answered.

"You boys need to learn some manners."

"You're lucky it was only us," the man holding his friend said. He looked as if he was having a hard time breathing.

"Who else would Thornberg have sent, if not you three?" I asked.

The one holding his side glanced at the others. His two partners looked back at him. A small crowd of Mexican-American gawkers was forming around us, causing my three assailants to look even more nervous. "You're gonna find out if you keep asking questions," the one I'd hit in the ribs finally said.

"You don't know who you're dealing with, buddy," the one who'd hung back muttered ominously.

I took a threatening step in his direction and he tripped over himself backing up.

"You guys should be in pictures," I said, turning and leaving the three of them standing in the middle of the crowd.

I continued down Fourth Street, a bit breathless and struggling to subdue my anger at the three punks and whoever sent them, which sounded as if it was the director, Brian Thornberg. When I arrived at the lot where I'd parked my car, Jim Stapleton was lounging against the antique MG's back fender.

"Now you show up," I said. "Where were you a few minutes ago when I needed you?"

"You know you can never find a cop when you need one," Stapleton replied. "What happened?"

"Some would-be security guys from the movie set tried to give me a warning."

"Christ all fucking mighty!" Stapleton said, his anger flaring. "You want to press charges? We can go get the little sons-of-bitches right now."

"Forget about it. They were just messengers. At least I know Lucia Chavez' claim that someone is trying to cover up her brother's death isn't a delusion."

Jim shook his head, looking at me with eyes squinted to block the sun. "You didn't listen to me, did you? You're still sticking your nose into this."

I shrugged. "One of my students lost her brother and I'm trying to help her understand what happened. A lot of people are trying to stop me."

He looked as if he was going to say something. Instead, he rubbed his hand across his face, then stared at the film of sweat on his palm. He pulled a handkerchief from his back pocket and wiped his hands on it. Jim was only five-feet-eight and once he'd entered adolescence, his wiry build had become muscular, but middle age had added about forty pounds of extra fat to his frame. "I told you before, the brass wants this wrapped up," he said. "It's publicity, legal issues, a lot of mucky-muck crap that's connected to big money, county influence, all that jazz. The movie studio wants to quiet any negative publicity and you and the Chavez girl are a thorn in their side."

"It's funny that we're a problem for them, but you're not. You're the cop, remember?"

"That's a low blow, Phin. Believe me, if there was something criminal to investigate, I'd be investigating it."

I pulled the folded note from my pocket. "You read Spanish?" I asked.

"Un poco," Stapleton said. He eyed the note warily. "What's this?"

I unfolded the paper and handed it to him. "Chavez' sister found it on her car's windshield after her brother's funeral."

Pink Carnation

He scanned the paper. The muscle on the side of his jaw began to pulse. "Shit," he said, then took the note between two of his fingers and reached with his other hand into his back pocket. He pulled out a folded, clean, white handkerchief, shook it out, and grasped the note with the handkerchief. "Who else touched this besides us?"

I hadn't even thought about fingerprints. "As far as I know just Lucia Chavez and whoever left it."

He folded the note and placed it inside his coat pocket." The sister could have written it herself, it could be a sadistic joke, or it could be the real deal. What's she say about it?"

"No clue, except she thinks it might be a friend. She's gonna ask around.

Does this change your mind about the case?"

"I'm not ready to reopen it as a murder case, if that's what you mean, but I'm gonna take another look at the whole thing. You've got my word on it, bro."

"Who's the old cop hanging around the set?" I asked." He kept giving me the fish-eye."

Stapleton chuckled. "You must mean Randy Fontana. He used to work for the department. He was the investigating officer on the original murders. The movie people have brought him in as a consultant. He's a mean old bastard. I'd stay away from him if l were you."

"Was Fontana on the set when the shooting happened?"

Stapleton shook his head in irritation. "I'm serious, Phin. Don't go any further with this." He glanced up at the sun and ran a finger around the inside of his collar. Then he loosened the knot on his tie. When he looked back at me, his face had softened. He reached a beefy hand out and slapped me on the shoulder.

"I promise I'll look into it, bro." He smiled his good-natured, professional smile. "You can go back to the university and leave things up to me."

"Thanks, bro," I said. "Already, I know I'll sleep better at night."

Six

"One man can make space for an orange tree, but it takes a whole village to clear a forest." My wife deftly chopped a large white onion, then gracefully sprinkled the tiny fragments among the mushrooms, bell peppers, carrots, and chunks of skinless chicken breast that were simmering on the top of the stove. She spoke with her back to me, while I surreptitiously admired the smooth curves of her hips and the shapeliness of her long legs, shown off by the thigh-length skirt she still wore after a day at work as one of Orange County's most sought after private CPA's.

"Huh?" I asked in professorial tones. I was sipping on a tall gin and tonic and standing in the open French door leading from the kitchen to the brick patio on the side of our waterfront Balboa Island home. The front of the house looked out on Newport Bay, which separated the island from the long neck of the peninsula on which sat the famous Newport Pier. I'd purchased the property in an almost even trade for the Marblehead Neck house I'd grown up in and which I'd inherited when my parents died. I'd gotten about one fifth the square footage and only half the view, but the perpetually sunny Newport Beach weather more than made up for the difference.

"In Vietnam we say that for one dollar you can spread a lie, but it requires a fortune to spread silence."

"I wish I'd said that," I said, taking a sagacious sip of my drink. "What does it mean?"

Kim turned her head in my direction, still stirring the vegetables in front of her. She raised one perfectly sculpted eyebrow. "Whoever is preventing these deaths from being investigated is very powerful."

A dim bulb flickered in the recesses of my brain. "Someone seems to be telling the Sheriff's department what to do and you're right, that means very big influence...not just money, but political."

Without turning, Kim asked, "Who?" In her left hand, she held two bamboo chopsticks, which darted among the simmering vegetables, pushing and turning them with small strokes, while with her right hand she flicked the pan rapidly back and forth across the hot burner.

"I don't know," I said. "I know that the movie studio wants things wrapped up because the director, Brian Thornberg sent me a clear message when he sicced his security crew on me. On the other hand, I don't know why the Sheriff's department would cooperate with a Hollywood film company."

"Do you think that the Chavez girl is right, that her brother was murdered?"

"I have a hard time believing a murder took place on a movie set. But Lucia is right about a cover-up of something, probably studio negligence."

"She sounds very angry."

I nodded. Lucia Chavez was a loose cannon and I was well aware of it. I wasn't sure that I could keep her in check, either in her urge to blame someone for her brother's death or her sometimes blatant attempts to seduce me in the process.

"She could get both herself and me in trouble if l can't keep her under control," I said. "I'd like to help her, but she makes it difficult."

Kim put a lid on the pan and moved it to a back burner. She ran her hands under the tap, and dried them with the small towel that hung at the end of the kitchen counter. When she turned, her eyes searched my face before she spoke. "What are you going to do?"

"The man I need to have a talk with is Brian Thornberg. He's made himself a prime suspect by sending those three goofballs after me."

Kim smiled up at me. She reached up and pulled my head toward hers. When I bent down she gave me a Vietnamese style kiss, sniffing delicately along my cheek. She pulled her head back. "You'll figure it all out," she said. "But I'm disappointed in Jim Stapleton. I'd hoped he would be more eager to help you."

"Me too, " I said. "In his job you can't always escape having to play politics."

This time Kim raised both eyebrows. "It is difficult for a man to serve two masters."

"Jim's my friend."

She shrugged and gave me a knowing look, but didn't say any more except to excuse herself to take a shower before we ate dinner. I debated another gin and tonic and then opted to pour myself a glass of 1997, Clos du Val Georges III, Cabernet Sauvignon and sat down at the dining room table, gazing through the front window at the evening boat traffic rounding the point to enter the bay. I kicked off my Sperry Topsiders before crossing the carpet; shoelessness indoors being an Asian habit I'd gotten used to since becoming married. The wine was soft, with a hint of California fruitiness. I didn't mind mixing my tastes, but I had a moment of regret that the gin had taken the edge off my palate.

I continued to mull things over until Kim reappeared, coming down the tall circular staircase leading from the upstairs master bedroom and bath. Her hair was still damp and her face was flushed from the hot shower. She wore Chinese style black silk lounging pajamas with a high mandarin collar and a slit up one leg that reached to her thigh, revealing her smooth skin, still pink from the shower. I stared and she dropped her gaze in characteristic Asian shyness.

While I sat enthralled with my beautiful wife, she refilled my glass of Cabernet and served the stir-fry for both of us. Her eyes sparkled. "You think too much, Anh," she said, using the traditional Vietnamese term of respect, and between husband and wife, endearment. When I reciprocated, I called her "Em."

"I know how to take your mind off such serious things," she said.

I glanced down at the smooth skin of her thigh as she crossed one shapely leg over the other. I had no doubt that she was right.

***

Lucia Chavez refused the chair I offered her and paced back and forth between the desk in one corner of my office and the tall half-oval window across from it. Her long dark hair was pulled back against her head and gathered in a tight bun, as if she was shedding her femininity in preparation for battle. Her thin, straight eyebrows were knitted together in a frown that brought creases to her young forehead.

"The movie studio is trying to pay us off," she said between clenched teeth. "They offered my mother two million dollars as so-called compensation for Ramon's death."

"Two million dollars is a lot."

She stared at me. "Two million dollars is nothing. I lost my brother. I want to make those bastards pay through the nose. What about Elmore? Did you talk to him?"

"Elmore is weird, all right. At one point he referred to Lisa Burke as Sally...the girl who the movie is about. He doesn't seem to be firing on all eight cylinders." I looked her in the eyes. "But I don't think he killed your brother."

"Why not?"

"He made no effort to deny his affair with Lisa. I don't think he cared whether anyone knew. But he's frightened by the deaths himself."

"Really?"

"That was my impression. He warned me that you and I should drop the whole thing."

She looked pensive. "Someone is trying to hide something. That's why the studio doesn't want my mother or me to ask any more questions."

"I think you're right about the studio, or at least Thornberg, the director." She sat down. Despite her pretense of rejecting femininity in favor of pugnacity, Lucia was wearing another short skirt and, as was her habit, she slung one leg over the other enough to reveal a whole lot of long, graceful thigh, though she seemed oblivious to this as chewed her lower lip in thought. "You think it's Thornberg who's trying to cover things up?" she asked, looking up at me.

"Thornberg was the one who sent the security people after me with a warning to stop asking questions. Elmore told me that Thornberg had an affair with Lisa Burke, also."

Lucia fingered the neck of her tank top. "Lisa got around."

"So did Thornberg. He was having an affair with your brother, too." Her face blanched." How do you know that?"

"Elmore said Thornberg and your brother were together the night before Ramon was shot."

She looked away, her face a mask.

"Do you think your brother could have been blackmailing Thornberg?" I asked.

Her tone was offended. "Ramon wouldn't do that. Maybe Lisa Burke was blackmailing Thornberg. Maybe the director decided to get rid of the blackmailer and the evidence at the same time."

"Maybe."

Her face was still expressionless. "How do we find out?"

"*We* don't," I said. "You're going to have to trust me, Lucia, to get the information from Thornberg myself."

She sighed and slumped forward in her chair. For a moment, she looked like a lost little girl. I was reminded that for all her anger, she was still just a nineteen year-old kid.

"Don't worry. We'll get to the bottom of this," I said. I hoped that I was right.

Seven

"You're wife is looking beautiful, as usual," Alfred Stonehill, the university president, smiled broadly as Kim and I entered the executive meeting rooms on the upper floor of the Faculty Club. It was the annual spring fundraising dinner and, as a professor, I was expected to make an appearance and charm a little money out of the invitees. President Stonehill grasped my hand. I was always surprised that he remembered my name.

"We have some excellent guests this evening, Phineas," Stonehill said, giving me a knowing wink. "I think some of them might be very interested in your research."

I was pretty sure that Slick Al, as I usually referred to Alfred Stonehill, had no idea what kind of research I did.

"Really?" I said, "Which aspect of my work particularly intrigues them, Alfred?"

Stonehill gave me a wink and jabbed the lapel of my dinner jacket with his index finger. "That's your job to find out, Phineas. I know I can count on you." Before I could compose a clever comeback, he'd already turned to the next guest. He was slick.

"There's a lot of big money in this room, Anh," Kim whispered as we threaded our way through the milling guests. Being a trained academician, I'd spotted a bar in the back of the room and was steering Kim in that direction. When we arrived at the bar, Janet Erskine Jones, my old flame and benefactor was immediately ahead of us.

"Are you here to give money or to squeeze it out of others?" I queried Janet's back.

The sexagenarian beauty swept around and blithely ignored me, grasping Kim by the hand. "I'm going to speak to you first, Kim, because I know that you're the polite one in the family." She smiled broadly, her exuberant beauty having diminished very little from the years during which I had dated her. "I can see that putting up with Phineas hasn't lessened your attractiveness one bit," she continued to Kim. "How are you?"

The two women exchanged small talk while I snagged a gin and tonic for me and an orange juice for Kim. I followed a strict rule to never order wine at a bar serving free drinks.

"You're a lucky man, Phineas. You're wife is darling." Janet said. With her gray-blonde hair and pale blue eyes, Janet could still be the center of attention and I appreciated her magnanimity toward Kim.

"The board is out in full force tonight?" I asked.

"As far as I can see. To answer your earlier question, we're supposed to contribute something ourselves and hit up all of our friends, all the while pretending that it's just a social event." She surveyed the room. "But I know it's for a good cause. You know that Brian Thornberg, the movie director is here?"

I felt my muscles tense as I scanned the room to see if I could spot the director. "He's a supporter of the university?" I asked, not seeing him anywhere in the vicinity.

"Alfred is hopeful. Thornberg apparently wants to use the campus for a couple of scenes in a movie he's making and Alfred thinks he can pull a few dollars out of him in the process."

It sounded like a typical Slick Al gambit. "Do you know Thornberg?" I asked Janet. She'd run around with a lot of the Hollywood crowd in her younger years.

She made a face. "Goodness no. I've heard terrible things about him. I didn't really even want him invited tonight. Michael Umstead felt the same way." Umstead was the President of the Board of Trustees.

"So who invited him?"

"Alfred ...and Jess Wolf. I don't think Jess knows Thornberg, but he doesn't have the same scruples some of the rest of us do when it comes to raising money." Wolf was another powerful member of Chandler's Board.

"Money's money," I said, hoping to impress her with my dazzling logic.

Janet frowned. "That's Jess' viewpoint."

I turned to my wife. "Wouldn't you like to meet a movie director, Kim?"

"I definitely think that you should, Anh. I think you and he will have a lot to talk about."

Janet looked confused, but I'd spotted Lucia Chavez across the room and all sorts of alarms were going off inside my head. Students were strictly forbidden from attending these affairs. I excused myself and slipped around the edge of the room until I was within a few feet of Lucia.

"What are you doing here?" I asked, sotto voce.

"Mr. Thornberg can hardly refuse to see me at an event like this." She retorted, her eyes flashing with defiance. She was dressed in an ankle-length black dress, made of some sort of satiny material and looking as if she had been poured into it. It was cut nearly to her hips in back and when she turned around, I could see that it revealed an almost indecent glimpse of the smooth, dark surface of her round firm breasts. Lucia's eyes followed mine as I took in her appearance.

"I guess the dress works," she said.

"It could work to get you thrown out of the university," I said, taking a stern parental tone, even though she probably was right. If Thornberg rang true to his reputation, he'd be a sucker for Lucia in that dress. "I'm telling you to leave and go home. I'm planning to confront Thornberg myself and I don't want you messing things up ...or taking any unnecessary chances."

She weighed what I was saying, and then gave me a reluctant nod. "You can have the first crack at him, but if you don't find out anything, then it's my turn."

"Go home," I repeated.

She smiled and melted into the crowd, the head of every man turning as she glided by.

"Lucia Chavez?" Kim asked, materializing at my side.

I nodded.

"She fits your description. She's dressed to kill tonight. Who's her target? Not you. I hope."

"Thornberg. She wants to ask him about her brother. She's liable to cause a scene and get herself thrown out of school, not to mention putting herself in danger if Thornberg really is guilty of anything."

"Have you found Thornberg yet?"

"Not yet." I scanned the room for the gray-haired director. I finally spotted him thirty feet away, talking to a thickset, rough-featured man with black hair—Jess Wolf—a member of Chandler's Board of Trustees. Wolf was probably 70, but plastic surgery had kept his features young, and he looked like a middle-aged Anthony Quinn. I knew almost nothing about Wolf, except that he was very rich, very influential, and gave an inordinate amount of money to Chandler and to a number of charitable organizations.

I nudged Kim and nodded in the direction of Thornberg and Wolf. "He's talking to Jess Wolf. I don't see Lucia near them, do you?"

"The woman with Mr. Wolf must use the same dressmaker as Lucia," Kim said dryly. I hadn't noticed Wolf's partner. She was probably one-third his age and dressed as provocatively as Lucia had been, only this woman was a bleached blonde. She had her arm entwined in Wolf's and the more I watched, the more I noticed that Thornberg was talking to the old man but the director's eyes were devouring the young woman like those of a hungry snake eyeing its next meal.

"Mr. Thornberg appears to be susceptible," I said. "He seems to be making a play for Wolf's girl."

"Mr. Wolf doesn't appear very disturbed by Thornberg's overtures, Anh."

"At that age and with that much wealth, you probably don't get disturbed easily."

Jess Wolf said goodbye to Thornberg and then moved away, but his date remained talking to the director.

"Maybe the young woman is Wolf's protégé and he's trying to get her into pictures," I said. "Anyway, now's our chance to talk to Thornberg."

Pink Carnation

I started moving toward the director and the young woman, pulling Kim along with me. I was too late. Michael Umstead, the President of the Board of Trustees had gotten to Thornberg ahead of me.

Umstead was the scion of one of Orange County's pioneer families in the high-tech industry. His father had begun an aircraft industry design and manufacturing business back at the beginning of WWII and had become one of the county's richest men. His son, Michael had taken over the business when his father died and the company's plants in Long Beach still churned out electronic parts for both military and civilian aircraft. Long Beach wasn't part of Orange County, but the family had resided in Newport Beach for over sixty years. Umstead was a sixty-ish, square-jawed, heavyset man and whatever he wanted to talk to Brian Thornberg about, it wasn't just pleasant chitchat. Their conversation was escalating into a shouting match. Umstead's face was red and he was swaying enough to imply that he'd taken one too many trips to the bar.

I held up Kim long enough for us to catch what Thornberg and Umstead were arguing about. Umstead was fuming about "exploitation" and Thornberg was shouting about artistic freedom and calling Umstead an industrial boor.

The blonde, who was now on Thornberg's arm, looked confused, but was nevertheless enjoying the confrontation. Thornberg reached out and tried to grab Umstead's arm, but Umstead threw the director's hand away and looked as if he was ready to square off. I started to move toward the two of them to prevent things from getting uglier, but again I was beaten to the punch. Randy Fontana, the old retired cop from the movie set, appeared from out of nowhere and grabbed both men's arms, holding them tightly enough that they both turned to him in shock and obvious pain. I couldn't hear what was said, but Fontana guided Thornberg away from Umstead and toward the door. The girl still clung to Thornberg's other arm.

"You all right?" I asked Umstead when Kim and I reached him. His face was still red with anger, but he looked as if he was trying to regain his dignity. "That sensation monger has no business being at a university function!" Umstead said to me, glancing at Kim and then looking down at the floor self-consciously.

"You know him?" I asked.

"I know about his movies and the kind of flagrant pandering to his audience's worst tastes that is his hallmark. I don't like him doing it in my backyard." He raised his head and looked at me. His eyes were slightly out of focus, probably from alcohol. "You're Routledge, aren't you? Psychology or Sociology or something... Janet's friend?"

I introduced Kim, and myself although we'd both met Michael Umstead at other such functions in the past.

"Sorry about all that," he said, glancing down at the empty glass in his hand and then over to the bar. "Guess I'll have another and then mix around a little. Good thing that old policeman was here to get rid of that bastard." He looked over at Kim and his face started to redden again. "Excuse my language, Mrs. Routledge. I guess I'm still a bit flustered." With that he moved off toward the bar.

"What do you think that was about, Anh?" Kim asked, grasping my arm.

I told her I didn't have the slightest idea. I was surprised that Umstead knew who Randy Fontana was, since I'd thought the old detective worked for Thornberg. "I'd still like to talk to Thornberg, if he hasn't gone home," I said.

"He'll be on his guard after his encounter with Mr. Umstead."

She was right. I wondered if Fontana was the one who'd ordered the three young security men to go after me. I might have to go through the old man to get to Thornberg.

The director and his bodyguard had gone out through one of the side doors that led to an outside balcony with a staircase descending to a garden behind the building. "How about if we find Thornberg," I said to Kim. "I might as well be the next one to attack him...before Lucia gets her chance, if she's still here."

"She's still here, Anh. I saw her watching the argument from over in the corner."

Pink Carnation

We had reached the door to the balcony. The cool evening air was refreshing after the closeness of the room. The night was still except for the soft sound of voices on the stairs below. Kim and I crept across the balcony until we reached the wall along its periphery. We peeked over the edge and looked down on the figures below.

Brian Thornberg and the young woman who had been with Jess Wolf were huddled beneath the stairway, barely visible in the shadows. The distance was only about twenty feet and if they'd looked up they would have seen our two heads peering over the balcony. Thornberg was holding his hands up to the girl's face. After a moment, he put his hands to his own face. They were snorting coke together. The two of them embraced.

Kim and I reflexively pulled our heads back and looked at each other. I felt my stomach tighten in anger "What a jerk Thornberg is," I said. "That freak has no limits on his behavior."

We headed back inside, only to be confronted by Lucia Chavez, standing on the other side of the door.

"I thought you were going home," I said.

"I'm not your daughter, Professor Routledge. You can't tell me what to do." She put on a show of arrogance, but then looked startled when she noticed Kim standing next to me, gazing at her with amused irritation. "Is this your wife?" Lucia asked, looking embarrassed.

"Yes," I answered. "Kim, this is Lucia Chavez, one of my students — one of my more challenging students."

Kim smiled at Lucia. "I'm very sorry about your brother, Lucia. My husband says he's trying to help you. He's a very kind man. I hope you appreciate that."

"I know he is," Lucia gulped. "I appreciate it." She looked around uncomfortably. Kim was still gazing at her with a benign but inquisitive stare. "Maybe I'll go home." Lucia said. "But Mr. Thornberg is still going to have to answer some questions," she added, returning to her more defiant mien for my benefit.

"She's a strong girl," Kim said as Lucia headed across the room, hopefully for the exit.

"And a little mixed up. But she needs my help."

Kim patted me on the arm. "And I'm proud of you for giving it, Don Quixote. What are you going to do about Mr. Thornberg?"

I felt my anger returning, like a hot balloon expanding in the pit of my stomach. "I'm going to put in my two-cents to President Stonehill about not accepting Thornberg's money or letting him film on campus and I'm going to tell Jess Wolf to rescue his girlfriend before she ends up being bagged by the campus police."

"You're going to call the campus police?"

"No. That would only embarrass the university. I'd like to find that Fontana character, though, and tell him to get his druggie boss out of here."

Kim went off to get us refills on our drinks and I spotted Jess Wolf talking to Alfred Stonehill. I approached the two of them. "Your honored guest from the movie industry is out snorting dope beneath the back stairs," I said, by way of injecting myself into the two men's conversation.

Stonehill looked irritated. "What are you talking about, Routledge?" He glanced over at Jess Wolf as if to apologize for the poor manners of a member of his faculty.

"Brian Thornberg is snorting coke on the back lawn," I said, turning from Stonehill to Wolf. "And I think it's your girlfriend who's doing it with him."

Wolf's alarm was visible. "I brought the young woman to introduce her to Mr. Thornberg," he said with a tight-lipped smile. "What she does is her own business, but this isn't the time or place for that sort of thing. I'll get her out of here."

I nodded and turned back to Stonehill. "I don't think you want a drug bust to occur during a faculty social gathering and you might keep this in mind when you consider inviting Thornberg on campus to film his movie."

Pink Carnation

Slick Al looked shaken. "Certainly. We can't allow something like that on our campus," he sputtered.

"You're very observant, Professor," Wolf said, giving me an appreciative look.

I addressed Stonehill. "Keep Thornberg's behavior in mind when you're dealing with him. He could bring trouble to this campus."

Stonehill nodded, a blank look on his face, as if he was still overwhelmed with the news about his prospective golden goose's misbehavior. I spied Kim heading my way with our drinks and I excused myself to meet her.

"I don't know what they're going to do about Thornberg," I said. "Probably nothing right now. It's time for me to go back and have a talk with him."

"What about the girl?"

"Here she is now," I said. We watched the young woman re-enter from the balcony. She was alone. She scanned the room and then, spying her former date still talking to President Stonehill, she joined him at his side, putting her hand around Jess Wolf's arm as though she had never left. Wolf's face was livid and he leaned close to the woman's ear and said something to her. She gazed at the floor.

Kim and I went back out the same door by which the young woman had just entered. Instinctively, we both went to the edge of the balcony and looked down to the garden. No one was to be seen, but we could hear voices raised in argument below. They were too far away for us to decipher anything except the angry tone. I thought I recognized Michael Umstead's voice as one of the two.

"Things get curiouser and curiouser," I said to Kim.

"I hope that's supposed to be Lewis Carrol and not pidgin Vietnamese, Anh."

"Answers to questions be like shafts of light from rainbow — fade to nothing as we approach." I put my hands together and bowed. "That's pidgin Vietnamese, Em."

Kim gave me a withering stare.

We descended the staircase that led to the overgrown garden below. The shouting match between whomever else was down there had stopped. The sound of approaching footsteps could be heard along the brick pathway that wound between the banana trees and palms.

Michael Umstead emerged from the trees looking startled to see Kim and me. At first he appeared panicked, then his demeanor changed to embarrassment, as he nodded curtly at the two of us while he tried to hurry past.

"Is Thornberg down here?" I asked.

Umstead looked surprised that I had spoken to him. "Oh, Routledge, hello. Hello Mrs. Routledge." He shook his head. "I haven't seen Thornberg."

"Weren't you just talking to someone?" I asked.

Umstead looked guilty, then his look was replaced by one of irritation. "That was Fontana. I was talking to Mr. Fontana. I haven't seen Mr. Thornberg since I talked to him earlier." He turned away and rushed up the stairs.

Kim and I exchanged mystified looks then we headed down the brick pathway. "I hear someone walking, Anh," Kim said, grabbing my arm to slow me. I stopped and heard the same thing, footsteps hurrying on the bricks, somewhere near the edge of the garden.

I shrugged. "Let's see if we can find Thornberg. I'd like to talk to him before he becomes occupied with someone else."

The lights from the windows above lighted the garden, and along the pathway were softly glowing lanterns tucked inconspicuously amid the thick foliage. Occasionally there was a brighter spotlight illuminating one of the palm trees for effect. I had the feeling of walking down a jungle path. Kim and I proceeded slowly, half expecting to come around a bend and find Thornberg in the midst of snorting coke. We rounded a corner and found Thornberg sprawled across the pathway.

"He's not breathing," Kim said, urgency in her voice as she knelt over the director's body. Kim had had first aid training in Vietnam and she immediately went into her crisis mode.

Pink Carnation

I knelt beside her and felt the director's neck for a carotid pulse. There was none, but his neck was still warm to the touch and I noticed that there were beads of sweat that hadn't dried on his forehead. He must have been dead only minutes. There was white powder on the edges of Thornberg's nostrils and on his hands. I'd been feeling panic, now I was angry.

Kim began CPR.

"He's overdosed," I shouted. "It's probably a heart attack. Maybe it's not too late. Keep up the CPR and I'll call the paramedics."

Kim was hunched over Thornberg's body. She motioned for me to go. Just inside the door at the top of the stairs, I almost collided with Randy Fontana. "Thornberg's had a heart attack," I yelled into Fontana's ear. "Get someone to call 911." I continued past him toward Alfred Stonehill, who was standing in the middle of the room, still talking with Jess Wolf.

I grabbed Stonehill's shoulder and spun him around. "Get the campus police over here. Thornberg's had a heart attack in the garden!" Stonehill looked flustered for a moment, then pulled a cell phone from his breast pocket and dialed the campus security. I looked for Randy Fontana. He was nowhere to be seen. Jess Wolf was looking at me with detached interest. His girlfriend appeared to be in shock.

When I got back to Kim, she was just giving up on the CPR. She stood up and looked at me with tears in her eyes. Her breath was coming in short gasps. "I'm sorry, Anh."

I felt my shoulders sag and my legs become weak. I reached over and put my arm around Kim. That's when I noticed Randy Fontana.

"Moron," Fontana said, looking down at Thornberg.

"Excuse me?" I said.

"He's a fucking moron. I bet he snorted a couple ounces of that stuff tonight."

"Don't you work for him?"

"I'm handling security for the film." Fontana's gaze fixed on me, as if he was trying to place where he'd seen me before. "Do I know you?"

"Your security boys tried to send me a message the other day...in an alley in Santa Ana."

He stared at me, and then looked back at Thornberg. "Fucking moron," he repeated, shaking his head.

The campus police had arrived and Kim and I had to answer a lot of questions. Pretty soon a host of detectives from the City of Orange and a county medical examiner showed up, putting us through the same questions. There was no evidence that Thornberg had been assaulted and the questions were pretty routine. Kim and I returned to the gathering upstairs, which, after a brief period of rubbernecking, was dissipating.

We said our good-byes to President Stonehill and to Janet Erskine Jones. Janet was talking to Michael Umstead, who looked as if the news of Thornberg's death had sobered him up. "I hope Alfred and Jess have learned a lesson," Janet said. "Everyone knew that Brian Thornberg was a drug addict. I can't believe we now have to endure the publicity of him overdosing on our campus."

"Do you think this means they'll stop making that horrid picture?" Umstead asked me, taking a large gulp of something dark with a minimum of ice in it.

He might have sobered up with the news about Thornberg, but he was trying his best to unsober himself.

I raised my hands in a gesture of ignorance. "I'll let you two console yourselves over Thornberg's loss. I hope neither of you is too overcome by grief."

Janet gave me a playful kick in the shin. "Come on, Phineas. Hollywood's loss is the world's gain, we all know that."

"Ta ta," I said, gathering Kim and heading for the door.

When we arrived at the coat check counter, Lucia Chavez was just putting on a long black cape over her svelte evening dress. She looked up with a guilty expression. "I'm just leaving," she said.

"I see that. Didn't we say goodbye a half hour ago?"

"I decided to take a little time to see how the other half lives," she said.

Pink Carnation

She was slurring her words. "What happened to Mr. Thornberg?"

"He had a heart attack. We'll talk about it tomorrow. Have you been drinking?"

"A little." She raised her hand in salute. "Pink Carnation strikes again! Maybe, Thornberg's heart attack wasn't an accident. Maybe it's payback." She looked at me with a sly grin, then turned and walked unsteadily out the door.

"Is she going to be OK?" Kim asked.

"I hope so," I said. "Kinda makes you wonder about Thornberg's heart attack, though, doesn't it. Maybe she had a point."

"Who'd want to kill Thornberg, Anh?"

I shrugged. "Probably a lot of people, from the number of them who seem happy that he's dead." We put on our coats and headed out the door. "Lucia's having a bad influence on me. I'm starting to see murders where there aren't any."

"You're just a romantic, Anh. "

"Then let's go home."

EIGHT

Brian Thornberg's death made the front pages of both the Orange County Register and the LA Times, the Times article being much larger and focusing on the director's Hollywood career. In both newspapers, his death was attributed to a heart attack with no mention of a drug overdose. The Times article went into some depth about Thornberg's rumored drug use and decadent lifestyle but made no connection between such allegations and the circumstances of his death, despite the fact that he was only fifty years old. President Stonehill called me at six in the morning to inform me that I had been mistaken about Thornberg's overdose and that the coroner had established that the director had died of a simple heart attack.

And the Pope sells condoms.

"Whatever," I said.

He also informed me that he'd gotten a report that one of my students had been at the fundraiser, drunk, and that there were rumors that I had some sort of special relationship with the student.

"I'm not going to dignify rumors by answering them," I said and hung up the telephone then went back to sleep.

When I finally woke up, showered, and drove to the campus, I found Lucia Chavez parked in the hallway outside my office door. She was sitting on the floor, her back to the wall, dozing. I crept past her and entered my office, got myself settled and started the coffeemaker, then went back and gave Lucia's foot a gentle shake. She awoke with a start.

"Have you got coffee?" she said, putting both hands to the sides of her head and pushing as hard as she could. I recognized the symptoms of a hangover.

"What am I, your home away from home?"

"Do you want me to leave?" she asked with an exaggerated pout. I opened the door and motioned for her to come inside.

"Now what?" she said, sitting down in a chair. She was still rubbing her temples and looking with longing at the dripping coffeemaker.

"What do you mean?"

"Thornberg is dead. How do I find out what really happened to Ramon?"

"I don't know," I said, picking up the coffeepot and pouring her a cup of strong black Kenyan coffee. She sipped the steaming coffee as if it were the most precious liquid on earth.

"You weren't supposed to be there last night," I said.

She gave a nonchalant shrug. "Because nobody wants students to see how their professors and Board members get drunk and loaded on drugs?"

"You got pretty drunk yourself."

"So what?"

"So I got a call this morning from the President of the university, complaining about it and wondering what our relationship was."

"Did you say we were lovers?" she asked, batting her eyelashes.

"I said that you were a misbehaving young lady who needed to be brought into line."

She looked as if she didn't know whether or not to believe me.

"At least I wasn't snorting coke under the back porch."

"How did you know about that?"

Her mouth curled in a sly smile. "I saw Thornberg and that bimbo in the garden. You and your wife did too."

"What else did you see?"

"That 'ho' gave more drugs to Thornberg before she left him."

I'd assumed that Thornberg had supplied the drugs to the girl, not vice versa. "You didn't miss much," I said.

She smiled triumphantly. "Rich people aren't so different from the rest of us."

"Did you see Thornberg have his heart attack?"

She looked shocked. " Do you think I'd just watch someone die and not call for help?"

I didn't, but I was reassured to hear it from her own lips. "I don't know if Thornberg was as important as we think. He had relationships with both your brother and Lisa Burke, but that's all we know about him, other than that he was directing the film in which they died."

She gulped more of her coffee, then slung one leg over the other and began swinging one foot. "If he did know anything, maybe that's why he's dead now."

"You mean you think your brother and Thornberg were both murdered?"

She looked at me with defiance. "Yes."

"Why do you think so?"

"Someone followed me home last night."

"Followed you home?"

She nodded. "Someone followed me from campus, right to my house."

"What happened?"

"I drove around the block to where some Santa Nitas live. When I pulled up in front of their place, whoever it was pulled up next to me in the street, but some Nitas came out with guns and they took off.'

"They? Did you see them?"

"It was too dark for me to see their faces. As soon as the Nitas came out they left."

The Santa Nitas were the most prominent gang in central Santa Ana. Despite concerted efforts from local and even federal law enforcement agencies to wipe them out, they'd been around since the 1940's and were the main reason that the LA based gangs had never made an inroad in Orange County. The SN's as they were called, had virtually owned their turf for more than fifty years.

"Did you have any problem with the SN's?"

She shook her head. "They like me, especially the Cordoza's, who head the gang. John Cordoza has the hots for me." She raised her eyebrows and gave me a provocative smile.

"You're playing with fire. The SN's are dangerous."

"I grew up with the Santa Nitas. John Cordoza is your age."

I frowned. "That makes him old enough to be your father."

She smiled back at me. "Does that make you jealous, Professor?"

Teenage girls can be very irritating.

I shook my head. "Like I said, you're playing with fire. The real question is who were those two guys? I suppose that Thornberg or the studio could have sent them before Thornberg got killed."

"My mother got another call this morning from the studio asking her if she'd made up her mind about the money. I told her to put them off, though I'm not sure if that's the right thing to do anymore."

"If they called, then they're still worried, even with Thornberg dead. You know the offer to your mother is worthless if Lisa Burke's family doesn't accept a similar one. The studio needs both families to agree to hold off on any lawsuits."

Lucia raised her eyebrows. "I wonder how much Mrs. Burke was told about her daughter's death."

"Have you talked to Mrs. Burke?"

"No," she said, "I've never met her. I know she's poor and she lives in San Clemente."

"Maybe we should both meet her," I said.

"I thought you were through helping me after last night."

"I should be, but I want to get to the bottom of this and I have to get back to teaching classes. With Thornberg dead, we haven't got many more sources of information. Maybe Mrs. Burke knows something."

"Can we go see her now?" she asked.

"It's as good a time as any."

NINE

Melanie Burke's mobile home was not one of the nicer ones in *Sea Breezes*, a sprawling trailer park tucked behind a hillside a few hundred yards from Interstate 5, just north of San Juan Capistrano. Painted a fading aqua and dirty white, the screen door on the front was torn along one edge and rust was eating away at the metal frame. A woven rubber mat said *Welcome*, but the corner of the mat above the final "e" had become disengaged and protruded almost an inch, waiting to snare the unobservant visitor. Lucia and I glanced at each other. I took a deep breath and knocked on the screen door's frame.

"Christ, just a minute!" came a voice, accompanied by the sound of water running and dishes clattering. The door swung open behind the ragged screen and a woman in her late forties or early fifties, thin as a rail, with hair hanging down on either side of her face in straight greasy strings, stood looking out at us, an irritated, questioning look on her face. She was wearing a powder blue jogging outfit made of a cheap, satiny material.

"This is Lucia Chavez, Ramon's sister, and I'm Professor Phineas Routledge. We called earlier?"

The woman appeared confused. "Of course," she finally said, brushing her stringy hair back with both hands. "I forgot you were coming. I haven't had time to clean up this morning." She pushed the screen door open. "Come on in. Excuse the mess."

Lucia entered cautiously, as though she expected the seediness of the woman's home to be infectious. I followed, having to bend to avoid hitting my head on the doorframe. Mrs. Burke gestured toward a couch that stood on one side of a ten by twelve-foot living room that looked more like someone's storage shed than a living space. Piled everywhere were cardboard boxes, some closed, most of them open and empty. I pushed the boxes on the couch toward one end and Lucia and I sat.

Pink Carnation

"Join me in a drink?" Mrs. Burke asked, disappearing into another room. There was the sound of dishes clattering. "I'm moving," she called. "The place is a mess. Anyone for a beer ...coffee?"

There was a dirty coffee cup on the table in front of the couch and two or three glasses parked on top of boxes; a few dregs of beer or something that looked like beer left in each.

"My doctor won't let me," I answered.

Lucia gave me a strange look and uttered a cold "no thank you." The sound of water running came from the back of the trailer.

"I'm packing everything up to move," Melanie Burke said, reentering the room with a cup of coffee in her hand. She was unsteady on her feet and had to catch herself with one hand against the wall. Some light tan coffee sloshed over the side of her cup and onto the worn carpet. Mrs. Burke gave a helpless shrug. "No sense worrying about the carpet now." From the look of the carpet it had never been the object of much worry.

The woman had brushed her hair and put on a dash of lipstick and rouge. There were circles under her eyes, and her skin, even through the rouge, was crisscrossed with deep wrinkles. She put her cup of coffee on the edge of the table, then removed a box from the seat of a rocking chair—it was an early American replica in faded turquoise with a worn painting of an eagle across the top of the backrest. After she retrieved her coffee, Mrs. Burke folded herself into the rocker and smiled over at us. Her eyes were slightly out of focus.

"You were friends of Lisa?" she asked, her glance shifting back and forth between the two of us.

"My brother was killed with Lisa," Lucia declared. Her voice had an irritated edge to it.

Mrs. Burke's face registered surprise, then she became teary. "It was terrible, wasn't it?" she said, blinking back her tears. She sniffed, and then took a long drink of her coffee, still keeping her eyes on Ramon's sister.

Lucia barely nodded. Mrs. Burke lowered her gaze and sniffed again. "Lisa was going to be a great actress," the woman said as she switched her attention to me. "She was meeting all the right people." She got up from the rocker and disappeared down a narrow corridor that led off from the living room.

"She's drunk!" Lucia hissed.

I held out my hands in a gesture of helplessness.

"Look at these!" Mrs. Burke reappeared from the darkness of the hallway carrying an armload of framed photographs. She plopped them down in the center of the coffee table in front of us. "You sure you couldn't use a drink?" she asked without sitting down. She hovered over the two of us. Her breath reeked of beer.

"My doctor..." I said, with a helpless shrug.

Lucia shook her head.

"Well, I will, if you don't mind," she said, exiting again in the opposite direction. The woman might not be healthy but she was a bundle of energy.

Lisa Burke was deliciously photogenic. She reminded me of Sandra Dee in movies from the fifties and sixties. That resemblance may have been why she was picked for the part of a late fifties debutante. A perfectly oval face, pink cheeked with a creamy white complexion, with large blue eyes framed by bright blond hair, looking out from each picture with an expression of innocence that could have melted the coldest heart. Most of the photos were of only her face, but one pictured her full-length, wearing the smallest of string bikini's, standing in a provocative pose next to a surfboard with the ocean breaking in the background. It was obviously a publicity photo... 'Gidget does Playboy.'

"Your daughter was beautiful," I said to Mrs. Burke, who had reentered the room, a glass of beer in her hand. I was surprised that she could find a clean glass, though maybe I was assuming too much to think it was clean. "You must be having a difficult time with the loss."

Her face became melodramatically sad. "I haven't been myself since my baby died." She held up her beer glass and nodded in its direction. "I don't usually drink this early in the day, but thinking about Lisa is more than I can take unless I have something to calm me down." Her eyes flitted from me to Lucia then back again. "The money can't replace my loss."

"Money?" Lucia and I asked in unison.

She drew back with a surprised look, and then shifted her gaze to Lucia, a shadow of suspicion crossing her face. "The settlement from the studio. They said the boy's—your brother's—family was getting the same thing. Aren't you?"

"How much are you getting?" Lucia asked, her voice flat, devoid of emotion.

"The amount isn't important is it?" Mrs. Burke had suddenly gotten soberly cautious.

"We don't care how much money you got, Mrs. Burke," I intervened "The Chavez family has been promised ample compensation from the studio, so long as there is no law suit. How about you?"

She drew herself up to her full frail height and took her third or fourth gulp of beer. "Why should I sue them? They've been generous to me. If I sue, I could lose and get nothing." She looked back and forth between the two of us, her face registering a mixture of anger and fear. "I don't want anyone prying into Lisa's death."

"What do you mean?" I asked.

She swung her head from side to side in an exaggerated manner, as if checking to be sure no one could hear what she was saying. "My daughter was pregnant." She hesitated for the effect. ""Do you think I want that printed on the front page of the newspapers?"

"She was pregnant?" I asked.

She gave me a knowing nod.

"How do you know?" I asked

"The medical examiner called me. Then the studio called and said they could keep it out of the paper. I think they were being very kind. They loved Lisa. Like I said, she had friends there." She rolled the last of her beer around in her glass and then tipped it up and downed it. She looked at the empty glass and shrugged. Without saying anything she stood up and zigzagged back to the kitchen. There was the sound of the refrigerator opening and then a can being popped open.

"I figure we have about three more questions before she passes out on us," I said to Lucia.

"I'm getting a house on the beach," Mrs. Burke said, returning to the living room. She sat down heavily in the rocking chair, putting both feet squarely on the floor to stop the chair's motion. "San Clemente Cove. Lisa always wanted me to live there."

"Who were her friends at the studio?" I asked.

Mrs. Burke appeared to be surveying her boxes, perhaps thinking about her impending move to the beach. She swung her head clumsily back in my direction. "What?"

"Friends. You said Lisa had friends at the studio."

She drew herself up with a proud look. "She knew Mr. Thornberg...and Mr. Elmore. They both took her out. Everybody wanted to go out with Lisa. She was beautiful."

"She dated them?"

She looked at me as if I was naive. "That's how young girls get in the movies. What? You think they just take screen tests and get picked from the crowd? Lisa ran around with the right people. They were going to look out for her." Her last statement brought her up short and all the wind seemed to go out of her sails. She sipped morosely on her glass of beer.

"Who was the father of the baby?" I asked.

Mrs. Burke gave me a vacant stare. There was a line of wet beer on her upper lip. "Who cares?" she gestured expansively, spilling some of the beer onto the floor.

She smiled and licked the rim of her glass. Then she looked up, a crafty expression on her face. "For the price of a beach house, I'm not going to ask any questions. As far as anyone's concerned, my baby died innocent." She took another drink and leaned back in her chair, closing her eyes and rocking back and forth. She held the near empty beer glass in both hands, resting it on her stomach. "I don't feel very good," she murmured.

"We'll let ourselves out, Mrs. Burke," I said. I had to pull Lucia by the coat sleeve to get her up. She was staring at the woman with loathing. Mrs. Burke didn't open her eyes.

As soon as we were out the door, Lucia was in my face. "Lisa Burke was pregnant! Are you going to tell me that her death was an accident?"

"What does her pregnancy have to do with your brother? And why would Thornberg be killed if he was the one trying to cover everything up?"

"Maybe my brother found out about it. He and Lisa were close. And if it was Elmore's baby, then Ramon might have told Thornberg. Elmore would have had to kill Thornberg as well as my brother to keep it a secret."

"Elmore wasn't even at the university fundraiser."

"OK," she said, irritated. "Maybe Thornberg really did die of a heart attack. But Elmore was covering things up when he talked to you. He didn't tell you anything about Lisa being pregnant."

We'd reached my car and I could hear the rush of traffic on the 1-5 in the distance. I opened the door of the antique MGA for Lucia. "Let's not jump to conclusions," I said. "Lisa Burke may not even have known she was pregnant herself. She obviously didn't tell her mother. And Elmore would have to be an idiot—which I'm not ruling out—to kill her in such an obvious fashion; and in a way which was guaranteed to require an autopsy, which would reveal the pregnancy."

Lucia got in the car and sulked.

I slid into the worn leather driver's seat and looked over at her. "We can't go off half-cocked, Lucia. Until I ask Elmore about the pregnancy, we don't know what it means."

"Maybe I'll ask him, when I see him," she said.

"Lucia..." I warned.

She went back to sulking. We drove in silence toward the campus. Interstate 5 was crowded as usual, but traffic cruised along at seventy miles per hour, even though a single miscalculation by one driver could cause a chain reaction accident that would take out eight to ten cars in one fell swoop. Lucia and I avoided much of the congestion by traveling in the carpool lane, where the pace was closer to eighty miles per hour. Even at that speed, a black SUV was closing fast on me from the rear. I had a solid wall of slower moving traffic on one side and concrete railing on the other.

"I hate SUV's," I muttered as I eyed the looming Ford Explorer in my rear view mirror. In my tiny MGA, our heads came to the top of the SUV's front bumper.

Lucia roused herself from her sulk and swung her head around. "The guys who followed me home were driving a car like that."

I looked in the rearview mirror. All I could see was the waffle-iron grillwork of the Explorer, bearing down on us like a Sherman tank. In a minute, the dark SUV's bumper would be touching the back of my car. I felt my heart racing.

"Damn!" I said, "those guys are trying to run us off the road!"

We were coming up on the exit to the Costa Mesa Freeway, which would lead us toward Orange and the campus. I couldn't slow down or I'd have the Explorer in the driver's seat along with me. As I kept one eye on the mirror and the other on the road, the SUV loomed larger and larger. My steering wheel was slippery from my sweaty hands.

I was almost to the exit ramp for the Costa Mesa Freeway. In a few seconds, the carpool lane would separate from the main highway and take off up the new elevated ramp that missed all of the congestion of the downtown Santa Ana exits, rejoining the main freeway just past Main Street.

I felt a knot in my stomach. I had only one choice.

I floored the gas pedal of my MGA, winding the small engine up to 6,000 rpms and inching the speedometer past ninety. The Costa Mesa Freeway exit flashed by and I followed the curve of the carpool lane around the corner and onto the approach of the elevated ramp. The Explorer lagged behind, and then surged forward. Just before I reached the concrete wall separating the incline of the carpool lane from the four lanes that continued below, I veered to the right, sending the little sportscar gliding through the air; all four tires off the ground. With a gentle slap we pancaked into the nearest lane of the four-lane highway. As soon as we landed, I hit my breaks to avoid rear-ending the tan Thunderbird ahead of me. Off to my left, the SUV continued up the elevated ramp.

"Jesus Christ!" Lucia said, next to me. Her face was white as a ghost's.

I grinned, despite my racing pulse and a feeling of lightheadedness. "England one, Detroit zero," I managed to say.

"I thought we were going to die," Lucia said, still shaken.

"Me too," I admitted, feeling my heart still hammering in my chest. I wiped one sweaty palm at a time on my pants. "That Explorer was trying to make us roadkill. Was it the same one that followed you home?"

"I think so, but I can't be sure. It was nighttime."

I moved over to the outside lane of traffic so I could exit before the main highway reunited with the carpool lane. Lucia's face was regaining its color. "Well we're rid of them for now. If hey show up behind us again, at least we'll know it was no accident."

TEN

When we arrived at the campus, Lucia looked drained and said she was going home. I still had an afternoon class to teach but first I put in a call to the studio to try to locate Elmore. I wanted to see if he could be more enlightening when he was faced with the news that his dead girlfriend may have been carrying his child. The studio said he had gone into seclusion after the death of Thornberg. They claimed to have no knowledge of his whereabouts. I did. I'd read in the society page of the paper that he was renting a house in Laguna Beach. It was a house I'd visited on several occasions in my bachelor days when an earlier tenant had hosted some of south county's wilder singles parties. It was gated, but there was a path up from the beach that I'd used for several productive trysts during my party-attending days.

I finished my four o'clock lecture on the relationship between father absence and the tendency to join gangs, a subject in which the data seemed evenly split between a clear-cut relationship if one studied African-American or White youth and no relationship if the culture was Latino or Asian. It was all very confusing and I hadn't the patience to unravel the threads of cultural differences that made sense of the findings for the benefit of my class. I left the bewildered students grumbling about my inconsistency and obscurantism while I grumbled to myself about their need to be spoon-fed pat answers to complicated questions.

The phone was ringing as I entered my office. Lucia Chavez had heard from the note-writer and he wanted to meet her. He was an old friend from her neighborhood. I told her we'd go meet him together. She might know the streets, but I was six foot six. She started to object, but I told her that in Vietnam they have a saying, 'to plow a rice field, you must hitch your plow to a water buffalo, not to a mouse.' She had no idea what I was talking about, but she invited me along. I didn't understand the saying, either.

Pink Carnation

Lucia and I met at Norm's (*We Never Close*) twenty-four hour restaurant in Santa Ana, about a mile from where they'd been shooting the courthouse scenes. Julio, her friend, had suggested meeting her in the parking lot of an abandoned bank building about four or five blocks away. A fat waitress in a pink uniform that was several sizes too small informed us that we'd have to order at least coffee to occupy the booth we were in while we waited for the appointed hour of the meeting. We obliged with two orders of coffee and I asked Lucia about the person we were about to meet.

"He wasn't really a gang kid," she said. "His family have always been Nitas ... his father, his uncle and his cousins. His family is the Cordozas, who live around the corner from me. They're the ones who came out and scared those men away the other night. The Cordozas run the Santa Nitas. Because he was a Cordoza, Julio was automatically a Nita, but he wasn't like the others."

"In what way?" I asked.

"He liked school and he was smart. He and Ramon used to study together when they were in junior high. I used to bug them. I had a crush on Julio. Later, I dated him a couple of times, but it didn't work out. He treated me like a kid sister. Now Julio wants to become a lawyer. He went to Santa Ana College for two years, and then transferred to one of the Cal States. I think he's a senior now. I'm not sure cuz we don't keep in touch. But every once in a while, he'll stop around to see me or Ramon."

"So what's his connection to the shootings, I wonder?"

"It's related to Raul Lopez, the boy who was killed back in 1959. Ramon was playing him in the movie. Julio said that his grandfather knew Lopez. His grandfather had some information about him. That's all he told me."

"Do you know anything about the grandfather?"

"Arturo?" She smiled fondly. "Arturo was one of the original Santa Nitas. He was one tough hombre when he was younger. Even now, nobody crosses him. He was always a kindly grandfather to Ramon and me, though. He raised Julio more than Julio's parents did. Arturo and Rosa, his wife, are like godparents to me."

"How about Julio's parents?"

"His mother took off when he was young. She was on drugs. I think she ended up dead somewhere. His father is John Cordoza." She blushed. "John's the one who's always after me. He's big in the Santa Nitas and he's tough. Same thing for Jorge, Julio's uncle. They're supposed to deal drugs. Both of them have been in prison. They ran a big car theft operation that got shut down by the cops. They both went to jail. Everybody in the neighborhood knew they killed the Chicano who informed on them, but they never got caught for that. The word is that they've killed others."

"You're playing with fire."

"I can't stop men having fantasies about me, Professor Routledge," she said with a sly smile.

She had a point but I gave her a disapproving look anyway.

"Let's focus on Julio," I said. "How will he feel about me being with you?"

She looked over at my camel hair Armani jacket, and then glanced below the table at my shiny Bruno Magli loafers. A tiny smile played around the corners of her mouth. "I guess he'll know that you're not from the barrio." Her face became serious. "He trusts me. I don't think it'll spook him to see that I've brought someone with me."

"We'll find out," I said.

We finished our coffees and got into Lucia's scruffy fifteen-year-old Toyota Tercel. Driving up in my shiny little restored '58 MGA might confuse Julio. The bank lot was only a few blocks away. We headed down Main and turned right at Washington then took an immediate left on Sycamore. We passed the East Santa Ana Police substation and turned toward the parking lot where Julio was supposed to be waiting. The lot looked deserted, but in the fading evening light he might be parked anywhere in the shadows of the tall, eight- story building. The bank building had been unoccupied for several years, and the sidewalks and outdoor walkways under its back porticos had become residences for the ubiquitous downtown street people. The giant brick-red dumpster that had been abandoned in the corner of the spacious parking lot was rumored to be a favorite spot for low-level drug deals. I didn't know if this was Santa Nita turf or not.

Lucia pulled her battered Tercel into the lot past the boarded up parking guard station, the wooden barricades of which had been turned into useless broken stubs sometime in years past. A black Camaro, about ten years old, was nosed into the deepening shadows near the entrance to the rear of the building. We drove across the faded crisscross lines of the parking lot, making a beeline for Julio's car. His head was visible in the driver's seat, but he didn't turn as we approached. Lucia pulled to a stop about twenty yards from the Camaro and we both got out. I could feel my heart pounding as I scanned the shadows. Julio still hadn't turned around. My legs felt weak and heavy as we approached the car.

The bullet hole in the driver's side window was obvious as soon as we stepped far enough into the shadows to see Julio clearly. So was the blood splattered across the front windshield and the passenger side window. The doors of the Camaro were locked. Lucia stood motionless, staring at Julio's still face, which was turned to one side, the eye on this side wide open. The bullet had made a small entry wound behind his left ear. I didn't want to see how large the exit wound was on the other side. My stomach was queasy, and I swallowed several times in succession to keep from vomiting.

"Have you got your cell phone?" I asked Lucia, my voice sounding as if it wasn't my own.

She nodded. Her face was white and appeared cast in stone.

"Are you all right?" I asked. As soon as I said it, I knew the question was absurd. I walked over and put my arm around her. She was stiff and unmoving. I tightened my hold on her. I could feel my arm shaking.

"It's like Ramon," she said, softly. She was shaking, too.

My shock was starting to wear off, and I could think more clearly. "We need to call the police," I said. The last light had vanished except for a dim street lamp on the corner. "Whoever did this could still be around."

She took a deep breath and began moving, walking the twenty yards back to her car where she unlocked the door and removed her purse and then her cell phone. She walked around to the passenger side and opened the door, then pulled a flashlight out of the glove box.

I took the flashlight and, flipping on a weak beam, swept it over the interior of the car. The amount of blood on the seat, the dashboard, and the opposite door and window was enormous. I could hear Lucia making the 911 call.

There was nothing on either the front or back seats, or as much of the floorboards as I could illuminate with the beam of the flashlight. Whatever Julio had meant to give to Lucia was either verbal or had been taken by his killer. The locked doors made me think that his message was verbal… which meant that it was sealed behind Julio's lifeless lips. I hard a siren close by, and I shut off the flashlight and handed it back to Lucia.

Two Santa Ana police cars turned into the parking lot, sirens dying as they slowed to a stop with red and blue lights flashing. They pulled up ten yards beyond Lucia's car and flung open their doors.

"Oh shit, here we go," I said.

Next to me, Lucia's face was a mask.

"Move back from the car!" The voice came through a loudspeaker on one of the cars.

Lucia and I stepped back a good ten feet. I turned and started toward the police cars.

"Stay where you are and show us your hands!" came the voice through the loudspeaker.

Lucia and I both froze, our hands held out to our sides, palms up.

A uniformed policeman emerged from the blackness beyond the glare of the cars' headlights. He didn't have his gun drawn, and his young, Hispanic face had an open, inquiring look. He held a long

Pink Carnation

flashlight, which shone a powerful beam, in one hand. He swept the beam over our faces, and then directed it at the car behind us.

"You the ones who called in the 911?" the young cop asked.

"We called," I said. "There's a dead man in the Camaro. He's been shot." Three other uniformed police walked past us to the car. They shined their torches inside, not touching anything. I could hear one of the men calling someone on his radio, static interrupting his voice, like a scene from *COPS*. Two of the officers began unrolling yellow crime scene tape. They were going to have a problem with crowd control in a moment. The curious were already starting to drift into the parking lot. A small knot of young men in baggy pants and loose T-shirts stood about forty feet back, engaged in animated conversation. A tall, skinny, black man with a well-groomed gray beard, but wild Don King hair, wearing a pair of too-big jeans held up by a rope, was wandering across the lot toward the car, pushing his shopping cart of belongings ahead of him. One of the policemen pointed a finger at him and shouted, "stay!" as though he was addressing a misbehaving dog. The homeless man gave him the finger but stopped moving.

The policeman who had addressed us watched the scene, shaking his head, as if he'd seen it all before. He motioned for us to come over to one of the police cars. When we got there, he pulled out a clipboard. Behind him, the other cops had pulled some plastic poles on wide bases from their cars and were fastening the yellow tape to the tops of the poles, cordoning off the area around the car. The homeless man began to wander away but more young people were coming into the parking lot, crowding up to the tape and craning their necks to see what was going on. They glanced over at us, probably hoping to see us cuffed and pushed into one of the cruisers.

"What were you doing here?" the young man, who identified himself as officer Mendez, asked after he'd gotten our birthdates, drivers license numbers, social security numbers, occupations, home addresses, and everything but our mothers' maiden names.

Lucia gave officer Mendez a silent stare.

"We were supposed to meet the boy who got killed," I volunteered.

Mendez gave Lucia a quizzical look, then turned to me. "You knew him, then?"

I nodded. Lucia gave no sign that she'd even heard the question. "Who is he?" Mendez asked.

I turned to Lucia. "Tell him, Lucia. We need police help with this."

She shot me a skeptical glance. "Julio Cordoza."

The cop frowned and looked at Lucia. "We know a few Cordoza's. He any relation to John or Jorge?"

Lucia frowned back. "John is his father."

The policeman began tapping his clipboard against the back of his hand. He swung his gaze from Lucia to me and then back to her. "So what was this, a drug buy?" he asked.

"Julio doesn't deal," Lucia answered. "He's a college student; so am I. We were meeting each other. This is my professor." Her eyes shifted in my direction.

The cop sighed and continued to tap the clipboard against his hand. Over his shoulder, the flashing lights of another police car entered the parking lot. This one was unmarked. Mendez stepped back.

Two plainclothes detectives emerged from the newly arrived vehicle. They were both about average height and weight, one of them well dressed in a sport coat and tie, creased pants and wing tips. The other wore jeans and a long-sleeved, white shirt, unbuttoned at the neck with a shiny necklace showing in a patch of dark curly hair. Mendez handed the clipboard first to one and then the other and they each signed in. The officer in jeans motioned for his partner to check out Julio's car while he looked over to where Lucia and I were standing.

"What have we got, Victor?" the detective asked, a look of studied boredom on his face. He appeared to be in his early forties with thinning black hair, a mustache, and a chin full of day old stubble.

Mendez made a show of surveying his notes on the clipboard. "One of the Cordoza boys got it in his car. These two called it in. They said they were supposed to meet him here." He made it obvious that he was only relaying our story, not necessarily believing it.

The detective looked over at his partner, who had opened the passenger side door and had his head over Julio's chest. Two of the uniformed cops were busy keeping the onlookers back and the third one was fiddling with the trunk. While we looked on, he popped the trunk open and shined his flashlight inside. He called to the detective who was examining Julio's body. "I guess they found something," our detective said, focusing his attention on Lucia and me. "Maybe you know what they found," he said, giving me a knowing look.

"Luggage?" I offered. "Spare tire? Jimmy Hoffa?"

The detective gave me a sour frown. "This is a dangerous place to be buying drugs," he said.

Lucia clenched her hands into fists. She gave me an, "I told you so," look.

"I'll bet it is, detective...?" I replied, waiting for him to supply his name.

"Coolidge," he said, taking the clipboard back from Mendez and perusing it.

The other detective was walking over from Julio's Camaro. He had something in his hand. It was a plastic bag with white powder in it. He held it up to Coolidge as if it were a prize. Coolidge nodded. He swung his eyes over to Lucia and myself. "Looks like somebody got to Cordoza before you could have your little seminar. You're lucky you didn't get here sooner. Drug deals don't always go they way they're planned."

I had a strong feeling about the way this deal was going and I didn't like it. "Somebody set this up to look like something it isn't," I said, hearing my anger in my own voice. "How about you call Jim Stapleton with the Sheriff's Department. He knows about us wanting to meet with the dead boy. He can clear this up for you."

Coolidge grimaced. "Don't get testy, professor. The Sheriff's department's already on their way. We called the SUAG unit when we found out it was a Cordoza."

Lucia and I glanced at each other. SUAG people were the last ones either of us wanted to talk to. "SUAG won't help," I said. "Call Stapleton."

I might as well have been talking to thin air. Coolidge and his partner ignored us while they discussed how much cocaine they'd found in Julio's trunk and their theory of what had happened, which sounded as if it was either a drug deal gone bad or a grudge hit by one of the SN's rival gangs. They were being careful not to disturb the crime scene until the medical examiner and crime scene team arrived. That meant that Julio was still sitting up in his car. I didn't know if they'd done a search of the body or not or if he was carrying the information that he'd planned to give to us. We were being pretty much ignored, except by the crowd, who seemed as curious about us as about the body in the car.

I asked Coolidge if we could sit in Lucia's car. She looked exhausted and I was getting tired of standing around, not to mention having a hard time controlling my anger. Coolidge agreed, which I assumed meant that we weren't considered suspects at the moment.

"Don't leave yet. Stapleton's on his way," Coolidge told us. I wasn't even aware that he'd made the call, but I felt relieved.

The SUAG team beat Jim Stapleton to the scene. Lucia and I stayed in the car while I watched a couple of plain clothes deputies, wearing the familiar blue jackets with SUAG printed in yellow across the back, get out of their unmarked car. As soon as they showed up, about half of the young people left the parking lot. Nobody wanted to get his head cracked for just standing around. The SUAG men swaggered over to where Coolidge and Mendez were standing. Mendez handed them the clipboard to sign in but Coolidge didn't offer to shake anyone's hand. The call to SUAG probably was obligatory but that didn't mean the Santa Ana cops welcomed the county boys.

My stomach tightened as I recognized the lumbering gait of the larger of the two SUAG officers.

"Damn!" I said to Lucia. "Tom Desmond from SUAG is here. He'd love to get something on me and now he's got his chance." I turned my head away from the huddle of policemen, but I knew it was to no avail.

As soon as my name came up Desmond would realize his chance for revenge had just materialized.

Lucia's face showed her surprise. "I thought you got along with the cops," she said.

"Most cops, including a lot of the SUAG people. But not Desmond and a few others who write their own rules."

Despite her look of concern, Lucia couldn't hide a smile. "Welcome to the club, Professor."

I gave her a grudging nod and glanced back at the cops. Desmond and his fellow SUAG officer were on their way to our car. I opened my door and stepped out. When push came to shove I preferred being two to three inches taller than my adversary. The advantage was mostly psychological, but it was real.

Tom Desmond had a sick grin on his face as he approached Lucia's car. "Out doing research on your own, Professor?"

Silence would have been the better part of valor, but, as usual, wisdom didn't win out. "I thought I'd drive around and see if they've cleaned up the police force yet, Desmond. I can see that they haven't."

Desmond had walked up close to my face but with my extra couple of inches, I looked down on him. I stepped forward, backing him up.

The sick smile disappeared. "Always the wise-guy, Doc. Well, you're in deep shit this time. I told Coolidge that we'd suspected for some time that you were using your research on delinquents as a cover for buying drugs." He stood with his feet spread and his arms hanging loosely at his sides, looking uneasy. The other SUAG officer looked confused. He wasn't used to confronting well-dressed middle-aged Anglos.

"I didn't get you before, when you bullied that poor kid who hadn't done anything," I said. "Make things easy for me this time, with a false arrest."

He shook his head. "It's not my case. I'll just tell Coolidge how helpful you are to cops." He looked over at Lucia, who had left the car and joined me. "This the Chavez girl who's brother got killed in the movie last week?"

I nodded.

"Nice operation, Doc. One of your students finds drugs for you and you're out banging another. Your university will be pleased to hear about this."

I felt a wave of heat spreading up my neck to my face. I'd had enough from this moron. I stepped forward and reached for the front of Desmond's shirt. Lucia grabbed my sleeve. "Don't waste your anger on this asshole, Professor." She spat on the pavement.

Desmond stiffened with anger, but he'd backed away and wasn't about to move closer. He gave us both hard looks, but from a safe distance.

I needed Jim Stapleton to get this clown out of my face and explain things to the Santa Ana cops, who would have jurisdiction in the case. I returned Desmond's hard look and brushed by him.

Stapleton's car arrived just as I reached Coolidge. Jim wasn't alone but I couldn't tell who his companion was, and when he stepped from the car, the other person remained inside. Stapleton gave me a rueful smile. I headed in his direction but he was already moving toward Coolidge. The Santa Ana detective and the two SUAG officers backed up to give the diminutive Chief of Homicide from the Sheriff's Department room. Even though the Santa Ana Police had jurisdiction at this location, it was clear who was the senior cop.

"Jimmy! How they hangin'?" Stapleton asked, slapping Coolidge on the back. He extended a hand to Desmond and his partner. Jim was working the crowd. "Jesus! Phineas, my favorite professor. I'm glad to see that you're here." Stapleton said, his greeting establishing our relationship in front of the others. Coolidge diverted his eyes from me but Desmond was seething. He could see his chance for revenge evaporating in front of him.

I didn't respond, except to smile at Tom Desmond.

"What have we got here?" Stapleton asked. "The professor and I have been working on something involving this Cordoza kid. Looks like someone else got to him before we did."

Pink Carnation

Either Jim was covering for me or he'd identified Julio Cordoza's fingerprints from the note I'd given him and he knew why Lucia and I were here.

"Looks like some kind of drug thing or maybe a gang hit," Coolidge answered. We called SUAG in just to follow protocol, being it's a Cordoza." The detective looked over at Desmond and frowned. He wanted to make it clear that he didn't need the anti-gang unit's help with the case.

"Probably a gang hit, since the drugs are still here," Desmond offered. He puffed out his chest and cast an angry glance in my direction. "I thought maybe the professor here came to buy from him. That would explain the drugs in the trunk."

Stapleton gave the SUAG officer a look of disgust. "You're better at cracking heads than at thinking, Tom. Phineas Routledge doesn't do drug deals. You oughta know that." He cast a sideways glance at me and winked. "Say, didn't you and Professor Routledge ride together once, Tom? You and he had a disagreement or two if I remember correctly. I sure hope that's not prejudicing you against the professor."

Desmond muttered something and looked at the ground. He turned away and walked a few yards toward his car, slamming a fist into his open hand. Stapleton laughed loudly, then turned back to Coolidge. "This is your case, Jimmy. Thanks for calling me and bringing SUAG in. I'm going to talk to the professor, if you don't mind. If you need him or the girl for something, just holler."

Jim slung his hand across my back as we walked away from the others.

He couldn't reach high enough to drape his arm over my shoulder. "What the fuck are you doing here?" he said under his breath as we walked over to Lucia's dingy Toyota.

I introduced Jim to Lucia and explained that Julio Cordoza had called her, identifying himself as the letter writer and wanting to meet. Lucia's face was a mask as she listened to me talk to the detective.

"He wanted to meet you here?" Jim asked her.

She nodded. She wasn't giving anything away to a cop, even a friendly one.

"Probably he had something else going on here first. From the looks of things, he was dealing drugs," Stapleton said, matter-of-factly, gazing back toward the Camaro with its trunk lid still open. The medical examiner had arrived, along with an ambulance, and there was a crowd around Julio's body in the front seat of the car.

"Julio didn't deal drugs," Lucia said through gritted teeth.

Jim gave her the once over with his eyes. Then his face broke into his most professional smile. "I guess he was a friend of yours, huh?"

Lucia gave him the once over herself. "Yes, he was," she said quietly.

"I think the drugs were a plant to make it look as if he was killed in a drug deal," I told Stapleton.

His look was skeptical. "A plant?"

"This is related to her brother's death," I said, "not drugs."

Jim looked back and forth between the two of us. "I'm sorry about your friend...and your brother, Miss Chavez," he said. "But this kid comes from one of the most notorious families in Orange County. Criminal activities go back generations with the Cordozas."

Lucia looked as if she wanted to say something, but instead she turned her back to us, looking over at Julio's car. The coroner's people were easing the boy's body onto a wheeled gurney.

"So this is just a coincidence that he gets killed before he can tell us anything?" I asked.

"That's the way it looks to me. Course, it's not my investigation. Maybe Coolidge will turn up something."

I told Jim about the car that had followed Lucia home from the university.

Then I described our near accident caused by the SUV on the freeway. "Why didn't you tell me about these things earlier?" Jim asked.

"What would you have done?"

Pink Carnation

A look of irritation crossed his face. "I would have told you to quit trying to do my job. You're putting yourself at risk and you're doing the same for your student here."

I glanced over at Lucia. She was staring off into space. "I guess we'll go then," I said.

Jim patted my shoulder and gave me reassuring wink. "Look, Phin, I promise I'll keep tabs on what Coolidge finds out about Cordoza's killing. I think you're wrong about this, but I'll keep an open mind." He looked over at Lucia, who was still avoiding looking at either of us. His face became serious "In the meantime, I want you to promise me that you won't do any more investigating on your own. The two of you could have been killed tonight."

I knew he was trying to protect me but I still felt as if he wasn't listening to us. "No promises, Jim. You just be sure your department doesn't drop the ball. I'm going to talk to Elmore again, but that's all I'm planning, for the moment."

Irritation flashed across his face then he forced a smile. "You're hard-headed, you know that?"

I smiled back at him. "It's taken you twenty-five years to find that out?"

His smile broadened and he jabbed me in the stomach. "How could I have forgotten?"

Stapleton checked with Coolidge and was told that it was okay for Lucia and me to leave. Jim gave us both one more fatherly warning about not carrying on an investigation on our own, and headed back to his vehicle.

Lucia and I got back in her Toyota. As we passed Jim Stapleton's unmarked car, I glanced over at the person sitting in the passenger seat. Something about the thick neck and large head outlined in the shadows from the police spotlights looked familiar.

Suddenly the figure's identity popped into focus. It was Randy Fontana, the old detective who was working as a consultant on the film.

Lucia and I drove to where my little sportscar was parked in Norm's parking lot. Lucia wasn't talking much. We were both still shaken.

"Julio was killed so he wouldn't tell us anything," Lucia said in a bitter tone.

"Whoever killed him knows that you and I are looking into your brother's murder. If we'd gotten there earlier, that might have been us who got killed."

"Do you want to stop?" she asked.

"I don't like risking you."

"It was my brother who was killed."

We rode in silence for about a block. Finally, Lucia spoke up. "Are you still going to visit John Elmore?"

"He's still the one with the best motive for killing Lisa Burke. But what Julio told your brother didn't have anything to do with Lisa or Elmore. It was about this character who died forty-five years ago, Raul Lopez."

"Can I go with you?" she asked. We were pulling into Norm's parking lot and I pointed out my car to her.

"I've already been called on the carpet for being involved with you outside of school. You need to go home and I'll talk to Elmore myself."

She started to protest but I interrupted her. "No arguing on this. I'll let you know what I find out tomorrow."

She didn't answer, and I could see that she wasn't happy with my decision.

I got out of the car and opened the door of my MGA. "Are you going home?" I asked.

"What do you care?" she answered spitefully. "As long as I'm not with you, your precious job will be safe." She backed her car away from mine. I watched her head her little orange Tercel back onto Main and into the evening traffic of busy downtown Santa Ana. The office workers from the suburbs had gone home and the cars going by were driven by Mexican-American drivers. Most of them were older American and foreign cars, bought sometime after their best years had expired.

Pink Carnation

Occasionally, a low riding, shiny Camaro or a souped-up pickup truck went by, vibrating with rap music or the sounds of Mariachi. Further down Main, the signs on all the shops were in Spanish. Lucia was a lot more comfortable in this environment than I was. I hoped her anger didn't lure her into doing anything foolish.

    I got into my car and turned the other direction on Main. I'd take the Costa Mesa freeway south to Newport Beach, and then grab the Coast Highway to Laguna Beach. I was going to go talk to John Elmore and that meant going back to the environment in which I was comfortable. No need to worry whether or not I might do something foolish. I usually did.

ELEVEN

It was past eight and Kim would be getting home from her workout at her club, expecting me to greet her. It was my night to cook, which usually meant Pizza Hut. The NBA playoffs were starting and the Lakers were an odds-on favorite to win the Western Conference this year. Kim would be anticipating an evening with the two of us curled up on the couch watching the game.

I phoned Kim and got her on her cell phone before she crossed the tiny bridge linking the island with the rest of Newport Beach. I warned her about the impending dearth of pizza at our house and suggested she might stop and pick up something for herself on the way home. I apologized for not being able to join her and told her about my hope to confront John Elmore in his Laguna Beach home. I didn't mention the death of Julio Cordoza.

Kim was disappointed that we couldn't watch the Lakers' playoff debut together. I told her to save me a seat, but not to wait up if I got home after the game was over. She worried that I was going to miss my dinner. I lied and said that I'd grab something along the way to Laguna.

The traffic began to thin as I sped along the Coast Highway, skirting the edges of the coastal parks that led down to the beaches and the dark Pacific stretching to the western horizon. There were only a few cars left in the parking lots along the highway, since most of the beaches closed at eight. I could see the moon hanging over the bluffs on the northern side of Cameo Cove. The surf was up and the waves were crashing white along the beach.

The California Riviera.

I slowed to pass the ultra-exclusive Emerald Bay community that bordered both sides of the highway. The next cove would be tiny Blue Bay, an even tonier gated community of multi-million dollar estates that hoarded access to its own private lagoon and white sand beach. In the summer, many of the residents would anchor overnight in the lagoon.

Pink Carnation

I'd done it myself a time or two when I was younger, and I knew that there was no fence on the ocean side of the enclave.

Announcing myself to Elmore via the guard at the gate was worth a try, since getting to the lagoon to approach his house from the ocean side was a problem I didn't want to tackle if 1 didn't have to. Not unexpectedly, Elmore's answer to the guard's query about letting me enter was emphatically negative. I thought I looked like I belonged in that kind of a neighborhood, with my camel Armani blazer, silk Evan Piccone tie, and my shiny little forty-plus year old sportscar. The guard looked at me like I was poor white trash.

I turned around and pulled back onto the highway. A quarter of a mile down the road was a field of tall grass that ran out to a grove of pines on a bluff overlooking the ocean sixty feet below. It was the most valuable piece of undeveloped land in Laguna Beach. The developer of Blue Bay Estates had reserved the prime piece of land for himself, but he'd died just as the last of the homes in the development had been completed and had never gotten to build his dream house on his piece of dream property. All of his wealth, including this piece of land, had been tied up in the courts for years, with his heirs fighting over each nickel and ounce of dirt, the old man having left no will or trust to guide the dispersal of his fortune. I shuddered when I imagined the dismal fate of his heirs: having been born rich and then actually needing to work for a living.

I pulled my car off the road and backed the little roadster far enough under the overhanging trees at the edge of the property that someone would have had to be looking for the car to find it.

The almost full moon enabled me to see the narrow, but well-worn dirt path meandering through the grass to the stand of pines. I'd brought the flashlight from the MG's glove box but I didn't need it until I reached the trees, whose overhanging branches blocked the thin shafts of moonlight and created a forbidding darkness, like the entrance to an impenetrable jungle. Because the pines ran to the edge of the bluff, I didn't want to wander around sightless. I switched on the flashlight and followed the path into the blackness of the grove.

The pathway down the cliff was steep; and in wet weather, even a heavy fog, it wasn't navigable. Fortunately, the dry, hot, Santa Ana days that we'd experienced recently had wrung the last drop of moisture from the soil and it crumbled in small dry clods that tumbled down the slope ahead of me like mini-avalanches. I gingerly made my way down the cliff, digging my heels into the arid dirt while I felt for the occasional bush or clump of grass to keep me from pitching headfirst to the beach below. Ascending the cliff had always been much easier, and I finally turned around backward and backed down, keeping my head turned to see where I was going.

Luckily, the tide was out. I had about ten yards of hard sand beach that followed the foot of the bluff around to the lagoon on the other side. The sand was ruining my Bruno Magli penny loafers, but at least I didn't have to wade through the surf with them. I could hear the waves crashing against the five or six rocks that protruded their round, guano covered heads from the water in a line that resembled a parade of small soldiers, starting about fifteen yards offshore. From the beach side of the bluff, I could hear the soft pounding of the waves and the drawn out hiss of the water running back across the sand, sounding like a chorus of snakes in the darkness.

When I rounded the head of the bluff and stepped onto the smooth, curved beach of Blue Bay, its white sand softly illuminated in the moonlight, I could see the concrete steps that led to the properties above. The house Elmore was renting was the first one at the top of the steps. My plan was to come across the back lawn and onto the patio, which, if I remembered correctly, was off of the dining room and kitchen.

Elmore was sitting, smoking. He sat in a wooden beach chair, half in and half out of the house, looking like a faintly glowing statue, propping the screen door open. I was able to creep across the neatly manicured lawn and onto the brick patio about ten feet away from him before he turned. When he saw me he panicked, leaping from his chair then backing inside the house and slamming the screen door, peering out like a trapped rat.

"What are you doing here?" he asked, the terror evident in his voice.

"This isn't an easy place to get to," I said, pulling his abandoned beach chair in front of the screen door and sitting down heavily. The climb up the stairs had tired me.

Elmore continued to peer out at me as though I was the devil incarnate. I wasn't sure he actually knew who I was.

"Phineas Routledge," I said, hoping to help him out, "the Third? Doghouse Reilly?"

"I gave instructions to keep you out," he said icily, though his voice still shook.

"I snuck in—used the sea route."

He glanced in horror at the stairs leading down to the beach, as if he'd suddenly remembered that he'd forgotten to close the back door.

"I'm going to call the police."

I figured he was bluffing. "Why don't you come out or I come in and we can discuss this?"

He turned away for a few moments, then returned to his spot behind the screen door, this time with a drink in his hand and cigarette hanging from his mouth. He removed the cigarette and took a hearty slug from the drink. Fortified, he turned his attention back to me. "How do I know you're not here to kill me?"

I cast a covetous look at his glass. *Some people are simply poor hosts.* "What are you talking about?" I said.

He didn't budge from behind his screen door. "Thornberg was killed. Maybe someone wants me dead, too."

"You think Thornberg was murdered?"

"Maybe."

"Why would someone want to murder him?"

He searched my face. "How would I know? He's dead, just like Lisa and that spic kid."

"Lisa Burk was pregnant with your child." Technically, I only knew that she was pregnant, but I could make a better point if I said the child was Elmore's.

Elmore's eyes widened. He took another gulp from his drink, and then lit a second cigarette, although he hadn't put the first one out.

"How do you know?"

"Her mother told me."

"I ...I didn't know," he stammered. He looked past me out to sea. I followed his gaze. Three or four small lights dotted the horizon; boats making their way up the coast or back to port before the night closed in completely.

"How about if either you come out or I come in?" I asked.

The writer gave me a suspicious look. He pushed the screen door open, tentatively.

I spread the sides of my sportcoat "No guns, knives, bombs."

Elmore cautiously emerged from behind the screen door. I got up from his chair and pushed it back over to him. He pulled it within a few feet of the retrieved another chair from the patio and sat down across from him.

"It's uncanny," he said.

"What's uncanny?" I asked.

"Sally Umstead; she was pregnant, also."

"Who?"

"Sally Umstead, the girl that Lisa was playing. The one who was murdered in 1959."

"I didn't know her name was Umstead. That's a big name in Orange County. The Umstead's pay for a big chunk of my university. Michael Umstead's on our Board of Trustees."

Elmore gave a small frown of indifference. "The family didn't want the movie made. They were afraid that the fact of Sally's pregnancy would come out." Suddenly his face became sad again. "I'm sorry about Lisa, and the baby." He took another drink and looked back at the dark ocean. A faint breeze rustled the tall palms. The wind blew toward the ocean; it was a lingering shadow of the Santa Ana wind that had been blasting down from the San Gabriel Mountains for the past week. The air was warm and dry. So was my mouth.

"You mind if l fix myself one of whatever you're having?" I asked.

Elmore looked startled. He started to stand, almost reflexively. "Sorry, I should have offered you something."

"Sit down," I said, exhibiting my characteristic graciousness. "I know where the kitchen is. A friend of mine used to rent this house."

"Of course," Elmore answered in a distracted voice. He was still staring off into the blackness in front of him.

I edged around Elmore and opened the screen door to the kitchen. A bottle of Tanqueray gin sat, half full, on the marble counter top. I opened the refrigerator and found an already opened bottle of Schweppes and, next to it, a lime. After opening only two cupboards I found a glass. The knives were conveniently placed in a wooden block on top of the counter. I filled the glass with ice, sliced off a sliver of lime using a meat-cutting knife that was much too big for the job, and poured in a half of a glass of gin, then topped it off with tonic water. When I returned to the patio, Elmore looked as if he hadn't moved.

"How secret was the fact that the Umstead girl was pregnant?" I asked.

Elmore pulled his attention away from whatever musings were occupying him and forced himself to look at me. "It was never reported in the paper. Old man Umstead paid off the cops and the coroner to keep it hush-hush."

"How did you find out?"

"I guessed; the same way you found out that I was the father of Lisa's baby." A thin smile crossed his face.

"How do you know you guessed correctly?" I asked.

"I interviewed the Umsteads when I was writing the script. The old man is dead but the mother's not and there's a brother who runs the family businesses. I talked to him, mostly. I told him that I knew his sister had been pregnant."

"What did he say?"

"He offered to pay me to keep it out of the movie ...and to sue me if I put it in."

"And...?"

"I told him to keep his money. I wasn't going to put in the script, anyway. Even the dead deserve some privacy." Elmore drained his glass and stood up. "Can I freshen yours?"

I was fine and I watched him go into the kitchen. The news about Sally Umstead had me thinking. The Umstead family had enough money and influence to put pressure on the Sheriff's department if they didn't want a lot of attention focused on an accident that would revive memories of Sally's murder. Had Ramon found out about Sally Umstead's pregnancy? Was he blackmailing the family? Michael Umstead was adamant about not wanting Thornberg to make a movie in Orange County. And Umstead and Thornberg had argued the night Thornberg had died.

My thoughts were interrupted by Elmore's return. He was drinking gin, but without ice and without a lime. Probably without tonic, too.

"Did Ramon Chavez ever ask you about Sally Umstead?" I asked.

He nodded, taking a short sip from his glass and making a little face. "He was full of questions. He was a lot more interested in Raul Lopez than about Sally, but he asked about both."

"Did he know about Sally's pregnancy?"

Elmore took another short sip and made another face. "I don't know. So far as I knew, I was the only one on the film who knew, except Fontana, of course."

"Randy Fontana, the old cop who hangs around the set?"

Elmore studied my face, as though he was trying to tell how much I knew. "Fontana was the detective in charge of the investigation back in 1959."

"So he knew about Sally's pregnancy."

He nodded. "Uh huh. I assume he's been well paid to keep quiet about it for the last forty years."

Pink Carnation

I remembered Elmore's discomfort when he'd looked over at Fontana the day I visited the set. "Was Fontana keeping an eye on things for the Umsteads? Checking on you?"

Elmore shrugged. He lit a cigarette. The breeze carried the smoke past me. I could smell the sweet odor of tobacco. "Fontana is still cozy with the family, especially the brother who runs things. Whether he's watching things for them, I can't say."

"Did Fontana tell you Sally was pregnant?"

More smoke drifted my way. Elmore's sips on his drink were less dainty and he wasn't making faces anymore. "No. But when I told him that I knew, he talked about it openly."

"Suppose Ramon Chavez found out about the pregnancy and tried to blackmail the Umsteads? Would Fontana step in and do something?"

Elmore smiled and flicked his cigarette ashes onto the bricks. The glowing embers swirled past me into the night. "You mean like shoot him during a movie scene? You should write novels, Professor."

It was dark enough he couldn't see me blush. Maybe I was getting carried away. "Would the Umstead's pay Ramon to keep quiet?"

"They offered to pay me."

"What do you know about Raul Lopez?" I asked.

"He was a poor spic kid. He'd had one or two run-ins with the cops, was a high school drop out who worked somewhere as a houseboy. That's probably where he met Sally Umstead. She liked to defy authority, especially her father's and the spic took advantage of that wild hair in her. Nobody knows how many times they saw each other. At least one time before the murder because he knocked her up."

"How do you know the child was Lopez'?"

Elmore took a long drink and carefully placed the glass on a wicker table next to him. He'd finished half of it already. "It's just an assumption. There was no DNA testing back then, so nobody knows for sure. Since it all got swept under the rug, it really didn't matter."

I told him about Julio Cordoza's note, the phone call to Lucia, and his murder. "The cops think it's a gang/drug thing but Julio's message was about Raul Lopez."

Elmore peered at me, each of us little more than an outline in the weak light from the house. "Goddamn it!" he said. "I shouldn't have listened to Fontana. He told me there wasn't anything to find out about the Mex kid, but Lopez must be the key."

"The key to what?"

"The murders of Lopez and Sally Umstead back in 1959." He stubbed out one cigarette and immediately lit another. "Some sadistic bastard killed a young girl, one that was pregnant to boot. For forty-four years he's gotten away with it. Why do you think I write about a crime like this? I want to find out who was responsible, even after all these years. And I want to catch the sonofabitch."

I remembered Elmore's own experience with murder. His mother had been killed when he was just a kid. She'd been raped and strangled. The case was still unsolved.

"Does Chavez' sister think that her brother found out who the killer is?" Elmore asked.

I noticed that he used the present tense. He was assuming that the murderer was still out there somewhere. "Frankly, she doesn't know what he found out, except it was about the murder and it involved Raul Lopez...and he thought that knowing it put his life in danger. I guess it did."

Elmore stroked his mustache, his eyes narrowed in thought. "The killer's worried. That's good. If he had to kill again to cover things up then he's bound to have left more clues." He rubbed his hands together.

"I thought you were worried that Thornberg's killer might come after you."

Elmore frowned. "Not if Thornberg was killed because of what he learned about Raul Lopez from Ramon Chavez. I didn't learn anything from the kid. It wasn't me who was cornholing the spic, it was Thornberg."

Pink Carnation

"You writers have a gift for words."

Elmore sounded determined. "I'm going to talk to Fontana! That old bastard didn't tell me all he knows about Lopez."

I was starting to feel better about Elmore. He was as determined as I was, except his goal was to solve a murder that occurred back in 1959, rather than less than a week ago.

"How about if we pool resources," I suggested. "You talk to Fontana. Lucia and I will find out what the Cordoza kid knew. We can talk to his grandfather. It seems to me that we've got a common goal here, maybe for different reasons, but we both want to find out what there is to know about Raul Lopez that is enough to kill for."

Elmore drew thoughtfully on his cigarette then sipped his drink. From the shadows that partially obscured his face, I could feel his eyes boring into me. "You've found out a lot in a short time, Professor. Not to mention getting to me when I tried to duck you." He nodded. "OK, I'll work on Fontana and you and the girl work on the spics."

"If we're going to be partners, you might lay off the reference to spics, especially around Lucia Chavez." I tried to stare him down but his face was just a dark shadow outlined by the backdrop of house lights behind his head.

"I can be politically correct when I have to be," he replied.

I glanced at my watch. It was after ten. "Maybe you'll call the gate so I don't have to swim around the point and climb back up the cliff."

He made the call. I declined his offer of a ride back to my car. A walk in the fresh air might get the smell of his cigarette smoke out of my jacket. Besides, Elmore was almost three sheets to the wind after that last gin and tonic. I left him sitting outside, smoking, his eyes half closed. He was either deep in thought or falling asleep.

When I reached the gate on foot, the old man looked surprised to see me. I was too tired to explain. I walked down the edge of PCH until I came to my little white roadster, still safely tucked into the trees on the side of the road. As I got into my car, a couple of passing autos slowed, probably wondering what I was doing in the bushes. One of the cars resembled Lucia's Tercel, but I didn't get enough of a look to tell. The other was a late model SUV, the driver of which raised his high beams, and almost blinded me. I waited a moment until the cars were safely around the next corner, then swung a U- turn and headed back toward Newport Beach. I kept my eyes on the rear view mirror to see if the Tercel would show up behind me, but it didn't.

I called ahead and Kim informed me that the Lakers had lost their first round game to Seattle. Nobody but Shaquille had been able to hit anything for the Lakers. Kobe racked up three fouls in the first quarter and sat out half of the game. Kim had saved some Pizza for me. She asked me how my evening had gone. I'd witnessed a murder, been accused of using one of my students as a connection for a drug buy, and struck a partnership with a bigoted, whacko writer. I told her that it couldn't have gone better.

TWELVE

I stayed up thinking about what had transpired that evening, downing a couple more gin and tonics, just to keep my mind from getting away from itself. I tossed around the idea that the Umsteads were behind the suppression of the Sheriff's investigation of the movie shooting and the more I thought about it the more likely it seemed. On the other hand, I didn't see any way that they could have been connected to the deaths of the two actors or that of Julio Cordoza, although Michael Umstead would have been pretty high on my list of suspects if it could be proved that Thornberg's death wasn't an accident. When I finally climbed into bed, Kim was asleep and I lay awake with the window open, listening to the sounds of the boats docked along the waterfront and trying to shut off my thoughts. The sounds of lines clinking against masts and hulls was musical and it reminded me of my childhood, listening to the night sounds from Marblehead Harbor through my open bedroom window. Sometimes Kim and I spent the night moored offshore on our boat, a steel-hulled, thirty-five foot '58 Chris Craft Roamer with twin gas engines that I'd inherited from my parents. As a kid, I'd cruised with my parents as far north as Maine's Christmas Cove and south to Mystic Connecticut and when my parents had died, the trim powerboat was the only piece of property that I couldn't bear to sell. I had it hauled across the country and it sat tied to the dock in front of my home. Kim had insisted on refurbishing the galley and it was now outfitted in custom ceramic tile, a new copper sink and shiny new appliances that matched the all-white paint on the hull and superstructure.

The gin was keeping me awake and I was sensitive to every sound. I recognized the familiar clinks and groans from my own boat and I suddenly became alert when their rhythm was interrupted. I heard the creak of footsteps on the boat's deck. It was probably just kids, who sometimes boarded the boats along the promenade, usually on a dare. I got up and padded downstairs in my pajamas. Cracking open the drapes on the front bay window, I peered outside; but nothing was visible except the boat against the dock. The promenade was barren in either direction.

Opening the door, I edged onto the patio, keeping my ears tuned for any sounds and my eyes glued to the Chris Craft. I thought I saw movement on the stem of the boat, a head bobbing up now and then. It didn't look like kids. I felt a cold chill down my back. Pushing open the gate that led to the promenade, I crept stealthily across to the dock, stepping over the little wooden gate, which had a squeak that would give away my presence if l tried to open it. A heavy-set figure was up against the hatch that led below deck. He was busy with the lock. I edged closer.

"What do you think you're doing?" I asked, stepping onto the deck about five feet forward of the intruder.

"I'm breaking into your goddamn boat." The man was almost my height and he was dressed in a dark T-shirt and dark pants. I couldn't make out much of his face but he was dark complexioned and thickly built. He let go of the lock on the hatch and backed away to face me. "You think you can stop me?"

It occurred to me that whoever this was, he might be on drugs—PCP or something like it. That might account for his brazen belligerence.

"Off the boat, buddy," I said, trying to talk to him in a normal tone.

"Why don't you make me?" He said, still not moving.

I felt my stomach tighten. I ought to retreat and call the cops, but I was getting pissed off. I took a step toward him, keeping my weight centered so I could move in either direction.

From the waist of his pants he pulled a knife—long, skinny, and shiny in the lights from the promenade. I was close enough to see his face now. He was a dark, heavyset man with a mustache, in his late thirties or early forties. He might have been Hispanic. His eyes looked past me.

"Grab him," he said.

Pink Carnation

I heard footsteps behind me and realized I'd been sucked into a trap. There were two of them! Just great. My heart was beating like a jackrabbit's and my mind was racing. If I hesitated, I'd have them both to deal with. I pivoted sideways to reduce my size as a target and aimed a barefoot kick at the heavyset man's chest. He staggered backward and I spun around and delivered a straight-arm blow to the Adam's apple of the second assailant, who was at least as big as the first. He dropped what looked like a gun and grabbed his throat with both hands. I felt a searing pain along my right side. The first man had recovered enough to stab me with his knife and he had his body up next to mine. I elbowed him as hard as I could in the ribs, and when I felt him move backward, I decided that wisdom was rapidly becoming the better part of valor and my safest bet was in the water, rather than on the deck, where these two clowns could still reach me. I lunged forward, taking one long stride and launching myself headfirst over the stern of the boat. I swam as far as I could beneath the surface of the shallow water, holding my breath until I felt my lungs were going to burst. When I finally surfaced fifty feet from the boat, the two men were standing on the stern, staring down at the water.

I took a deep breath and dove again, this time heading back toward the shore but trying to stay away from my own dock. It was difficult in the murky, black water, but I finally felt, rather than saw, the shadow of my neighbor's boat above me and off to my right. Just in time. My arms and legs were starting to feel as though they had lead weights attached to them. I swam back to the surface and edged my way along the waterline of the sleek sailing yacht until I came to the bow. Peering around the bow of the yacht, I could just make out the two men clambering off my boat. They walked to the end of the dock and scanned the water once more, then turned and crossed the promenade to the street.

When they'd disappeared around the edge of the house, I waded ashore and followed them. I made it around the house just in time to see a dark SUV disappearing down the street. I felt a sharp pain in my side, which I thought was the effect of being winded, until I pressed my hand against my ribs underneath my soaking pajamas and felt something warm and sticky.

I woke Kim, who looked at my wound and declared it superficial, spraying it with antibiotic and bandaging it. The knife had barely broken the skin. I called the Newport Beach Police, who were there within minutes and I told them the whole story. The police surmised that I had foiled the men's robbery plans but I wasn't so sure. My two assailants seemed far too aggressive for mere thieves. It felt to me as though they were out to get me; that the robbery was just a way to lure me out to the boat. I kept that theory to myself. The police made me visit the hospital emergency room where Kim and I waited for half an hour before a fuzzy-cheeked young physician concurred that my wound was superficial and replaced the bandage that Kim had given me. When we got home and finally made it back to bed, it was nearly four a.m. When I woke up the next morning, I had a mild headache and a major pain in my side. I had no need to be on campus until my class at four, so I put on a pair of shorts, sat outside in the sun, tried to keep from bumping my side where the bandage was, and drank strong coffee. Kim offered to stay home and take care of me, but I told her I didn't want to feel like an invalid just because I'd had a scratch. As usual, she was up, had jogged the five or so miles around the perimeter of the island, come back and showered and dressed before I was even out of bed.

The Santa Ana wind was dead but the sun felt warm, even in the cool morning air. The encounter with the hoodlums on the boat made me feel as if I'd become a target. But every time I tried to focus my mind on the attack, I started to drift off, and my thoughts became jumbled and surreal. I had better luck focusing my attention on the morning parade of sailboats, mainsail's down, jibs fluttering languidly, using their inboard motors for power while they made their way past my front patio and around the point of the peninsula, like so many brightly colored cars on an amusement park ride -heading off for a day's pleasure. The more I

Pink Carnation

thought about someone violating my own boat, the angrier I became. I tried to close my eyes and let the sun relax me.

The telephone rang, but I didn't move, and I let the answering machine do its job. I could hear the voice on the line; it was Jim Stapleton. He said it was urgent but I wasn't ready to rise and face another crisis, so I finished my cup of coffee before I shuffled into the kitchen and grabbed the portable phone. I returned to my spot on the patio, straightening my chair, and positioning myself just right with respect to the sun before finally dialing Jim back.

"You were at John Elmore's last night?" Stapleton asked without so much as a "good morning."

I grunted an affirmative.

"What time did you leave?"

"Ten or so," I answered, a sense of foreboding starting to build. "Why? What happened?"

"Elmore's dead. He was stabbed to death in his house in Laguna Beach sometime before midnight last night. A neighbor found the body on the patio this morning."

I felt weak. My head was filled with a rushing sound, like a river was drowning my thoughts, pulling me under its surface. It was difficult to focus my attention. I had been talking with Elmore less than twelve hours before. We had agreed to work together. Now he was murdered? I couldn't understand how that could be. "Do the Laguna Police have any leads?" I asked.

There was a pause on the other end of the phone. "Blue Bay Estates are an unincorporated area. This is gonna be a Sheriff's department case."

"You mean you're doing the investigating?"

"Not me personally, but it's in my division. Someone's gonna want to talk to you."

"Me? Last night I got attacked and stabbed in my own house and now I'm going to be questioned about a murder?"

"What are you talking about?"

I told him about the attack on the boat.

"Dammit, Phin, I told you that you need a security system for that boat."

"Thanks for the sympathetic ear, bro. Did you say Elmore was stabbed?"

"With a knife from his own kitchen. And the assailant left some of his own blood on the patio."

I was in deep manure. I looked down at the bandage on my side and remembered Elmore's knife that I'd used to slice the lime for my drink. The knife seemed humungous in my memory; just the perfect implement to slit someone's gullet-whatever a gullet was. My fingerprints would be all over it. My head was still spinning.

"What do I do next?"

"Talk to the investigating officers. You can do it in my office. I'll be here—on your side. I mean it, Phin." I could hear the emotion in his voice. It made me even more worried.

"I'm going to call someone, then I'll be right down," I said.

The ache in my side was gone. When I thought about John Elmore, I felt something cold in the pit of my stomach. Elmore was unique: a genius as a writer—a classic case of sublimation. I'd also misjudged him, taking his aloof manner as callousness, rather than the schizoid preoccupation that it was. Elmore was engaged in a doomed quest to protect the vulnerable women of the world from sadistic predators. But he was always too late; left to solve the insoluble crime years after the horror had occurred and compelled to repeat his obsession again and again until he finally became a victim himself. I was stunned and saddened by his loss.

Even before I called Bill Hoskins, my lawyer, I called Kim. She wasn't in her office and she didn't answer her cell phone, so I paged her. Within minutes she called back. I told her about Elmore—and my surreptitious entry into his house, my sharing a drink and slicing a lime with a kitchen knife that probably was the murder weapon.

Pink Carnation

Kim offered to call Bill Hoskins and come herself if I wanted. I told her I'd call her afterward and tell her what happened. I was assuming I wouldn't be making the call from a jail cell.

When I arrived at the Sheriff's Department administrative building, I expected everyone to stare at me, like those criminals you see on television, hustled to their cars, holding their coats over their heads to conceal their faces. To my relief, no one took any notice of me. I told the sergeant at the front desk that I had an appointment with Jim Stapleton and he logged me in, then let me pass.

"Should I have worn orange?" I asked, unbuttoning my tweed jacket and taking a seat in one of the leather chairs in front of Stapleton's desk. The top of his desk was clear except for an in-box and an out-box, both about half full of papers, and one more stack of folders on the far front corner of the desk away from my chair. Behind him, on hanging bookshelves filled with large black books of legal codes, were pictures of his wife, Karen, and two daughters, Amy and Tina. I'd been best man at Jim and Karen's wedding. I was godfather to both of their daughters. A small pale ivy-like plant grew from a white ceramic container, its leafy tendrils cascading over the sides of the pot and hanging a foot or so below the shelf. I'd sat across this same desk many times in the past, but this time it felt different. This time I had a cold feeling of apprehension in the pit of my stomach.

Jim looked crisp and fresh, dressed in a light wool suit, gray, with thin stripes of blue. His collar was starched and his tie in place. He looked ready to sell me a policy of life insurance. "You're not even officially a suspect," he answered. "You're probably the last one to see Elmore before he was killed, other than the killer, but right now Jarvis and Mellons just want to ask you questions."

"That's what you guys always say," I said. "Can I talk to you as a friend, or are you officially involved?" I asked.

"I'm just a friend, unless you tell me you murdered him. Short of that, you can tell me whatever you want to. People know my relationship with you, Phin. They're not going to press me about anything you tell me in confidence."

I told him everything that had transpired between Elmore and myself—except the part about my using the kitchen knife. No sense tying the knot around my own neck.

"What did you and he talk about?" he asked.

"Lisa Burke was pregnant. Her mother told me." He nodded; evidently the pregnancy wasn't news to him. But then Melanie Burke had said that she'd found out from the coroner, so Jim must have gotten the same information. "I wanted to see how Elmore would react to the news."

He leaned forward. "And...?"

I glanced over at the small silver-encased clock on the file cabinet in the corner. Jarvis and Mellons should be along any minute and my lawyer still hadn't arrived. "Maybe we'd better talk about this some other time. When do the bad cops arrive? My lawyer still isn't here."

Jim's intense expression melted. "Sorry. You're right. Mellons and Jarvis will be here any minute. If you want to wait until your lawyer's present, I'll phone and stall them a while longer."

At that moment, Bill Hoskins appeared at the doorway. I introduced him to Jim and thanked him for coming.

Bill Hoskins looked the part of a lawyer. He was slim, balding, and in his mid-fifties. He wore glasses, a bow tie, and a seersucker suit that was gray with pinstripes. He was probably wearing suspenders under his jacket. His shirt was crisp and white, his wingtips so highly polished, that they reflected the lights from the room. He looked like Gregory Peck in *To Kill a Mockingbird* and I suspected that the resemblance was deliberate. Bill's face was rounder—Henry Fonda playing Gregory Peck. He spoke with the slow easy-going manner of Fonda.

"I'm not really a criminal lawyer, Phineas. I can advise you this morning, but you'll be wanting me to call in someone else if this is serious."

I looked over at Jim Stapleton. "Is this serious?"

Jim looked back and forth between Hoskins and me. "A man was murdered and you were the last known person to have been with him."

"Could be serious," I said to my lawyer. "Are they going to arrest me this morning?" I asked Jim

"I doubt it. At this stage of an investigation it's not usual to arrest someone unless they've got strong evidence."

Hoskins started to say something but I interrupted him. "What kind of evidence would that be?" The bad feeling in the pit of my stomach was starting to spread throughout my body, like a metastasizing cancer.

Stapleton looked at Hoskins before answering. "Eyewitness, fingerprints on the murder weapon. They found blood that they've already identified as coming from someone other than Elmore. Apparently there was a trail of it leading out of the house."

I felt the bandage on my side. "Blood and fingerprints?" I was envisioning leaving the room in handcuffs, telling Jim to call Kim and tell her what happened to me as I was being taken across the street, booked and thrown in the slammer with the rest of the thieves and murderers. Hoskins gave me a worried look.

"I was there...I touched things. I also got stabbed last night." I said.

"You got stabbed?" Hoskins asked, a hint of accusation in his tone.

"I was attacked last night on my boat." I gave a helpless shrug. "Sorry about the timing."

We all sat while Stapleton put in a call to the detectives who were investigating.

Jim Stapleton began drumming his fingers on the polished top of his desk, a frown on his face. He was staring straight ahead, preoccupied. Bill Hoskins appeared relaxed. But then Bill always appeared relaxed. I was envisioning myself in shackles.

Stapleton's door was open and the two detectives suddenly appeared. Stapleton introduced us all. Paul Jarvis was only an inch or two shorter than me and outweighed me by a good fifty pounds, most of which was probably muscle, judging from the size of his shoulders and arms, but some of which protruded as a well-stuffed belly. He looked to be in his early or mid thirties, with a big serious face, a large square jaw, short-cropped hair and a broad, walrus mustache. He wore a short-sleeved polo shirt, open at the neck. His pants were starched and lightweight cotton and he had on a pair of cheap loafers, scuffed around the heels. Holstered on his belt was the biggest pistol I'd ever seen. Jarvis looked us over with noncommittal eyes and stuck out his hand to each of us, unsmiling. When his gaze found Jim Stapleton, he frowned outright.

Rudy Mellons was the older of the two detectives. He carried no gun and took his time shaking each of our hands. Mellons also wore no coat but I recognized the labels he was wearing. His soft, cream-colored cotton shirt was Armani, as was the figured maroon tie he wore with it. His slacks were Joseph Abboud and his tasseled soft leather loafers, which shone with the same radiance as Bill Hoskins' wing tips, were Kenneth Cole. I figured he was either on the take, or he had a rich wife. Mellons's face was lined and tan, his nose bigger, more veined and pock-marked than it should have been for anyone who hadn't consumed large quantities of alcohol at some time in his life. He was gray and balding, probably in his mid-fifties.

"You mind if we take Mr. Routledge down the hall to one of the conference rooms?" Jarvis asked. He addressed Jim Stapleton, who, even if he wasn't investigating the case, was still Jarvis' superior. When he spoke, Jarvis' voice was surprisingly congenial.

"Professor Routledge would like his lawyer present and, as his friend, I'd like to be here myself." Stapleton smiled and looked back and forth between the two detectives.

Jarvis' frown broadened and his back stiffened. Before he could speak, Mellons jumped in. The older detective's voice had a rougher edge to it than his partner's. "That's fine with us, Jim. If you don't mind, though, we'd like to keep the conversation between the Professor, his lawyer and us. Those ground-rules gonna work?" Mellons' jaw was set. He was ready for an argument.

Jim raised his hands in a gesture of submission. "No problem."

Pink Carnation

"When were you at Elmore's house last night?" Jarvis asked me, his voice casual. For the first time, he had a friendly look on his face. I'd thought Mellons would do most of the questioning and Jarvis would do the beatings. Maybe that part came later. Mellons was sitting with one leg over the other, his creased pants pulled up neatly to avoid wrinkling. He had a small note pad on his knee. He was frowning and unscrewing an expensive looking gold pen.

"I got there about 8:30 or so. Right after I left Detective Stapleton in Santa Ana." I threw in the reference to Jim with the vague hope that it would make it seem as if what I was doing was semi-official. I glanced over at Jim and he nodded. Neither Jarvis nor Mellons seemed to notice. The latter had apparently given up on his fancy pen and was writing with a cheap plastic one.

"Did you have an appointment with Elmore?" Jarvis asked.

"Not exactly," I said. "I tried to get an appointment but his secretary couldn't locate him." In a minute I'd probably tell him that my dog ate my invitation.

Jarvis gave me a small smile. I suspected that I was being led down the garden path, but I was desperate enough that the smile still made me feel good.

"What happened when you tried to get in the compound to see him?" Jarvis asked.

"He acted as if he didn't want to see me, but you know how writers are. They're basically shy people."

"But you got into the compound anyway, on foot."

"I'm a big fan."

"How did Elmore react when you appeared at his door?"

"He was surprised to see me. After his initial reaction to me being there, he got friendly. He even asked me to have a drink."

"And did you?"

"Yes."

" So there should be a glass with your prints on it?" Jarvis looked at me, his eyebrows raised in question.

I realized that I'd said too much. "Yes," I said, swallowing. "Did you touch anything else while you were there?"

I looked at Bill Hoskins. I hoped he was good at reading desperation in his client's eyes.

"My client's not denying touching anything but I'd rather he not answer that question right now."

Jarvis raised his eyebrows in surprise. Over to the side I heard Mellons make an inarticulate grunt. I glanced over. He was staring at me, nodding his head.

Jarvis looked over at Bill Hoskins. "You know it makes your client kinda suspect in our eyes when he can't answer simple questions about what he did at the murder scene."

Bill smiled back. "I'm sure my client is willing to answer your questions. Since I'm not really a criminal lawyer, I'd just rather have him not answer until I've gotten him an attorney who knows more about this sort of thing. It's my reluctance, not his, Detective."

Jarvis nodded. He knew he'd been outmaneuvered. "Elmore called the gate and asked them to let you out. Why didn't he give you a ride back to your car?"

"I wanted to walk. He was a little drunk."

"So you walked back out, through the gate, and down the road to your car?"

I nodded.

"What time was that—when you left Elmore's house?"

"Ten-thirty or so. I looked at my watch right before I left."

"And what time did you get home?"

"Before eleven."

Jarvis reached up a large hand and scratched his neck in thought. He looked over at Mellons, then back at me. "The killer left some of his blood at the scene. You don't happen to have any open wounds on your body do you?"

"Wounds?" I asked, as though I suddenly had no idea what language the detective was speaking.

Pink Carnation

"Knife wounds." Jarvis said patiently, not lowering his eyes from mine.

I winced. "You know it's the silliest thing, but I actually do."

The two cops both leaned forward. "You do?" Jarvis said. He must have thought that this latest revelation was too good to be true.

I told them about the attack on the boat, explaining that the Newport Beach Police had a record of the whole thing.

"Kind of an amazing coincidence, isn't it? You getting stabbed the very night Elmore is killed and his attacker also appears to have been stabbed. What do you think, Rudy?" Jarvis looked over at his partner.

Mellons was shaking his head, frowning. He slapped his note pad against his thigh. When he looked up, he looked at me, then at Bill Hoskins, still frowning. He caught Jarvis's eye and shook his head again. He was a bundle of negativity. "I think the Professor and his fancy lawyer think they're dealing with a couple of yokels. Routledge hasn't told us anything we didn't already know, except that he probably left fingerprints and blood at the scene of the crime. He gives us some cock-and-bull story about getting attacked on his boat, and he and his lawyer act like they think we're gonna swallow all this bullshit."

Mellons looked over at me with a sour look. He rubbed the end of his pen with his thumb. "We can arrest you now, Professor Routledge or we can wait a day or so, until the fingerprints and blood samples come through. I'm inclined toward now. I think you're a smart-ass who thinks he can get away with murder."

Bill Hoskins looked stunned. It wasn't the polite maneuvering between lawyers that he was used to.

I should have been frightened, but the detectives' arrogant attitude had grated on me. I felt my muscles tighten and my face getting hot. "You obviously haven't got diddly-shit as far as evidence goes, Detective, " I said, staring Mellons down. "If you arrest me on what I just told you, I'll sue your ass off."

Jarvis smiled, watching his partner to see what he would do.

Casey Dorman

Mellons stood up, angrily slapping his notepad against his thigh. He looked over at Detective Jarvis. "I love it when someone tries to threaten us. It's the kind of thing we remember later."

"Watch it, Rudy," Jim Stapleton said. He was leaning back in his chair, his eyes narrowed as he watched the older detective, who was standing facing Hoskins and me. "Remember where you are."

Mellons glared at him, clenching his jaw, but saying nothing. He looked over at his younger partner, but Jarvis just sat in his chair, his face a bland mask.

Stapleton cleared his throat. "Seems like I heard that there were some things taken from Elmore's house — even from his person. Makes it kind of look like robbery might have been the motive." He looked over at me, an inquisitive look on his face. "You need a new Rolex, Phineas?"

I tapped the crystal on my own Rolex. "Mine seems to be working fine." Mellons clenched his jaw so that the muscle in his cheek stood out. "You two are a great comedy team. Let's see how funny the professor is when he's looking out from behind bars." He looked down at Stapleton, a deep scowl creasing his alcoholic face.

Jim looked up at Rudy Mellons, a hard smile playing around the corners of his mouth. "I guess the captain might be upset if he heard you booked someone in a robbery-murder case and your suspect had no motive for robbery."

Mellons rubbed his hand across his mouth in a savage gesture. He shifted back and forth on his feet, like a boxer looking for an opening, and continued to glare at Stapleton.

"Let's go, Rudy," Jarvis said, standing. "Let's do a little more homework before we go off half-cocked." He looked over at me. The congeniality had left his face and he stared at me with a hard, serious look. "I got a feeling the fingerprints and blood samples are gonna show us something."

Mellon's shoulders slumped. He looked down at me with disgust. I smiled back. The two detectives left the room without saying goodbye.

"Was that a gag or did I really come close to being arrested?" I asked Stapleton.

"Mellons might have done it, if Jarvis didn't stop him. They haven't got enough to arrest you and the robbery angle really points in another direction. You've got zero motive." He looked up at the ceiling for a moment, thinking. "If your fingerprints are on the weapon though, or your blood type matches the blood at the murder scene, they could pull you in. At least you'll be high up on their suspect list, which you probably are already."

His words didn't make me feel any more comfortable. "What do I do?" I asked.

Jim looked at Bill Hoskins, who was listening attentively. "Bill, you'd better find Phin a criminal lawyer, just in case." He looked back at me. "I think I can convince the captain that arresting you doesn't make sense."

His words relieved me. "You think it was just a robbery? Remember, Julio Cordoza was killed too...and Brian Thornberg."

Jim shook his head, a look of irritation crossing his face. "Don't even go there, Phin. Thornberg died of natural causes and the Cordoza kid was killed in a drug deal. Elmore getting killed after you talked to him was just a freak coincidence."

Bill Hoskins looked confused. "Anybody care to give me a clue as to what you're talking about?" he said.

I gave Bill a brief synopsis of why I'd been at Elmore's and my interest in the deaths of Ramon Chavez and Lisa Burke.

"Sounds like a matter for the Sheriff's Department, not you," Hoskins drawled.

I looked over at Jim Stapleton. He was smiling. "It's your lawyer's advice, Phin. You ought to take it."

"Thanks," I grumbled. I got up to leave. "How long before they get fingerprint results?" I asked Stapleton.

"Not long. They would have printed the murder scene this morning. If your prints are on file with Cal ID, they'll know in a matter of hours. If not, they'll have to bring you back in and print you and probably take a sample of your blood. They need probable cause for that, but they've probably got enough evidence for that already. If your lawyer hadn't been here they would have done it this morning."

Great. My fingerprints were filed with the Psychology Licensing Board, which meant that Cal ID would have them, too. I could feel my apprehension returning. My stomach was churning and, as I moved toward the door, I had to concentrate on placing one foot in front of the other. I looked back at Bill Hoskins. "Get me a lawyer."

Thirteen

Kim was able to meet me for lunch before I had to get to the college for afternoon meetings and my class. We picked a spot near the campus but not too far from her afternoon appointment in Anaheim. The historic section of the city of Orange was one of the oldest residential and business areas of the county. It had always reminded me of a small, midwestern town—something out of Thurber—more than Southern California. At its hub was a roundabout with a miniature park in its center. Tom Hanks had sat on a bench in that park, waiting for a bus and musing about life and chocolates in *Forrest Gump*. The area was dotted with restaurants, antique shops, bookstores, and century old Watson Drugs where you could purchase prescriptions, sundries, and burgers and floats from the old fashioned soda fountain in the back of the store. A little out of the main shopping area and nestled among the stately early nineteenth century houses that made up the district was P.J.'s Abbey, a converted one hundred and ten-year-old church, with vaulted ceilings, stained glass windows, and a quiet ambiance that was conducive to conversation. Kim and I had a lot to talk about.

My story about Mellon's threat to arrest me produced one of Kim's rare flashes of anger. She was ready to fight for her man. "The police are being very ignorant, Anh!"

"I told them that they should be looking for a one-armed man, but they wouldn't listen."

"I'm serious, Anh." Her anger changed to concern. "You really could be arrested?"

"I suppose if they find my fingerprints on the knife that was used to kill Elmore, they're going to have to do something."

"But your fingerprints are on the knife."

"I used a knife to cut a lime for my drink. I'm assuming it's the same knife.

"You couldn't have gone without, a lime?"

I stared at her in disbelief. "In a gin and tonic?"

She looked pensive for a moment. "Elmore's the second person who's been murdered since you started looking into those movie deaths."

I nodded, taking a sip of the 1997 Joseph Phelps Insignia table wine I'd ordered to fill in the gap before my pork loin sandwich arrived. Kim was having a salad and water.

"Elmore was robbed—personal stuff. It sounds like an opportunistic murder, although Blue Bay isn't the kind of place a robber wanders into by chance."

"There's an old Vietnamese saying, 'if one pig is missing, perhaps it wandered away. If two pigs are missing, look for a thief.'"

"What?" I said. "You mean my pork loin's been purloined?" I scanned the room with mock suspicion.

Kim gave me with a withering look.

"Both Julio and Elmore became interested in learning more about the Pink Carnation murders. Both of them are dead. It's too much coincidence, Anh."

"Let's not forget Brian Thornberg. He's dead, too." I didn't remind her that if the attack on the boat had been successful, there would have been another murder—mine. "Elmore had been looking into those Pink Carnation murders for some time." I continued. "That was the whole plot of his script. But if someone was worried about Elmore, why not bump him off right at the get-go—save time and bullets?"

The waitress interrupted us with our food. A thick slab of lean pork stuck temptingly out from the edges of my sandwich. The sliced baguette in which it was encased was still warm—crisp on the outside and soft and light inside. The Abbey had its own bakery and the bread was half the allure of its sandwiches. Being mindful of the deleterious effects of undernourishment on cognitive processing and being acutely aware of my need to maintain my razor-edged mental prowess, I asked the waitress for another glass of wine then stuffed two large steak fries in my mouth. I watched Kim take small, precise bites of her Caesar salad, then a slow, measured drink of her water. She could risk the chance of starving her brain but not I. I bit off one delicious corner of my sandwich.

Kim looked over at me, a somber expression on her face. She reached across the table and rested her hand on mine. "You have to be careful, Anh. You're very precious to me."

This is where I should be muttering, "I'm not worthy."

"You don't mind being married to a murder suspect?" I asked.

"I always knew it would come to this," she answered, patting my hand. She became serious again. "Do you think the attack on the boat the other night was part of all of this?"

I took a bite and nodded. "I think so. Those two guys seemed more interested in doing something to me than in robbing the boat. But maybe I'm imagining things. Maybe Jim Stapleton is right that I've become paranoid about this whole thing."

Kim shook her head. "I don't think so. Elmore's murder was no coincidence. You asked him about Raul Lopez and from everything you've told me, Raul Lopez is the key to this."

"The common thread between Ramon Chavez, Julio Cordoza, and John Elmore is that each of them was trying to find out more about Lopez. Elmore had given up looking into Lopez until I told him about Ramon and Julio."

Kim swallowed another small bite of Caesar Salad while I wolfed down chunks of pork loin sandwich that would have choked a horse – a carnivorous horse.

"And Elmore was killed within an hour or two after you told him," Kim said.

I stopped chewing. "Elmore was pretty drunk. He said he was going to talk to Randy Fontana, the old cop who was in charge of the original Pink Carnation investigation."

Kim had stopped eating and was watching me. "Would Fontana kill Elmore?"

"Fontana looks as if he would kill anybody," I said.

"You said Elmore was drunk. Maybe he threatened Fontana in some way – like said he was going to dig deeper rather than take Fontana's word for things."

Kim's scenario made sense. "But would Fontana hop right in his car and drive over and knife Elmore?"

"If Elmore told him that you'd just been there, and especially if he'd told him how you got in, Fontana might have thought that you'd be the one who was blamed."

"I'm glad you're not advising the killer," I said.

Kim folded her napkin and pushed her plate away. "I think you should call Jim Stapleton and tell him about Fontana."

"Fontana was with Jim earlier in the evening."

"With Jim?" Kim asked, looking confused.

"I saw him sitting in Jim's car when he came to the scene of Julio's murder."

"What does that mean?" she asked.

"I don't know. But if Fontana was with Jim earlier, then it's not very likely that he killed Julio. That means that either Fontana didn't kill Elmore either, or there are two killers." I shook my head. "I don't know, maybe Jim is right. Maybe it's just two pigs wandering away. No connection, no plot, just coincidence."

Kim shook her head. "No. We might be wrong about Fontana, but this was no coincidence." Her grip on my hand tightened. "That's why I want you to be careful. But call Jim Stapleton. You need him to help."

I nodded and signaled the waitress for the check. Mundane as they were, Kim and I both still had jobs to go to.

***

When I called Jim Stapleton, he made no attempt to hide his anger. "Jesus Christ, Phin, can't you leave it alone?"

At least I knew I had his attention.

"What am I supposed to do, wait around until your two dim-witted detectives arrest me? Fontana was the last person Elmore planned to talk to when I left him. If he called him up, Fontana might have come straight over."

"And picked up a kitchen knife and stabbed him, took his watch, his credit cards, and his cash," Stapleton said. "Give me a break."

"Mellons said he thought the robbery was a ruse."

"He was talking about you, Phin. The robbery was real and it's your best argument that the killer wasn't you."

"So are you going to tell me what time you left Fontana last night?" I asked with dogged determination.

"Goddammit!" Pissed would probably be the best description of Stapleton's tone. Extremely pissed might even be better.

"Well?" I said.

"I dropped him off at his house about ten o'clock. He lives in Silverado Canyon. You know where that is?"

I knew it was up in the Cleveland National Forest and miles from Laguna Beach. Silverado Canyon was populated by hermits, bikers, a few artists, one or two wealthy estate owners—and I guess one retired detective. Make that one retired murderous detective as far as I was concerned. "Way out in the boonies. Do you mean it's too far to drive to be able to get over to Blue Bay or that hayseeds from Silverado don't kill people? What's your point?"

"It's a long way. Anyway, Fontana's SUV is in the shop. That's why I was ferrying him around. So unless he hitchhiked back to Laguna Beach, I don't see how he could have gotten to Elmore's house last night."

"A lot of murderers are hitchhikers. I saw that on *True Crimes*."

Stapleton's toned softened to the level of garden-variety irritation. "You can be a pain in the ass, bro. Let the Sheriff's Department find the killer. You just make sure you've got yourself defended. That lawyer of yours couldn't argue himself out of a paper bag. You're gonna need somebody who's done criminal cases. That's where your energy should be going."

Maybe he was right. Maybe I was focusing on Fontana so I wouldn't think about the trouble I was in myself. "Any word on the fingerprints?"

"Not yet. There were prints but they haven't identified them yet."

Great. It would only be a matter of time before they identified my prints on the knife. I still wasn't mentioning my use of the knife to Jim, although I wasn't sure why. I'd talk to a lawyer first.

"It's starting to look like an ordinary robbery," Stapleton went on. "Not much was taken, except what Elmore was carrying. Someone went through most of the drawers of the house looking for things, but none of the big stuff like a stereo, TV, silver, was taken. The theory is that the killer was on foot. He could only take what he could carry. 'Course Mellons still thinks it was you."

"Asshole," I commented.

"First Class," Stapleton added. "But he can be a pit bull when he's after someone. Get yourself a good lawyer."

"Thanks bro," I said, hanging up, less enlightened than when I'd started. At least I'd had a theory before. Now I was left with a couple of wandering pigs. And my fingerprints all over the murder weapon.

Fourteen

Lucia Chavez wasn't home and she hadn't called me, which was odd, given that Elmore's death was all over the newspapers, radio, and television and Lucia knew that I was headed to his home when I'd left her the night before. The Orange County Register carried a front-page story, complete with a picture of Elmore and of course an interview with the always charming and informative Rudy Mellons.

The detective mentioned "assorted articles taken from the house and from the deceased's person." He gave provocative hints that "we have a suspect, who was known to have been with the deceased close to the time of death, but we're not releasing any names or making any arrests at this time."

I loved copspeak, with phrases like "the deceased's person." I rolled the phrase around on my tongue a few times, linking the words with a few of my favorite people, like President Stonehill and of course Detective Mellons himself. I began to develop a feel for it. But I was forgetting that I was a suspect. Perhaps I should quit working on my elocution and start spending more time smelling roses and gazing at sunsets before I was carted off to the dungeon.

I'd hold off on the rose smelling for a while because, as life always has it, the mundane and tedious had to take precedence. I had a class to prepare. I reviewed my notes on treatment strategies for juvenile offenders. Boot camp and *Scared Straight* approaches were popular with right wing politicians, the moral majority, and other varieties of sublimated sadomasochists, but in truth they made kids worse, providing role models of harsh, cruel, and sadistic mentors that young, incarcerated, first offenders emulated out of fear.

The bleeding hearts and the soft-headed liberals preferred counseling but the various approaches that had been tried—from teaching social skills to replacing never present attachment figures—had no effect whatsoever. The picture was bleak except the answer, which probably should have been obvious, was sitting there in front of everyone's noses. An ounce of prevention was worth a pound of cure.

The most effective preventive measure against delinquency was a combination of preschool and parent training for children from high-risk situations when they were toddlers. Project Headstart did more to combat delinquency than all the juvenile halls and psychotherapy put together. The problem was, you couldn't predict with any precision who would become a delinquent when he or she was still a toddler, so Headstart or similar programs, enriched by heavy training of the parents in parenting skills, had to be given to massive numbers of poor children. That cost money. In a society where people would rather vote for politicians who sponsored legislation to restrict teenagers' access to Dungeons and Dragons and MTV, or institute dress codes at school to combat delinquency, it was hard to convince anyone that the best method to fight delinquency was to increase funding for preschool programs for the poor.

I reviewed my material and vowed, as I always did, just to present the facts and not get up on my soapbox to rail against society's astigmatic point of view on social issues. It was a vow I hadn't yet been able to keep, but there was always a first time.

It was nearly four and I made one last call to Lucia but she still wasn't in. I left another message for her to call me as soon as she could. If she waited until tomorrow, I might have to give her my number at the county jail. At any rate, there were young minds to mold. I headed across the quad to Lander, the ivy covered hall opposite my office in Macmillan. Despite the late afternoon hour, the quad was crowded with students hurrying to what was the last class of the day for most of them. I had on wide wale corduroy pants, my still gritty Bruno Magli loafers that I'd worn across the sand the night before, and a tweed sportcoat, appropriately wrinkled and only waiting to be covered with chalk dust. With my briefcase stuffed full of notes and articles, the majority of which buttressed the points I planned to make in my lecture, I looked the perfect professorial type. I had to admit that the smug sense of

Pink Carnation

superiority that comes with lecturing naive students on a topic I'd spent several years studying buoyed my spirits. Feeling self-satisfied, I smiled at the students I passed as I strolled down the wide brick path leading from one building to another. It crossed my mind that I might be overdoing the happy professor demeanor because several of the students were eyeing me peculiarly.

When I reached bottom of the steep brick steps leading up to the tall, red, mahogany doors at the front of Lander Hall, I realized the students were doing more than giving me quizzical looks. Several from my class were coming down the stairs as I was going up. A skinny, freckle-faced boy, who always asked irritating questions about the most obvious points, stared at me so hard he nearly tripped and fell down the stairs. Most of the other students bent their heads, looked at each other or to the side, and avoided my gaze.

When I reached my classroom door, I realized the reason behind the students' behavior.

Taped to the closed door of the classroom was a letter-sized sign bearing the Dean of Arts and Sciences' name. In bold typeface was the announcement that my Psychology of Delinquency class was cancelled for today, but would resume tomorrow with Dr. Michael Thorne, who I'd never heard of, teaching the class. The announcement contained no explanation for the change.

I stood staring at the announcement. I felt my face starting to burn and my breath coming in short bursts. My first thought was that somebody with the Sheriff's Department had gotten to the Dean. My second thought was that my first thought pissed me off royally. I didn't care whether the whistle blower from the Sheriff's Department was Tom Desmond or Rudy Mellons—and I was sure it was one or the other of those two—I was pissed that my college would remove me so unceremoniously and unfairly.

I beelined across campus to the front porch of Administration Hall, yanking open the wide oak door so savagely that several students stared wide-eyed, as if a wild man had just burst into the building. I took the winding staircase leading up to the administrative offices on the second floor, two steps at a time.

"Where is he?" I asked Greta Hundley, Dean Kastner's middle-aged secretary. Greta was the university's unofficial chief of protocol. She was a model of decorum in every situation to be encountered in an academic environment. Dealing with a crazed, oversized, psychology professor bursting into her office looking ready to commit mayhem and bodily harm on her boss wasn't a situation she'd ever anticipated, however. She backed away from me toward the door to her superior's office, her eyes wide with terror. "Th...the Dean's in a meeting," she managed to get out between stentorian breaths. She used her padded tweed secretary's chair like a bullfighter's cape, turning it back and forth in small, semi-circular sweeps, ready to interpose it between us if I mounted an attack. Her frightened gaze darted between me and the space on the carpet in front of the chair, as if trying to estimate the distance between my present position and the most likely spot I might strike. "Where?" I asked, taking a threatening step toward the fifty-year-old woman, sensing that I'd have greater success sticking with terror than attempting reason.

"Board room," Greta answered, inching the chair a little more to the left so that it remained between us.

I glanced down, as though I was considering kicking the feeble chair out from between us and doing whatever dastardly deed was driving me to the state of agitated lunacy that she had concluded I was in.

"Thank you Miss Hundley, " I said.

The Board Room was for meetings of the Chandler University Board of Trustees and I wasn't surprised to find more than half of the Board members, as well as the Dean and the university President, sitting in their usual chairs, all gazing at the door, as if they'd been waiting for me to appear.

"Come in, Phineas," President Stonehill said, a disingenuous presidential smile on his face. "We've been expecting you."

"Really? I thought you all gathered here every day and just stared at the door with your brains disengaged."

Pink Carnation

Stonehill frowned. In his shiny expensive business suit, and with his short, no nonsense haircut, Stonehill had the well-fed robust look of a successful businessman, which was just what made the successful businessmen who sat on the Board of Trustees feel comfortable. Nobody wanted an egghead running an institution of higher education. Slick Al tried to regain his smile but his eyes remained as cold as ice. He was probably envisioning my head being severed from my body and served up on a platter to the Board by a dancing girl. "I hope you're not going to make this more difficult than it needs to be, Phineas."

"Trust me. I lie awake at night thinking of ways to avoid causing any of you any difficulty. But removing me from my class without consulting me is taxing my goodwill."

I surveyed the Board, who were arrayed around one end of a large oval table, Dean Kastner and President Stonehill seated at the two ends of the group nearest me. Only four of the six members were present. At the apex of the semicircle I recognized Michael Umstead, the Board President, with his graying hair, his large, strong chin, and steel gray eyes. I knew from the faculty get-together that Umstead had a volatile temper. On his left was Dr. Simon Flowers, a wealthy ophthalmologist who advertised his laser surgery aggressively in the media, but rarely had any input at board meetings. Flowers was the kind of small, bald-headed man on whom a hefty set of horn-rims would have added some dignity. Unfortunately, he'd had one of his own surgeries and now he just looked like a pale, pop-eyed nerd. His only reason for being on the Chandler Board was probably to vote for books with finer print so he could ruin the eyesight of the next generation of Orange County citizens.

Next to Flowers was my old flame, Janet Erskine Jones. She smiled an embarrassed smile and looked away. I could see that if I could work her guilt, I might be able to dredge up an ally. Next to Janet was the lackey, Dean Kastner. On the other side of the table was the oldest member of the Board, Jess Wolf, the multimillionaire who was reputed to own much of the real estate in downtown Santa Ana. Despite his robust facial appearance, the product of countless plastic surgeries, and his obviously dyed, bushy, black hair, Wolfs thin, bony hands betrayed his age. They were dotted with liver spots and had a constant tremor. He wore a large diamond ring on the little finger of his left hand. Next to Wolf was the weasel, President Stonehill.

I stared accusingly at each of them—except Janet, toward whom I aimed a winsome smile. No sense alienating a potential ally.

"You're a suspect in a murder case," Michael Umstead boomed in a strong Boardroom voice.

"What on earth could you be you talking about?" I asked.

Umstead frowned.

"You don't know you're a suspect?" Janet asked. Beneath the wrinkles she allowed to show in her tanned outdoor skin, her strong, handsome face could still launch ships. No wonder I'd fallen for her—me and dozens of other men. She gave me a look of concern, and then cast a dismissive glance at the others. When she turned back to me, her eyes had softened, a hint of her former fondness showing through.

"I've been a witness to two recent murders," I said, looking only at Janet. "No one ever said I was a suspect." I looked at the rest of them, and then came back to Michael Umstead, listening intently with an ugly frown on his face. Umstead was in his sixties. I did some quick calculating. He would have been in his early twenties, and probably in college when his sister, Sally was killed.

"Who told you that I was a suspect?" I asked, my eyes still locked on Umstead. I assumed this whole charade had something to do with discouraging me from further investigations into his sister's death.

"We were informed by the Sheriff's Department," President Stonehill answered for the group. "We were also told that you, along with a student, with whom you apparently have a personal relationship, have been interfering in their investigation."

Even Janet's eyes held an accusatory look after Stonehill mentioned Lucia. I hoped I wasn't going to become the object of the fury of a woman spumed. Stonehill's source sounded like Tom Desmond, with SUAG After I made Rudy Mellons' suspect list for Elmore's murder, the opportunity to sabotage my career at the university must have been too much for him.

"You've been misinformed," I told Stonehill. "I haven't interfered with any Sheriff's Department investigations. Lucia Chavez is a Chandler student whom I formerly counseled. She came to me because her brother was killed while making Thornberg's movie. She couldn't get any information from the Sheriff's Department so I intervened on her behalf. Assistant Chief of Detectives Jim Stapleton is a friend of mine."

Michael Umstead's eyes widened when I mentioned Lucia's brother being killed making the movie.

"I want to know who you talked to at the Sheriff's Department," I continued. "I think you've been drawn into a personal vendetta one of their people has against me."

"We can't divulge that information," Stonehill said, looking at me with a superior presidential look.

Umstead smacked his lips and drummed on the tabletop. He wasn't the kind of man who enjoyed someone dictating to him. None of them were. I gave Janet a hopeful look. Maybe she could mediate between us.

"We confirmed that you are an official suspect in the Elmore case, Phineas," Janet said, glancing at the others and frowning. "A Detective Mellons provided us that information. He's not releasing that news to the press, at least for now. But if it should come out later that the university had been informed and took no action, well, we're concerned about the public reaction."

"As I remember, this is the same university that invited a hop-head movie director on campus in order to cajole him into donating money. That same director OD'd on drugs in the middle of a faculty fundraiser." I gave Alfred Stonehill a pointed look. "Of course he was snorting the drugs with a guest of one of you," I added, switching my attention to Wolf. "I think you've got a lot more worries than me when it comes to public reaction about this school."

Umstead glared at Stonehill and Wolf.

115

"Would you consider a voluntary cessation of your teaching duties until this whole thing is cleared up?" Umstead asked. He opened and closed his fist. His scowl was back. Come to think of it, the scowl had never left his face. He looked around the room for suggestions.

Old man Wolf stirred for the first time. He rubbed his blotched bony hands together as if he were enjoying himself. "Professor Routledge makes some interesting points, even at my expense," Wolf said, chuckling. " I've never been one to give in to vague accusations and innuendo, which appear to be the substance of the complaints against the professor. However, I believe it's within our rights as the Board of Trustees of this university and with in loco parentis responsibilities for its students, to ask the professor to desist from extracurricular activities with a student. Especially a student whom he is supposed to be counseling. And especially when the police have warned us that that professor's activities with that student have brought him under their suspicion. I believe we have that responsibility to the student and to the student's family."

No wonder the old coot had made millions.

Umstead nodded with an appreciative look toward the old man. "Mr. Wolf is right. Will you agree to that much, Professor Routledge?"

"I'm afraid I can't. I don't deny what Mr. Wolf is saying but Lucia Chavez needs my assistance. I'm not going to turn my back on her."

Old man Wolf looked at me with a sad smile. "I wish you didn't feel that way professor, though I admire your loyalty to your student. But you force us into a decision. It wouldn't be right for us to let you continue teaching at Chandler under those circumstances."

"Then make your decision," I said.

Michael Umstead couldn't conceal the smile that crept onto his face. He looked over at President Stonehill. "I recommend that we suspend Professor Routledge from all of his duties connected to Chandler and that he not be allowed to work on campus until the professor agrees to sever his personal relationship with this student in compliance with our request."

Pink Carnation

Umstead played hardball. Maybe I should just come out and tell him that I already knew that his sister had been knocked up by Raul Lopez and that this whole rigmarole wasn't really necessary.

Umstead looked around for a show of hands. Kastner and Stonehill couldn't vote. There were two more board members who weren't present, but those who were there constituted a quorum. A simple majority would seal my fate. Wolf raised his hand a few inches off the table. Dr. Flowers was prompt to raise his too. He looked both mystified and relieved that something had been decided. Janet looked at her three fellow board members and shook her head again. Her hand remained on the table. It was good to see that an old love still meant something.

"You don't need to clear out your office, Phineas, but take everything you need to be able to work at home. You'll have to stay off campus until this gets resolved. And that includes the counseling center." President Stonehill shook his head with regret. "I hope you come to your senses soon, Phineas. You're throwing away a valuable career."

I searched around for something appropriate to say. "Fuck you," would have confirmed their opinion of me as rebellious and irresponsible. "See you in court," sounded almost as ridiculous, so I said it.

Fifteen

"We're going to have to initiate an austerity program, Em," I told Kim. She'd known something was wrong when my "Hi Lucy, I'm home," had lacked its usual enthusiasm. "No more designer shops and specialty stores. We're going to have to limit ourselves to Nordstrom's and Nieman Marcus."

She looked at me with a solemn expression. "In Vietnam we have a saying: 'Even a Mercedes will do in a pinch'."

"I'm glad you understand, Em," I said. Financially, the job made no difference one way or another in terms of our standard of living, but being suspended was both a blot on my career and an insult to my integrity as a teacher. More importantly, the board's action was a clue that Lucia and I had gotten too close to finding out the truth. And it must be a truth that involved one of the board members. From what I'd found out from John Elmore, Michael Umstead was the most likely candidate.

"What have you heard from Lucia?" Kim asked.

"Nothing. And that worries me. She must have heard that Elmore got killed. You'd think she'd want to talk to me."

"Have you called her?"

"Twice," I said. "There was no answer at her house. I'll try again before I go to bed. Maybe she and her mother have gone out."

Kim put her hand over my shoulder and massaged my neck. We were sitting on the couch in our living room watching the evening boat traffic moving in a slow, ragged procession down the bay. I had a glass of 1995 Beringer Private Reserve cabernet in one hand and the other hand on Kim's soft thigh. My bare feet were up on the coffee table. Kim had already showered and changed into her silk pajamas, which she did as soon as she got home unless we were going out for the evening. It was a Vietnamese habit. Walking around the house in my PJ's at that hour still made me uncomfortable, but I'd changed into a pair of baggy shorts and a garish Hawaiian shirt as a way of signaling the end of the workday and a transition to a more relaxed mode. After today's Board meeting, it looked as though I'd be staying in that mode for some time.

I was doing my best to unwind but my anger kept getting the better of me. "I'd like to find a way to expose what a bunch of weak spined lowlife's comprise the Chandler Board — all except Janet, of course," I said, draining my wineglass. "But I think that Umstead's the one who's behind getting me suspended. He wants me to lay off digging up dirt about his murdered sister."

"Why don't you talk to him, Anh?"

"Who?"

"Talk to Michael Umstead. If he's suspending you because he doesn't want you to find out about his sister then tell him you already know. He might not be so eager to punish you if he's aware you know about his sister's pregnancy already."

"You don't mean threaten to tell about his sister do you?" I looked at Kim with curiosity. Threatening someone was not in her repertoire of techniques for dealing with people, but when it came to protecting her husband, she might recommend almost anything. Or, I thought with horror, perhaps living with me was starting to rub off.

Kim looked askance. "Anh," she said with disappointment in her voice. "Of course I don't mean for you to threaten Umstead. I just mean that if he knows you're keeping the secret of his sister's pregnancy, he will see that to punish you is absurd. He's afraid of what you'll find out and he needn't be."

I raised an eyebrow, or made an attempt to. Without a mirror, I couldn't tell if I was raising an eyebrow or just producing a nervous twitch. "He'd better fear me if he's behind any of the deaths that have occurred." I put down my glass and raised my fist to my forehead, flexing my bicep.

"You're my hero, Anh," Kim said, feeling my muscle. "But instead of flexing, why don't you pick up the phone and call Michael Umstead."

I let my arm drop limply to the couch. "Now?" I asked, meekly.

"The sooner you straighten this out, the sooner you'll have your job back."

"The austerity program is getting to you, eh?" I gave her a knowing nod.

"Make the call, Anh," she said.

Michael Umstead surprised me with his cordiality. He invited me to his house. In another half-hour the Lakers and Sonics were going to begin their second playoff game. Why did this always happen? But if I didn't keep my nose to the grindstone trying to clear myself of Elmore's murder, I'd be watching the rest of the playoffs from a jail cell. I said I'd be right over. Kim gave me an approving smile, but she worried that I was going to miss dinner. I left the house munching on a roast beef sandwich that was so thick I kept picking pieces of roast beef off my lap all the way to Umstead's house. I'd changed into a pair of Dockers slacks, a short-sleeved polo shirt, a light wool, forest green blazer, and put on a pair of socks and newly polished loafers. Other than the roast beef crumbs, I looked spiffy enough to meet the President of my university's Board of Trustees.

Michael Umstead and I weren't exactly neighbors but he still lived in Newport Beach and only about a mile and a half from Balboa Island. Santa Ana Heights, where the Umstead family residence was located, was an enclave of about a dozen sprawling estates, sitting side by side on a bluff overlooking one end of Newport's Back Bay. Upper Newport Bay was the body of water's actual name, though the locals referred to it as Upper Back Bay.

To complicate things further, the residents of Santa Ana Heights had renamed their neighborhood Bayview Heights Equestrian Community, I suppose disliking any mistaken association between their pricey homes and the mostly lower class and Hispanic city of Santa Ana less than a mile away. No one would have confused the two. Each of the palatial homes in the Heights, with its luxurious grounds, stables, riding rings, and so forth, would have taken up several city blocks in Santa Ana.

Pink Carnation

It took me a while to remember how to get to the Heights. I'd seen the houses plenty of times when Kim and I walked around the Back Bay or visited the Ecology Park below the bluffs. We'd had to dodge piles of horse manure left by the residents' horses along the hiking trails. Many of them rode around the bay on the weekends when those less fortunate were strolling along the nature paths that provided access to the tidal flats and marshes that edged the water.

As I approached the golf course, whose presence off to my right reminded me that I was nearing the narrow, unmarked road that led to the Heights, I noticed a black SUV two car lengths behind me. The vehicle looked familiar, though I didn't think it was the Explorer that had tried to run Lucia and me off the road the day before. I slowed to let the driver pass, but he slowed to match my pace. When I turned on my blinker to signal that I was about to turn down the road that led to Umstead's mansion, the SUV's turn signal began blinking also.

I turned off my turn signal and cruised by Umstead's road. The SUV did the same. When I circled around and came back toward the same spot from the opposite direction, he was still on my tail, still about two car lengths back. I turned into Umstead's road and pulled to a stop.

The SUV rounded the corner going a good thirty miles and hour and the driver slammed on his brakes to avoid rear-ending my parked car. He swerved then gunned his engine and sped past on the shoulder on the opposite side of the road.

I tried to make out the driver. There was only one man in the vehicle and, if I had to bet, I'd put my money on him being Randy Fontana. Whoever it was continued at break-neck speed until he squealed around a corner a quarter of a mile further down the narrow road and was lost from sight.

I put my car in gear and resumed my search for Umstead's house. No houses were visible from the street, only high fences and forbidding gates.

The Umstead residence was marked by an ornate "U" centered on a heavy, black, wrought iron gate, which barred access to a narrow graveled road that disappeared over the crest of the gentle hill that topped the bluff. No house was visible from the road. After pulling my MGA up to the gate and waiting less than five seconds, the gate slid open. The wrought iron receded into an opening in the gray stone fence to which it was attached. I pulled through the gate, shivering a little when it silently slid closed behind me. I had a sudden vision of Jonathan Harker entering the gates to Count Dracula's Transylvanian castle.

The gravel on the entrance road had been recently raked. This was the kind of residence that employed a lot of people who ended up with a lot of time on their hands; time to rake driveways, wash the limo, groom the horses, screw the mistress—oops—I was getting carried away. It crossed my mind, though, that maybe Raul Lopez had worked for the Umstead family back in '59. He'd had to have met Sally Umstead somewhere.

I rolled down my window and listened to the soft crunch of the gravel under my tires as I followed the road toward the crest of the hill. Ahead of me, the slate roof of the house rose above the hilltop, like the image of Camelot appearing over the horizon in front of Sean Connery and Julia Ormond in *First Knight*. The house looked gigantic, even to someone who'd grown up around massive New England "summer homes" that were the size of small hotels. I passed six garage doors before getting to the house proper, where a shiny black Mercedes S500 sat under the porte-cochere. I pulled up in back of the Mercedes. In the distance, beyond the end of the house, I could see a row of small barn-like structures, which I assumed were the stables.

The front door was massive and painted black, as was the trim around all of the windows. The rest of the house was covered with shingles, painted a dull gray, enhancing the country-house appearance of the place; California Country House—wood rather than stone. I looked for a doorbell button but couldn't find one. In the middle of the door was a well-worn steel knocker in the same ornate "U" shape as the insignia on the front gate. I was reaching to grab it when the door opened and I stood face to face with Michael Umstead.

Pink Carnation

He put out his hand and we shook. "Any trouble finding the place?" He asked.

"No. I just looked for the lawn where the 747's were landing."

He gave me a slight smile at the same time motioning me in the door. "It is a bit big, especially for this day and age."

We had entered a foyer, lit by a spectacularly large crystal chandelier. Ahead of us, the floor dropped three steps and there was a long hallway leading to two very tall, closed doors. The walls were papered in small figures against a federalist blue background. The wood trim around the doorways was something dark—walnut or mahogany. The floors were wide pine, darkened from decades of wear. Umstead began walking down the hallway toward the double doors. I followed next to him. Our footsteps echoed off the wall. Occasionally, to either side of us there appeared rooms, possibly parlors or libraries. They were unlit, so I couldn't tell exactly. I looked for anyone else home.

"I live here with my mother," Umstead said as if in answer to my musings. "I'm divorced and my kids are grown and scattered. My mother insists on keeping the house. She says it keeps the family together, although it hasn't. When she's gone, I'll sell it, although I don't know who could afford anything this big except maybe Bill Gates or a Mafia Don."

"I thought Bill Gates was a Mafia Don," I said. He smiled again, with a certain sadness, I thought.

The tall, double doors opened to a magnificent sunken living room with three shallow steps descending to a vast floor. The room was rectangular and we entered at the midpoint of one of its long sides. Opposite was one long floor to ceiling window with deep blue velvet curtains drawn three quarters of the way open. The floor was highly polished wood rather than carpet, but large, worn, Persian rugs were scattered around, strategically placed under clusters of furniture: a sofa and chairs surrounding a coffee table in one corner, an all white grand piano, it's cover raised, sitting in the middle of the floor at another end of the room, several chairs surrounding it.

Umstead stood to one side and gestured toward a pair of wingback chairs situated in front of the window. The chairs were angled to face each other obliquely but still have a view. Between them was a round cherry table with an inlaid pattern of lighter wood. When we reached the chairs, we both paused. I was fascinated by the view. The Back Bay shone in the evening light far below us but not so far that I couldn't make out an Egret wading along the edge of the water, fishing for dinner. The pathways for hikers and joggers were invisible from this viewpoint so nothing marred the pristine scenery.

"Beautiful," I said.

He walked to one end of the window and threw a switch. The area in front of the window was flooded with light, revealing a sweeping lawn, with an occasional white chair, a fountain in the very center, and at the edge of the bluff an octagonal gazebo. The whole scene looked like something out of *The Great Gatsby*.

"This was once the busiest social scene in Newport Beach," Umstead said, a dreamlike expression on his face as he stared at the expanse of lawn in front of us. "When I grew up here, we had parties every summer weekend. We'd go sailing in the morning and then back here for lunch, cocktails for the adults, and often music in the evening-right about this time. My mother was the social organizer for Newport Beach in those days." He stopped and looked down at his shoes, then he raised his eyes to me. "We stopped the parties after my sister was killed." He switched off the outside lights. There was nothing in front of us except blackness. Slowly the water and trees started to reappear. It was too dark now to see the Egret—if it remained.

Umstead walked over to where I was standing. He motioned for me to sit. "Would you like a drink? I can call for one. I'm going to have a scotch."

I thought he must have a pretty good set of lungs, if he was going to call from here. I hadn't seen another soul so far. I said I'd take a gin and tonic or, if that wasn't possible, a beer. He walked back to the window and pulled on a cord. I hadn't seen any one do that except in the movies.

Pink Carnation

But there was a Hollywood quality to the whole place—fifties Hollywood. Maybe his mother would turn out to be Gloria Swanson. I waited for Eric Von Stroheim to appear and take our orders.

Umstead sat down next to me. Before either of us could say anything, a stout middle-aged woman in a flowered housedress entered the living room. She marched over to where we sat and gave Umstead an obedient and inquiring look.

"Oh hi, Irma, " he said in a casual tome without smiling at her. "Thank you for coming. This is Professor Routledge from Chandler University. He'd like a gin and tonic and I'll have a scotch."

She smiled at us both and left.

"Irma's the cook and does most of the housekeeping. But she's an even better bartender."

"And your mother is here?" I asked.

Umstead had a direct gaze. His face didn't reveal much, except the hint of sadness that I'd seen earlier. "Mother can't get around very well. She uses a walker, but she's fallen a few times and broken some bones. She mostly stays in her rooms upstairs. I had an elevator installed about five years ago, so she can come down if she wants to, and she does when she has her friends over. But she's ninety-one and she's outlived most of her contemporaries."

"That's too bad. My parents died in their early seventies, within a year of each other. Not a good prognosis for me, but perhaps fortunate for them."

This wasn't quite the conversation that I'd expected but I sensed a genuineness beneath his words that urged me to respond in kind.

"You're from Massachusetts, if I remember correctly." He looked at me with that same direct, unrevealing look. He'd done some homework to know my birthplace, although I suppose it was on the employment documents I'd filled out for Chandler.

"I was born there, but I've been in California since I was in my teens." I no longer had any idea where the conversation was going. Maybe we were supposed to become bro's or something.

He nodded. Irma came back with a tray of drinks. She'd added some cashews and crackers in shallow, cut crystal bowls shaped like leaves. I remembered that my parents had had similar dishes for candy when I was small. Irma deposited the drinks, complete with monogrammed coasters, and the snacks, on the little table between us. Umstead thanked her and she nodded and left.

I wasn't sure who was supposed to start our real conversation. Umstead took a cashew and popped it in his mouth, chewing while he looked out the window. I took a sip of my drink. Irma would have lost money as a bartender. She must have just passed the bottle of tonic over the top of the glass. I'd have to keep that in mind before I got looped and began babbling like an idiot.

"I wanted to clear up a possible misapprehension, in case you had it," I began. Umstead tilted his head in my direction, ready to listen. "Lucia Chavez and I have been trying to find out more about her brother's death. Lucia doesn't think the shooting during the movie was accidental. She got a tip from a friend that it wasn't, only that friend has since been killed. John Elmore was dating the girl who got killed. In fact, she was carrying his child."

Umstead's face blanched at my last words. He took a quick gulp of scotch. "The girl who was playing my sister was pregnant?" he repeated.

"Elmore thought it was uncanny, too, given that he knew that your sister was pregnant, also." I waited for the bomb to explode.

Umstead's eyes narrowed. His expression went from shock to suspicion. "Elmore told you?"

"Only because he was taken off guard by the coincidence, just as you were. He didn't know that Lisa Burke, the actress playing your sister, was pregnant until I told him. He had no plans for revealing your sister's condition. Nor have I."

Umstead nodded, as if he understood. "You mean you have no plans as long as I give you your job back."

"No. I'm not threatening you. I just didn't want you to be under the impression that you needed to stop me from looking into your sister's

Pink Carnation

death because of what I might find. I wanted you to know that I already knew about her pregnancy."

He glanced at the ceiling. "I've kept it from her for forty years," he said.

"Your mother?"

He nodded. "She still thinks Sally was innocent. Mother's life was centered on my sister. Sally was her life. I was closer to father and that was fine with mother. Sally got everything mother could give..." he took another gulp from his glass, "... and she took it."

"It must have been difficult keeping a secret for so long."

He lifted another cashew from the crystal bowl and slid it into his mouth. I reached over and grabbed a handful, throwing them into my mouth three at a time.

"It wasn't really much," he said, shaking his head. "Father managed to get the Sheriff to keep the information confidential when it happened. If they'd had a trial, it could have been a problem with the coroner's report, but since no one was ever caught, there was no trial. I thought it was a closed issue until Elmore came up with his screenplay."

"He told me you offered to pay him to leave the fact of the pregnancy out of his script."

Umstead looked out the window. He looked even sadder than before. "What was I to do? At least Elmore was decent about it."

"Why didn't you stop them from making the movie?"

He looked at me, surprised. "How would I do that?"

"Didn't they have to get permission from the Supervisors or someone to shoot the movie in Orange County?"

He shrugged and took another quick swallow from his drink. It was almost all ice at this point. "I suppose they did. But I don't have any influence with the Board of Supervisors. I live in Orange County, but my business is in Long Beach. Even my campaign contributions, which aren't really much, mostly go to LA county politicians."

I sipped cautiously on my gin and tonic. If Umstead was on the level, he wasn't the powerhouse in Orange County politics that I'd thought he was. But there was still the matter of Randy Fontana. Elmore had told me that Fontana had been in the pay of Umstead for years.

"I guess I was under a misapprehension. I thought that businessmen like yourself controlled most of the local politicians."

He got up and walked over to the window and gave another pull on the silver cord. When he sat back down, he said, "I'm not one of those businessmen. But you're quite right that there are some with that kind of power, even on our Board."

"Who?"

He looked out the window again. When he turned back in my direction, he had a polite smile on his face. "I've probably said too much. And if I said anything more, it wouldn't be pertinent to your case anyway."

I took a longer sip on my drink. "Fair enough," I said. "Speaking of my case, I hope you understand that what I'm doing with Lucia Chavez does not constitute anything improper between a professor and a student."

He looked around uncomfortably, searching for Irma, I think. It occurred to me that he was an alcoholic. I remembered how he was drunk at the faculty fundraiser. Maybe that's why Irma was used to fixing such potent drinks. As if in response to his discomfort, Irma appeared. She had a new scotch on her tray. She took the old glass and replaced it with the new, glancing over at my still three-quarters full glass then leaving us alone.

Umstead took a long drink, then held the glass between his two hands, like a protective talisman. "Your association with the young lady outside of school gives an impression of something improper. And you are a suspect in a murder case. As a Board, we have to do something." His voice had taken on some of its boardroom quality. I guess we were no longer just a couple of guys getting loaded together.

If I pushed, he'd only become more rigid. It didn't appear that he was going to rescind the Board's decision. Maybe I could use our meeting to find out more about the Pink Carnation murders. "Let's forget it then. I'll abide by the Board's decision. I'm just glad that I've had an opportunity to tell you what's really going on." I raised my glass in a salute and took a long drink. He reciprocated.

"What can you tell me about Raul Lopez?" I asked.

His expression darkened. He glanced again at the ceiling, as if wanting to make sure that his mother couldn't hear us. When he spoke, his voice was hushed. "Lopez was a bastard. He was an opportunist who took advantage of Sally."

"You knew Lopez?" I asked.

"Not really. He worked for some of the wealthy families down here. I don't remember which ones anymore. Sally must have met him at someone's house or when he was serving at a party. I don't believe Mother ever hired him, but I can't be sure of that."

"How long had he been seeing your sister?"

Umstead looked down at the floor. "I don't know. Sally did a lot of running around. She wasn't the innocent that mother thought she was."

"You mean that Lopez wasn't the only one she went out with?"

"Sally was very nice looking—and fun. She had boyfriends from our social group but she sometimes strayed beyond. More than one time I had to rescue her when she got drunk and stranded in a dangerous situation."

"But she must have dated Lopez more than once if she was pregnant with his child."

Umstead looked surprised. "His child? Why do you think it was his baby?"

"Wasn't it?"

He shook his head and took a drink. "It could have been almost anyone's. That's how Sally was."

"But I thought you blamed Lopez."

"I blame Lopez for Sally's death. She was supposed to be at a country club dance. Lopez was working for the club that night and she took off early with him. Someone must have had it in for him. A boy like that...he was a gang member, you know. No one was trying to kill my sister." He looked consumed by emotion. After about a second, he shook himself and looked over at me as if to see if I had any more questions.

"Randy Fontana was in charge of the case. I understand you paid him to keep quiet about Sally's pregnancy."

He put down his drink and eyed me with suspicion. "How do you know that?"

"Elmore told me. He confronted Fontana about it."

He shook his head and frowned. "Elmore told you a lot."

"I thought I saw Fontana tonight, on my way here. He passed me just down the road from your gate."

Umstead appeared surprised. "Really? I wonder what he was doing on our road?"

"Following me, I think."

"Whatever for?"

"I thought you might be able to tell me."

"You mean you thought I was having him follow you?"

"Somebody is. Are you still paying Fontana?"

Again he looked surprised by my question. "Not to keep an eye on you."

"Then for anything else?"

"Such as what?"

"To keep the pregnancy a secret. To keep the news from coming out over the last forty years."

"My father paid him when he first heard about the baby. After that, he came to father a few times and hinted that someone was looking into the case and maybe he needed a little money to keep the records away from whoever it was. After about ten years that stopped. He never approached me since father died."

It was my turn to be surprised. "You're not paying him to keep an eye on the people making the movie?"

"Fontana?"

"He's a consultant on the film."

"I didn't know that. I knew that Elmore talked to him extensively when he was writing the script but I didn't know he was connected to the movie."

"Fontana interceded when you and Thornberg began arguing at the faculty party. Was he working for Thornberg, then?"

"I hadn't thought about it. He wasn't working for me. Thornberg seemed as surprised to see him as I was, though."

"You seemed awfully angry at Thornberg that night."

"He was a sensation-monger who would only cheapen Sally's memory. Stonehill was an ass for inviting him to the university."

"It was Stonehill's idea?"

"Who else's? Neither Janet Erskine Jones nor I wanted him there."

"Jess Wolf seemed friendly with Thornberg."

Umstead started to say something then evidently thought better of it. He picked up his drink and jiggled the ice. The scotch appeared to be gone. He glanced over at the window cord, as if debating whether to call Irma and ask for another. Instead, he looked at his watch, then at me and gave a wan smile. "It's getting late."

I'd worn out my welcome and reached nothing but dead ends. Umstead wasn't going to reinstate me on the Chandler faculty and he knew zip about Raul Lopez or any details about his sister's death - except that maybe Sally Umstead's baby wasn't Lopez' and maybe the night that they were killed was their first date. Things made less sense than they had before I'd talked to him. I swirled what was left of my gin and gin around in the glass and decided to leave the rest. I had to cross water to reach my house and I had a history of difficulty with that sort of thing. I thanked Umstead for his time, and said he needn't show me to the door. When I left the living room, he was headed for the window cord to summon Irma.

When I pulled back onto the little road that led from Umstead's house to the main street, I saw a pair of headlights come around the corner where I'd last seen the SUV. I slowed to see if I was going to have a tail again. This time, whoever it was came slowly down the road as far as

Umstead's gate, then turned in toward the gate. I stopped and watched as the driver waited for the gate to open then drove inside. Michael Umstead was having a late-night visitor. If it was Randy Fontana, then Michael Umstead wasn't as forthcoming as he'd appeared to be. I backed down the road as far as the gate, but the SUV had already disappeared over the crest of the hill.

    I was tired of sleuthing. I put the car back in gear and drove home.

Sixteen

The Lakers had come back with a vengeance. Shaquille O'Neal had a monster night with 46 points and 22 rebounds. Kobe and the rest of the team had played well and the Supersonics, even playing at the top of their game, had no chance to stay with the high flying LA team.

Kim provided me with an account of the highlights as soon as I got home. My highlight reel was a little less stellar. I told her that Michael Umstead was a sad old man who sat in his creaky old mansion, pickled himself in scotch while reflecting on the people he'd lost over the years, and was too ineffectual to have quashed a murder investigation or orchestrated four deaths himself. The only thing he wasn't too ineffectual to do was to get me suspended from teaching at the university.

"Then you'll have plenty of time to find the murderer and clear yourself as a suspect, Anh," Kim said, rubbing my shoulder to reassure me. She was snug under the covers in our bed, her favorite spot for watching television; and I was lying on top of the covers next to her, still in my shirt and slacks. "You'll fix things," she said. "I have all the faith in the world."

How many jobless murder suspects had a wife who would say that? I gave her a Vietnamese kiss on her cheek, the softness of which always amazed me, and even now threatened to distract me from doing the things that had to be done.

"The only flaw in Umstead's story is that I think Randy Fontana followed me to Umstead's house tonight and then came back to visit Umstead after I left."

"What does that mean, Anh?"

"It probably means that Umstead is a liar."

"But you thought he was being honest."

"Who knows? Maybe he was honest. Maybe Fontana was headed to his house to put the squeeze on him and when he saw me headed in the same direction, he decided to wait until I left."

"You can't figure it all out right now, Anh. Maybe you should come to bed." She winked one eye, wickedly.

Reluctantly I rolled off the bed. "I'm going to try Lucia one more time first, Em. I'm worried that I haven't heard from her. Keep my spot warm."

I dialed Lucia's house and this time her mother answered. She was distraught. Lucia had not been home since sometime yesterday. Mrs. Chavez had called the police but they wouldn't do anything about a nineteen-year-old who'd only been away from home for a day. The thought that something might have happened to Lucia made me sick to my stomach. My guilt at letting her stay involved in the case made my knees weak. For a moment I was unable to speak.

"Dr. Routledge?" Lucia's mother inquired. "Are you all right?"

I reassured her that I was all right. I'd do some checking on Lucia and call Mrs. Chavez back in the morning.

I hung up and returned to the bedroom. Kim took one look at my face and asked what was wrong.

I told her about Lucia's disappearance.

"Do you think something's happened to her?" Kim asked.

"Her brother, Thornberg, Julio, Elmore, all of them are dead and now she's missing. It's not good, Em. I'm going to call Jim Stapleton and let him know. Maybe he can get his department to do something."

She nodded.

I called Jim Stapleton at home.

"I'll do what I can," he said after I told him about Lucia's absence. "It's Santa Ana jurisdiction but they won't do anything this soon. Most likely she'll show up at home tomorrow, but there's been enough funny coincidences about this case that I'm not assuming anything."

I felt my shoulders sag in relief. I'd been worried that he would slough Lucia's absence off as he had my other suspicions about the case. I felt better knowing he was willing to get involved. I thanked Jim and hung up. I told Kim that Jim had promised to look into Lucia's disappearance. She was relieved and patted the side of the bed.

Pink Carnation

"You need to relax, Anh. Take a long hot shower and come to bed."

"Good advice, Em. I'll have a nightcap, too."

She looked at me through half-closed eyes, a dreamy smile on her face. "I'll be waiting for you."

I fixed myself a gin and tonic, weaker than the one Irma had made me, and set it within reach while I steamed myself into lassitude in the shower. I left the door to the bathroom cracked open so Kim could hear me serenading her with the old favorite, *Who's Your Little Who-zis?* By the time I was finished, my skin was starting to pucker and the gin and tonic was gone. I stopped singing, toweled off and returned to the bedroom. Kim's eyes were closed, but I noticed that her pajamas were neatly folded on the nightstand next to her side of the bed. I slipped under the covers and she reached over and ran her fingers down my stomach and beyond.

"I thought you'd never come to bed," she murmured, her skin feeling cool next to mine.

"You couldn't wait to feel me next to you?" I murmured, becoming aroused.

"I couldn't wait for you to stop singing, Anh."

***

The next morning I called Mrs. Chavez. She still hadn't heard from Lucia. Her news made me even more worried, but I tried to reassure her by telling her that my friend from the Sheriff's Department had promised to look into Lucia's disappearance.

"Someone has already called, Professor Routledge," she said in heavily accented English. "A Detective Mellons. He asked me questions about where Lucia was the night before last and when she had last been home. He wanted to know the names of all of her friends."

I felt my back stiffen and the blood rush to my head. I couldn't believe that Jim Stapleton had involved Mellons in looking for Lucia. Mellons had the sensitivity of a doornail and he was probably prejudiced against Lucia because of her association with me, anyway. I called Jim at his office, furious.

"Did you tell Detective Mellons to interview Lucia's mother?"

"No, of course not."

"So who did?"

"Nobody did. Mellons is investigating Elmore's murder. The lab finally matched the prints on the murder weapon. They belonged to Lucia Chavez. Besides that, the blood types matched."

To borrow a phrase from Archie McNally, my flabber was gasted. "Somebody must have planted Lucia's prints," I said. "I bet it was Mellons who found them."

It was Stapleton's turn to be pissed. "Oh come on, Phin. Don't accuse my department of planting evidence. Mellons is an asshole, but he's a good cop. If he says her prints were on the knife, they were on the knife."

"That's just great! What happens now?"

"Mellons hasn't given up on you as a suspect. He thinks you and the Chavez girl are in cahoots. He's still got your admission that you were at the murder scene and he's got more prints on the murder weapon, but he hasn't' run them yet. He's out to get you, bro. For now the Chavez girl is gonna get picked up as soon as anyone can find her. She's been charged with Elmore's murder."

The blood was still pounding in my head. I could feel beads of sweat on my forehead. "Mellons is an asshole," I said." He's wasting time. For all we know, the real killer has already gotten to Lucia."

"Well at least nobody's going to do anything to her if she's in custody," Jim answered. "You'd better tell her to come on in, bro."

"I don't know where she is, *bro*," I snapped.

"Geez, don't get so testy," Jim answered. "I'm on your side, remember?"

"Sorry. At the moment, it doesn't feel as if anyone's on my side—or Lucia's."

"It'll all get straightened out," Stapleton said.

Pink Carnation

I hoped he was right. I hung up and considered my options. Lucia was a hothead and she didn't always use good judgment, but I refused to believe she would resort to murder. The problem was, if she hadn't killed Elmore, why was she missing? There was only one answer. Someone had decided to silence Lucia before she could make any more inquiries into her brother's death. The most likely scenario was that whoever it was had also killed Elmore and planted the evidence against Lucia at the crime scene. That they'd found traces of her blood at Elmore's house scared the hell out of me.

Whatever Julio Cordoza's grandfather, Arturo had told his grandson, and Julio had then told Ramon Chavez, appeared to be what had started this whole string of killings. That meant I had to talk to Arturo Cordoza. That meant going into Santa Nita territory and finding the old man. I called Lucia's mother.

Mrs. Chavez was even more upset than before. She still hadn't heard from Lucia and the Sheriff's detectives had been back with a warrant for her daughter's arrest. I asked her if I could come over and talk.

Lucia lived northwest of the Santa Ana town center. The city was seventy-five percent Latino with a median family income of less than thirty-five thousand dollars. In fact, in the area in which Lucia lived, the median income was less than half that and the Latino percentage shot up to over ninety. It was in this area that the Cordoza's and other families, who belonged to the notorious Santa Nita gang, reigned.

I pushed my little 1500cc roadster up to 90 mph, then peeled off the freeway and headed west, past Main and Norm's where Lucia and I had waited for our ill-fated meeting with Julio Cordoza, and then deeper into the Santa Ana barrio. Soon the neighborhood became residential, filled with small, one-story wooden houses, most with fences around them, some of which had spiked iron tops and wrought iron gates. There were occasional empty lots and some of the wooden fences and stone walls that abutted them had gang graffiti sprayed across them. The little stores that popped up now and then advertised their goods in Spanish and had wire grates across their windows and doors.

When I turned onto the side streets I was surprised by how neat the houses were kept. This wasn't like entering Bedford Stuyvesant or even Watts. Despite a crime rate that was astronomical for Orange County, people still took pride in their homes in this neighborhood. Young mothers sat on their porches with babies on their laps, and older folks were working in their yards. Unlike the central downtown area of Santa Ana, I didn't see any homeless wandering around or sleeping in doorways. A group of young men, most of them with shaved heads, baggy pants and T-shirts, lounged on the porch of a home on one of the corners and gave me a long hard look as I drove by.

Lucia's house was a small, one-story frame structure with white, wooden, clapboard siding, the paint peeling in places, and what had once been bright blue trim around the windows, but which was now blue-gray and dusty. There was a small front porch and, unlike the majority of its neighbors, the Chavez house didn't have either a chain-link or spiked fence around it. Either the family was too trusting or too poor to invest in security. The lawn was green and a sprinkler was making lazy circles over the tiny carpet of grass. The lawn hadn't been mowed for a while. Maybe that was Ramon's job.

Mrs. Chavez came to the door before I could ring the bell. I could have picked her out of a crowd as Lucia and Ramon's mother. She was slim, like her children, and had straight black hair with significant streaks of gray in it. She had Lucia's narrow face and deep-set eyes. In her case, she had dark circles under her eyes, making them look tired and defeated, rather than haunting and mysterious. She had Ramon's finely chiseled features; more delicate than Lucia's. She was wearing a long wrap-around skirt and an oversized peasant blouse. I entered the house, watching her rub her hands together nervously as she led me into the living room.

"I feel like someone is trying to destroy my family," she said, gesturing toward a small, flower-print couch. "Ramon was so happy making his movies. He was excited about meeting movie stars and making money. Then the movies took him away from me." She sat in a

Pink Carnation

demure posture on the front edge of a large easy chair, her knees both pointed sideways, and her hands resting on them as if to be sure her skirt covered her legs. Every once in a while she brought her hands together and began rubbing them in agitation, then, catching herself, placed them back on her knees. Her eyes were trusting and large, but frightened. She made an effort to smile, but her fear was stronger. "Lucia was angry about Ramon's death," she went on, "but she wouldn't kill anybody. Not Lucia. I don't even know who this John Elmore person is."

I explained about Elmore's position with the studio and his relationship with Lisa Burke, the girl who'd been killed at the same time as Ramon.

Mrs. Chavez was surprised. It was clear neither Ramon nor Lucia confided in her. "I'm worried, Professor, Routledge," Lucia's mother said, looking at me with imploring eyes. "Lucia hasn't called since yesterday afternoon."

"I'd like to talk to Arturo Cordoza," I said. "Does he live near here?"

"Arturo?" She looked startled.

I told her about Arturo giving some information to his grandson, Julio, and Julio passing it on to Ramon. "I think that whatever Arturo told Julio could be the key to this."

"The key? I don't understand. Does Arturo know where Lucia is?" Mrs. Chavez looked confused.

I shook my head. The whole story was too complicated to explain. "I think that your son might have been killed because of what Julio told him, and what Julio's grandfather told Julio."

She gave me a searching look. "Do you think that Ramon was killed on purpose, like Lucia said?" She'd stopped smoothing her skirt and leaned forward as she spoke.

I nodded. "I think so. And Julio and Elmore were killed to cover up things further."

I'd expected a gasp or at least a look of surprise. Instead, her shoulders sagged and she got a faraway look in her eyes. "Then Lucia could be dead, too," she said.

"I need to talk to Arturo Cordoza," I repeated.

"Arturo lives on the next block, just around the corner," she said. "He's an old man, a drunk. I don't know what he will tell you." Her fear had turned to discouragement.

"Do you think he'll talk to me?"

She nodded. "I will call him. He will do it for Lucia. He loves her like he loved Julio. Watch out for Arturo's boys, though. John and Jorge are bad men. I don't think they will bother you if they know you are Lucia's professor. Lucia is like their family." She shook her head. "But those Cordoza boys are bad people."

"And Arturo? I thought that he was a leader in the Santa Nitas?"

A smile flickered across her face. "Arturo is old. He still gets respect, but he doesn't lead anymore. He just stays home and drinks. Arturo took care of the neighborhood. His sons don't do that. When my husband was killed, Arturo helped me and made sure that Ramon and Lucia got what they needed. The Santa Nitas were different when Arturo was younger." Her face saddened again. "Now they are just criminals."

I thanked her for her help and told her that I would let her know if I found out anything about Lucia and she should do the same for me. She agreed, but by her eyes, I could tell she had already lost hope.

"I am afraid I have lost my daughter as well as my son," she said.

I started to protest, but she reached out and grasped my forearm in her hand. "Tell Arturo that someone is killing my children—and his grandchild. Tell Arturo to help you."

"Will you call him before I get there? Explain who I am?" I asked.

She nodded.

"Then you can tell him," I said.

I followed her directions around the corner to a small, wood frame house in the middle of the block on the next street. A wrought iron fence, too low too keep out anyone with serious intentions, surrounded the house. Roses were planted in a three-foot wide garden area that followed the inside of the fence around the house. The gate was closed but not locked. The house itself was white clapboard, like the Chavez house, and

Pink Carnation

the paint was peeling a little in places. The low, peaked roof was shingled in green asphalt tiles that looked relatively new. In front of the house were parked a white, low-riding late model Chevrolet pick-up truck and a dark blue Ford Explorer. I took a long look at the Explorer, trying to decide if it was the one that had tried to run me off the road or that had visited my house two nights earlier. I decided I was becoming paranoid.

Two short steps led up to a wide front porch that was enclosed by a low wooden wall. A group of chairs, including an upholstered easy chair, a couple of metal-framed kitchen chairs, and a swinging rocker were at one end of the porch. Two young men were sitting on the kitchen chairs. They both looked as if they were in their late teens. They each wore the typical Chicano "uniform" of baggy jeans and T-shirts. Their heads were shaved. The two of them glanced at me then looked over at the two older men sitting on the other two chairs.

One of the older men had a wide collared shirt, the most striking royal blue I'd ever seen. He wore a necklace that was visible even from where I stood on the street. His hair was slicked back in sort of a western pompadour, with a large Elvis Presley wave in front. He was smoking, with one leg crossed over the other, the creases on his black slacks carefully in place. I couldn't see his eyes because of the dark sunglasses he wore, but he had a wide salt and pepper mustache.

The other man looked about the same age, which would have been in their late thirties or early forties. He was dressed more like the younger men, except his shirt was a sleeveless tank top with an orange Harley Davidson logo on the chest. His stomach was massive, but so were his shoulders. Down both arms he sported tattoos; swirls and writing that looked like the kind of graffiti that's found on downtown walls and buildings. His hair was dark, like the other man's and balding in front. In the back he had it pulled into a ponytail He also had a mustache, longer than the other man's. Unlike the other, he wasn't wearing sunglasses and I could sense the hostility in his eyes all the way across the yard.

I walked up to the gate and looked from one of the older men to the other. "I'm looking for Arturo Cordoza," I said.

There was a long pause while I got the once over from each of the four. The younger two looked eager to see what the older ones were going to do. I must have resembled a sacrificial lamb.

"You the professor?" The one in the sunglasses asked. He'd said professor as if it were the punch line to a joke. His gold necklace shone in the sun. The younger men looked at him and smiled in appreciation of his wit.

"I'm the Mary Kay Jewelry salesman," I said, looking at his necklace. "Are you the lady of the house?"

His smile disappeared. "Are you some kind of wise-guy?" He got up from his chair and started across the porch in my direction. As he passed the other older man, the latter held out one thick arm in his path.

"He's here to see the old man," the one in the sleeveless undershirt said.

Fancy pants stopped moving. He looked at me. "You're lucky, Professor. You've got a big mouth."

"We can talk jewelry later," I said. I pushed past the gate and walked up onto the porch. The door was open but the screen was shut. The odor of cooked bacon wafted through the open doorway. I knocked on the screen's frame.

A round, brown face, wrinkled with age and worry, appeared from the darkness beyond the screen door. The face belonged to a small woman, almost as broad as she was tall, her gray hair pulled back except for loose strands sticking out at odd angles. Her upper lip had a thin mustache, darkened in small clumps by perspiration. She wiped her hands on a dishtowel and looked me up and down with suspicion.

"Is your husband home?" I asked.

She gave me another suspicious look, then opened the screen door just wide enough for me to get through. She pointed down the hallway.

I gave her a sympathetic smile. "I'm sorry about your grandson," I said. I didn't know whether she understood me or not, but she nodded.

Pink Carnation

The front door led into a small anteroom on one side of which was a hallway leading to a well-lit kitchen. Down the direction she'd pointed was a living room. The room was neat and comfortable looking with old, well stuffed furniture—two large easy chairs and a sofa surrounding an eight-by-ten Persian carpet. A picture of Jesus, one of those in which his piercing eyes seem to follow you around the room, hung on one wall and a cross was hung on another. Against the far wall was a large, black, big-screen television set. Mrs. Cordoza motioned for me to sit on the sofa. I sank into the furniture's deep stuffing and hoped that this wasn't how the Santa Nitas captured their rivals. Trapped by an antique sofa!

I heard Arturo Cordoza coming before I saw him. Something or someone was clumping down the hallway toward the living room. When the old man appeared, I realized that the clumping was because one foot was held three inches off the floor behind him, while he moved along on a pair of heavily padded wooden crutches. The injured foot was covered in a clean white stocking and was either swollen or heavily bandaged under the stocking. His eyes were intense and hard as he stopped at the entrance to the living room and looked at me.

I struggled up from the clutches of the sofa. The old man's gaze followed me, as if he was watching a tall building being erected.

"Jeesus Christ !" he said, looking up at me.

I held out my hand and introduced myself. Cordoza clumped across the room and shook my hand. He smelled faintly of beer. He wore faded jeans, and a large beer gut stretched his white T-shirt across this belly. His face, sporting a big, droopy mustache, was lined by age and weather, and his nose was enlarged by alcohol. It was the friendly face of a hard drinker, but it was also a face that could probably turn cruel at a moment's notice. I was reminded of Wallace Beery in the old movie about Pancho Villa. Cordoza wore his hair long on the sides, almost to his shoulders; but had little on top. His hair and his mustache were a salt and pepper gray. He was an older version of the man on the porch in the Harley shirt.

I sat back down on the sofa and Cordoza lumbered over to a well-worn easy chair and lowered himself gingerly into it, protecting his foot. In front of the chair was a small footstool, which he fussed with for a moment, then when he was satisfied that it was positioned just right, he grasped his pants leg and pulled his bad foot up to rest it on the stool.

"Gout," he said, looking over at me and pointing to his foot. "It comes and goes. I just have to wait for it to go."

We sat there looking at each other. Cordoza looked like a rough but kindly old grandfather and from what her mother had told me, that was the relationship he had with Lucia. But I had been warned about the dangerousness of the Cordozas and I was leery of violating whatever protocol was supposed to govern our interaction.

"Thank you for allowing me to come to your home," I began.

He nodded. "You are welcome. I understand that Lucia is missing." He looked at me for confirmation.

"She's been gone since yesterday. The Sheriff's Department suspects her of killing someone, but I'm afraid something has happened to her. She and I were looking into her brother's death." I looked over at him. He was watching me with interest. I took a deep breath. "We think it might have something to do with your grandson."

"I understand you were with Lucia when she found Julio." The old man continued to gaze at me.

"I'm very sorry about your grandson, Mr. Cordoza," I said.

His expression hardened. "Someone must pay for his death," he said, matter-of-factly. His face relaxed. "Julio was a good boy—not like my sons. He was going to become a lawyer. Julio never got into trouble when he was a child. Did Lucia tell you that?"

"Lucia said Julio was a good boy."

"The police say it was either drugs or that one of the other gangs shot Julio." Cordoza looked toward the window. He was again angry. He had a look that I was sure could still strike fear in those who knew him. "If it was another gang, Julio's death would be avenged by now. My son's would start a war. But nothing..." he held out his hands in an empty gesture. "This is something else."

"Why do you think he was killed?" I asked.

The old man frowned and dropped his gaze to the floor. "I made a mistake. I thought no one cared about this thing anymore." Cordoza raised his eyes and looked at me with a flat stare. "Julio asked me about Raul Lopez." He started to lean forward, but his bad leg stopped him. He reached down and pulled back the bottom of his pants where they touched the top of his foot. Gout could make even the slightest touch painful.

"I knew Lopez,' Cordoza continued. "We grew up together and were both Santa Nitas back when there weren't very many of us. Raul was a little like Lucia's brother Ramon. He wanted out of the barrio. He took jobs with the rich white families and dated their daughters when he could. It was not surprising he was with a white girl when he was killed."

"Do you know why he was killed?" I asked.

Cordoza looked at me, his face sad. "There are things I can tell you, but many people have died because of this knowledge."

"I need to know," I said. "Ramon and your grandson were killed because of that information. Lucia may be in danger because of it."

He nodded his head in agreement. "From this moment on, your life will be in danger, too, Professor." He took a breath and continued. "Raul Lopez worked for the Erskine family," he gave me a steady look to be sure I was getting every word he was saying. "The family owned most of the land from Santa Ana south and they had a large ranch that began in what is now Tustin. Raul was a houseboy at Mr. Erskine's home." He said it as if I should recognize the significance of what he'd just told me.

I looked back at him with what must have appeared to be blank expression.

"Mr. Erskine was killed the week before Raul died," Arturo said.

I did a little figuring in my head, trying to narrow down which Erskine he was talking about. It was probably, Winthrop, Janet Erskine

Jones' uncle and the youngest of the three grandsons of old John Erskine, who had established the family's massive landholdings back in the late 1800's. A few years after Winthrop's death, the ranch and the company that had been formed to develop the land had been sold to the current owner, who soon became the richest man in Orange County.

"Are you talking about Winthrop Erskine?" I asked.

Cordoza's nod was solemn. "Mr. Winthrop Erskine." A hint of reverence for the County's most famous family was still discernible in the old man's voice. He must have grown up at a time when the Erskine's virtually ruled the county.

"How did Mr. Erskine die?" I asked.

Cordoza's voice became quieter, as if he was still uncomfortable discussing the topic out loud. "The Sheriff said it was a suicide. Mr. Erskine was said to have shot himself." He looked at me and shook his head." Raul was there. Mr. Erskine was murdered in his own home."

"Lopez witnessed it?"

Cordoza shook his head." He didn't see it happen. He saw men leaving the house."

"Who?" I asked.

The old man raised his hands in a gesture of helplessness. "He didn't know them. He told the Sheriff's deputies about them, but Raul was afraid. He was afraid the men would come back and kill him. A week later he was dead."

"They arrested gang members from Los Angeles," I said. "Is that who Raul thought killed Erskine?"

Cordoza's face twisted in disgust. "Shee..it!" he spat out. "The Sheriff knew those Chicanos didn't do it. There was no war going on at that time and Raul was not important enough in the Santa Nitas for anyone to kill him like that."

"Who do you think it was?" I asked.

Cordoza rubbed his chin then stroked his mustache. "Raul said they looked like Las Vegas people."

"Las Vegas?" I repeated. "You mean Mafia?"

Pink Carnation

He shrugged. "Mafia's in the movies. Back in those days we just called them Las Vegas people."

"Lopez told the Sheriff's men about the Las Vegas people?"

"Raul told them everything."

"Did the Sheriff's men question you after Lopez was killed?"

"Only about his being in the gang."

"They never mentioned the Las Vegas people?"

He shook his head." They only asked about other Chicano gangs."

"So the Sheriff's people were covering up?"

"Go back and read the old papers...the stories about Mr. Erskine's death. Raul is never mentioned. The Sheriff just said it was a suicide."

"You really think it might have been Las Vegas people who killed Erskine?" I asked Cordoza again.

He smiled a little. "You don't believe it, I can see that." He paused. "We have a lot of killings in Orange County, you know that? We have always had a lot of killings. The Sheriff's department is not very good at solving these murders. They simply blame them on the Chicano gangs." He shrugged again. "It works well. People are killed and we get blamed for it, then the Sheriff and the police get more money to spend on hassling us. But the killings go on."

"You mean someone else has been killing people in Orange County...and blaming the gangs?"

"We kill some, but we don't kill so many."

I'd never heard of Mafia involvement in Orange County but the old man had no reason to make anything up. After all, it was his grandson who had gotten killed for knowing what he'd just told me. But why would anyone continue to cover up a forty-year-old murder? And who that was involved back then would still be around now? "Do you know Randy Fontana?" I asked.

The old man sat up then caught himself as he winced with pain from his foot. "I know that bastard. Why do you ask me about him?"

"He was in charge of the Lopez murder investigation. He's also working on the movie in which Lucia's brother was killed. He's a consultant about the original crime."

Cordoza's eyes were bright. "I didn't know Fontana was still alive."

"Did he talk to you about Lopez back then?"

"He was the one who asked about Raul being in the Santa Nitas. We all knew Fontana back then. Everyone was afraid of him."

"Was Fontana involved in the investigation of Mr. Erskine's death?"

Cordoza shrugged. "I don't know. I only know he asked me about Raul."

"What are your sons doing about Julio's murder?"

The fire left the old man's eyes. It was replaced by a dull sadness. "My boys do nothing. One of them is Julio's father and the other his uncle. They blame it on the police. They say they can't do anything."

"Did you tell them about Lopez?"

"My boys don't listen to me anymore." He adjusted his foot, then sat back and let out a long sigh.

"But Julio listened when you told him, didn't he. And he told Ramon Chavez."

The old man shook his head with regret. "I should have kept the secret a little longer. I thought no one cared any more." He looked up at me "What can you do?"

"I can check out whether Fontana was assigned to the Erskine case. If he was, then he's the one behind this. I have friends with the Sheriff's Department who can help me do the checking."

Cordoza continued to shake his head. "You can't depend on the Sheriff's Department for this. Fontana is one of them. No one is going to help you with this."

I got up and thanked Cordoza for his help. I said goodbye to the old woman. She smiled and said something I didn't understand in Spanish.

When I walked outside, the two young hoods and the older, well-dressed one in the sunglasses were still on the porch. The latter took off his sunglasses and gave me a long hard stare. I pointed to his necklace and mouthed the word, "lovely."

The fourth ne'er-do-well was leaning against the front fender of my MG, his hands hanging loosely at his sides. The tattoos on both arms writhed like snakes as he flexed his muscles. I wondered about asking him if he could flex his stomach the same way, since it had a much more impressive bulge than his sizable biceps. I assumed he was one of the Cordoza juniors—either John or Jorge. This one looked like the old man, except he hadn't yet gotten gray. The beer gut was the same.

"You think you can find my son's killer, Mr. Professor?" the younger Cordoza sneered. He must have heard some of the conversation from the front porch. If this was Julio's father, then he must be John Cordoza.

"I'm going to try,' I said, looking him straight in the eyes. I walked up to within a couple of feet of him but he didn't move. The gallery on the front porch cast eager glances at each other.

"My father lives in the past. He thinks everything is connected to something that went on back in his days." Cordoza was still leaning on my car, watching me curiously.

"This time your father might be right," I said.

"And this is your business?" Cordoza straightened up. His look was insolent.

"Yes, it is," I answered." And it seems as though it ought to be yours." Anger flashed in his eyes and he stepped toward me. I didn't move.

Cordoza looked as if he didn't know what to do, then he relaxed and shrugged. "Go ahead and tilt at windmills if you want," he said.

The literary reference was surprising, although it was appropriately Spanish. Maybe John Cordoza was more complex than he appeared. He stepped aside and I walked around to the driver's side of my car.

"Lucia Chavez is missing," I said.

For a heartbeat Cordoza shed his macho act. "Lucia...Julio's friend who used to play here at the house?"

"She said someone followed her home the other night and one of you scared them away."

Cordoza's face still showed concern. "I thought they were just punks following a pretty girl."

"They may be the same ones who killed your son."

He glanced over at his friends and his brother on the porch. He walked over to my side of the car, his eyes dark and serious. "You tell me if you find out who did this," he said. "You tell me if I can help Lucia." He held my gaze. "You find the person, Professor and I will take care of him for you."

"Not for me, Cordoza," I said, getting into my car. "Julio was your son. You need to do it for yourself." I shut the door and started the engine. John Cordoza stood there looking at me as I pulled away.

Seventeen

I called Lucia Chavez' mother to find out if she'd heard from her daughter. She hadn't. I assumed that meant the Sheriff's Department hadn't found Lucia, either. I called Jim Stapleton, just to find out. At any rate, I wanted to go through the Sheriff's Department records on the Erskine case and find out if Raul Lopez was mentioned as a witness — and if Randy Fontana was assigned to the case. Jim Stapleton could get me access to the records, assuming that they went back that far. Stapleton wasn't in and he didn't answer his page. I left my cell phone number on his answering machine.

If I couldn't get access to Sheriff's records, my second choice was the newspaper archives. I called the Orange County Register only to find that they didn't allow public access to their archives. A not-so-friendly receptionist directed me to the Santa Ana Public Library, which did have archives that were open to the public.

The library was crowded, mostly with women and old men browsing among the aisles of books or seated in front of antique looking computer monitors. A young man with orange hair and an effeminate manner directed me downstairs to the microfilm department.

Two girls in their twenties — one African American and the other Hispanic — sat behind a counter looking up at me as I descended. From the anticipation on their faces, they must have been starved for customers. The black girl, skinny and wearing large thick glasses, apologized for the condition of the microfilm machines and then, in the officious tone of a burgeoning bureaucrat, informed me that I would have to pay a one dollar deposit for a lens and sign a form indicating my name, address and phone number. I asked her what the street value for used microfilm lenses was, but she didn't get it.

The three machines, which must have been at least thirty years old, were conveniently located in their own little room along with the archives of the Orange County Register and two large tables for reading

Casey Dorman

Sharron, the black girl, found the microfilm containing all of the Registers for the first quarter of 1959, then showed me how to install the lens, thread the film into the machine, and push the button to move the film forward or back. This process made a sound like two old-fashioned washing machines having a wrestling match. The machine had a tendency to hesitate, then jump forward, moving through several pages at once. I practiced using a light touch on the forward button.

The first headline was a shock. I hadn't remembered that January 1st, 1959 was the day that Fidel Castro had marched into Havana. The lead story identified Castro as a rebel leader whose ragtag band of soldiers had come down from the Sierra Maestra Mountains and ousted Fulgencio Batista, the former President turned dictator. In the next several months Castro would nationalize all of the main industries, thereby alienating the U.S., and then declare himself a Communist in the Russian mold.

I hit the button and the machine jerked forward. Headlines, advertisements, brightly colored comic strips all zipped across the screen in front of me as I looked for a headline that mentioned the death of Winthrop Erskine. I experienced the odd sensation of having entered a time machine. The upcoming presidential race was mentioned, with Richard Nixon and John F. Kennedy being the front-runners for their parties. Conflicts between the United States and Russia in Berlin were heating up and I remembered that in another year or two the famous wall separating East and West Berlin would be erected. The machine groaned and creaked like a tired wagon as I tried to manipulate the forward and backward buttons to insure that I didn't miss anything. The news of the death itself should have occupied a banner space at the top of the front page, but I didn't know the exact date. At the beginning of the second week of January, I struck paydirt. The headlines carried the news of the unexpected death of Winthrop Erskine, the head of the County's most prominent, wealthy, and powerful family. The coverage was disappointingly brief, making me wonder if it was the family's influence or the Sheriff's Department, or even some more sinister third party, who had squelched the story. As it was, the account was sufficiently provocative to raise my eyebrows, even forty-four years later. According to the Register story, Erskine and his wife were alone in the house on a Sunday afternoon. He was located in a basement room and apparently shot himself—not once, but three times. And with two different guns. The first two shots were with a sixteen-gauge shotgun into his stomach. When that didn't kill him, the story said he dragged himself across the floor to a cabinet containing a .22 caliber handgun and placed the next bullet in his temple. Through all of this, his wife didn't hear a thing, and only found his body when she went searching for him to answer a telephone call. There was no mention of a Mexican-American houseboy being on the premises and, in fact, the Sheriff's Department detective in charge of the case was quoted as saying, "Mr. and Mrs. Erskine were home alone at the time." The detective's name was Randy Fontana.

The remainder of the story chronicled the Erskine's family's rise and dominance over land ownership and agriculture in Orange County. Winthrop Erskine's wife indicated that her husband had been depressed for several weeks but she didn't reveal why. Erskine was lauded as a philanthropist and visionary land developer. The next day's paper had news of the funeral and contained a brief reference to the coroner's statement that the two shotgun wounds to the abdomen had preceded the bullet to the temple and the official ruling for the death was suicide. The Sheriff's Department had concluded their investigation of Erskine's demise even faster than they had closed up the recent deaths of Ramon Chavez and Lisa Burke. I searched in vain through the local news, feature stories and advertisements on the rest of the pages of the paper and then through each of those for the next few days but there was no more mention of Winthrop Erskine in any of them.

I plowed on, fighting the temptation to digress into the era of my parents. When I reached Saturday's front page, another death had captured the headlines. This time it was Sally Umstead's. I stopped the paper's movement and began to read.

The debutante's murder had garnered even larger headlines than Winthrop Erskine's suicide. There was a large portrait picture of Sally, looking hauntingly similar to the pictures Lisa Burke's mother had shown us of her daughter. A smaller picture of Raul Lopez was less striking; showing him looking uncomfortably dressed in a too big suit coat, a wide tie, and his long hair slicked down flat to his head. The story detailed their brutal murder. Each had been shot once in the head while they parked in Sally's Cadillac convertible in the middle of a vast orange grove on the Erskine Ranch.

Randy Fontana was again the detective in charge of the case. Fontana gave no interview this time, but the story mentioned that the Sheriff had said that they "were pursuing all possible leads," which probably meant they didn't have a clue who the killer was. The remainder of the story was about Sally and her family. It was revealed that she had been accepted to Mills College in northern California and was to enter in the fall after graduating from high school. The family was described as long-time Newport Beach residents and Sally's father was the owner of a manufacturing company that made airplane parts, mostly for the United States Air Force. Michael and Sally were the only two children. In 1959 Michael was a junior at USC. Raul Lopez was described as being nineteen years old and a former student at Santa Ana High School. Nothing was mentioned about his current employment nor any connection between Lopez and the Erskine family.

I cranked the machine forward through the remainder of Saturday's paper to the Sunday edition. There was a continuing story about the Sheriff's department exploring Lopez' ties with local Mexican-American gangs. A mention was made of upcoming funeral arrangements for Sally Umstead. The editorial section of the paper contained a column deploring the reach of violence into Orange County and implying that the influx of Mexican- American gang members from Los Angeles—the Zoot Suit influence—was to blame. Reading the story, I could feel the momentum building for the community to find a scapegoat for the

Pink Carnation

killings— a momenturn that crystallized their fears about the growing Hispanic presence in the county.

It wasn't long before the scapegoat was found. By Tuesday's edition of the paper, Detective Fontana had announced that arrests were "imminent" in the Umstead-Lopez murders and that they were related to Lopez' gang connections and a supposed gang war that was raging between the local Mexican-American youth and those from Los Angeles. It was a war that Arturo Cordoza had told me had not existed. On Friday, the front page of the Register contained the pictures of three menacing looking Mexicans, who were identified as the suspects in the killings. All three had been arrested and were in the Orange County Jail. The murder was now described as a gang retribution for some earlier infringement on the LA gang's territory by Lopez' gang. Sally Umstead was an innocent bystander who happened to be at the wrong place at the wrong time. The Register's Editor-in-Chief called for a crackdown on gang activity in Orange County, lest the area become a violent war-zone like its larger, uglier neighbor to the north.

Two days after their arrest, the Mexican-American trio was let go. The news that they had been in jail in Riverside County the night of the murders was enough to free the three youths, although there were no editorials deploring white suburban panic nor apologizing to the Mexican-American community for the rush to judgment. In fact, the Sheriff's Department vowed to continue pursuing the "Mexican gang connection" and the editor of the Register continued to call for action to deal with the gang problem brought on by the influx of immigrants.

The story petered out. I cranked the machine forward and was occasionally rewarded by tidbits in which the Sheriff's Department announced that leads were still being pursued, though there were no more promises of imminent arrests. My eyes were getting tired and my head was dizzy trying to keep up with the newsprint whizzing across my field of vision and then skidding to a stop as I thought I found something of interest. I'd learned enough to raise Randy Fontana to the top of my list of suspects in the Burke/Chavez and Julio Cordoza murders and maybe John Elmore's and Brian Thornberg's, too.

I fumbled with the microfilm, rewinding it and prying it from the machine so I could wrap the rubber band around it and stuff it back in the box marked January-April, 1959. I had less success disengaging the lens from the machine. I gave up and called Sharron over. She deftly turned the lens counterclockwise and it fell out into her hand. She gave me a condescending smile and suppressed a giggle. I thanked her and asked for my dollar back.

It was time to go after Randy Fontana.

Eighteen

I tried Jim Stapleton again but he still didn't answer. I called Kim on her cell phone to tell her I was going to the Sheriff's department to wait for Stapleton.

"Anh, the Sheriff's deputies are looking for you. They want to arrest you for Elmore's murder."

I felt blindsided by the news. I had almost forgotten than I was still under police suspicion. Suddenly my palms were slick with sweat. I felt like my strength had just been taken out of me. I did my best to focus. I thought about Randy Fontana and I thought about Lucia Chavez.

I asked Kim if they'd found Lucia yet.

"I don't think so. They're looking for both of you."

My mind was racing. I knew what I had to do. "I'm going to Silverado Canyon, Em. The person behind this is Randy Fontana. Try to get hold of Jim Stapleton and tell him I need him to come to Fontana's house."

"Shouldn't you wait for Jim?"

"He's a detective," I said. "If there's a warrant for my arrest, he'll have to bring me in and deal with Fontana later. I'm not going to sit in jail and wait for someone else to discover that Fontana's the killer."

"What are you going to do, Anh?"

"If Fontana's the killer, then there must be some clues at his house. I'll find something. I'm sure of it." I hoped my plan didn't sound as lame to Kim as it did to me. "Remember the Vietnamese saying, 'you can't catch a fish by climbing a mountain'?" I asked.

"You made that up, Anh," she said.

"OK, maybe I did. Haven't you got an old Vietnamese saying that's appropriate?"

"How about Oy Vay?"

"It fits," I said. "Just keep trying Stapleton, Em. He knows where Fontana lives. Tell him to get there as fast as he can."

Silverado Canyon was in the hills that stretched eastward from the valley that contained the millions of people who populated Orange

County. I took Santiago Canyon Road, a winding, two-lane highway that stretched from the city of Orange to Rancho Santa Margarita twenty miles to the south. The dizzying population explosion that had turned most of Orange County into crowded tracts of identical houses and four lanes of slow moving, bumper to bumper traffic came to a sudden halt at the line of hills on the west side of Santiago Canyon. Driving down the two-lane highway, it was as if I had gone back in time to a period when only sprawling sheep and cattle ranches and pine forests made up the land south of Los Angeles.

Silverado Canyon and Modjeska Canyon were the two largest branches off of Santiago Canyon. Modjeska Canyon got its unusual name from a famous Polish actress who had migrated to Orange County in the late 1800's. In the mansion she had built, she entertained dignitaries from all over the world, who made the trek by train and wagon from the ports of Los Angeles or San Francisco. Silverado was a tiny mining community that had flourished briefly. When the mine ran out, the miners' homes were replaced by small ranches, which were now run by country types who raised horses, artists who enjoyed the beauty of the forests, steep bluffs, and the winding creek that flowed down the center of the canyon. The canyon was also home to one or two eccentric millionaires who preferred to isolate themselves from the frenetic pace of the rest of Orange County, and to a substantial population of underemployed roughnecks and bikers who lived dirt cheap in their small shacks, mobile homes, or in a rented room in the one dilapidated motel that still stood on the road leading into the canyon. Entering Silverado Canyon was more like visiting Oregon or West Virginia than being ten miles away from the sophistication of Irvine and Newport Beach.

It was late afternoon and the sun was bright but the shadows of the western hills were starting to touch the bottom of the canyon. I drove the winding curves past riding stables and small, old houses set back into the hillside until I arrived at a widening in the road containing the Silverado General Store, a post-office, gift shop, hardware store, and two restaurants

Pink Carnation

Outside the General Store, a knot of men sat around a large wooden cable drum, drinking beer from cans. Besides the five men, who were dressed in jeans, boots, and T-shirts or western-style long sleeved shirts, there were three dogs lying on the store's raised wooden front porch. All eyes, including those of the dogs, looked up at me when I pulled my shiny '58 MGA roadster up next to the two battered and dirty pick-up trucks, one sixties-looking VW van, and a chopped Harley Davidson parked in front of the store.

I knew that Fontana lived in Silverado Canyon, but I didn't know where. The post-office would have been my best shot at getting his address, but it was past five and post office employees were punctual about quitting time, if nothing else. My next best bet was one of the local businesses or the group of loungers on the front porch of the General Store. As I passed by them on my way into the store, my country-like, "howdy gents," didn't get any reaction but a snicker.

The acne-faced boy at the counter didn't have a clue who I was talking about when I asked him about Fontana, even when I described the old man. If Fontana lived in Silverado, he must be a regular at the store but the teenage boy's blank expression when I asked him about Fontana made me think the kid wouldn't recognize his own sister if I described her to him. Nevertheless, I also gave him a description of Lucia—just in case—and drew another blank.

I bought a six-pack of Budweiser and ambled out onto the front porch. Only the dogs looked over at me as I planted myself against the store's doorframe and peeled off a beer. The boys were discussing how, after the last rain, one of the local horsemen had gotten his trailer stuck in the mud when he tried to back it down a slippery hill from his house to the highway. Agreement was unanimous that the basic problem was that the driver of the SUV that was hitched to the horse trailer was a "townie." I glanced down at my shiny Bruno Magli penny loafers and thought about walking around the parking lot scuffing them up with dirt. I wondered if Armani made a western-style shirt. I doubted it. At least I had a Budweiser in my hand and not an Anchor-Steam or St. Pauli Girl.

When the conversation lulled, I plopped the five remaining Buds in the middle of the cable-spool table and announced that each one could help himself. Nobody bothered to ask why and in less than ten seconds there was nothing left on the top of the table but a plastic holder with six empty holes. Three of the guys lifted their cans toward me in salute and I knew I'd made the right move. I asked if any of them knew Randy Fontana.

"Old guy, used to be a cop?" The man sitting closest to me turned his head in my direction to ask the question over his shoulder. He had shoulder length hair that still bore the impression of the hatband from the western hat sitting on the table in front of him. He was wearing a faded red T-shirt over a slim but muscular frame and his arms were tanned the color of copper. He looked to be in his late twenties or early thirties.

"That's him," I said, still leaning against the doorframe. "I'm trying to find out where he lives."

"You a friend of his?" the same young man asked. The others all had their attention on him.

"Not exactly," I said, feeling my way through the conversation. "I just need to know where he lives."

"You a cop, too?" The question came from the man opposite the one who'd been doing the talking. This time the speaker was older. He had a mustache and a short ring of hair around a large bald spot that was tanned and shiny. He wore a checked shirt that was open at the collar with tufts of gray hair sticking out below his neck. He pulled a Marlboro Light from a box in front of him and lit it with a black plastic lighter. He stared at me with clear gray eyes, waiting for my answer.

I shook my head. "I'm not a cop."

"He's too tall for a cop," one of the others, a young kid still wearing his cowboy hat and not looking old enough to drink, said. The rest of the group laughed, except for the older man across from me who kept looking at me with his steel-gray eyes.

Pink Carnation

"You drove all the way up here to see somebody without knowing where the man lives?" the man asked, still piercing me with his stare.

I thought about offering the explanation that I was a townie, but decided against it. "I figured somebody around here would know him," I answered.

"That old man is a shit-head," the kid with the cowboy hat said. He looked as if he'd had too many beers. He grinned and looked around the table for approval. There were a couple of nods and one of the men laughed out loud. It wasn't the one who'd been questioning me. The latter smoked and frowned, looking around the table at the others as if they were lame-brained.

"I said I'm not a friend of his," I said evenly, looking at the older man.

"Third house after the bridge on the other side of the creek, down by water," the man said, nodding his head toward the bridge at the end of the parking lot.

I nodded back. "Much obliged, pardner."

The third house on the creek side of the road was a low affair, built of broad, horizontally placed redwood boards with wooden paned windows and a shake roof that had become the repository for a variety of small tree limbs and pine needles. From the road, I could see the railing of a rear deck sticking out from behind the side of the house. There was no garage and no car in the driveway. Across the creek I couldn't see anything but a vague outline of buildings through the trees. I drove a little further up the road until I turned a corner that hid my car from view, then parked in the trees and walked back along the narrow gravel road.

No one answered my knock on the door, and thankfully, there was no sound of a barking dog from inside the house so I walked around the edge of the house to the back. I could hear the gurgling of the stream and when I rounded the corner, I could see the shallow water meandering among the trees about twenty yards away at the bottom of a steep slope. There was no basement level to the house, but a wooden deck, supported by three concrete pillars, stuck out toward the water. It looked as if there were a couple of lounge chairs and a portable barbecue but not much else sitting on the deck. I reached up and grasped the waist-high railing, and hoisted myself onto the deck.

French doors with small glass panes led from the house onto the deck. I picked up a large metal fork from next to the barbecue and with one quick stroke, poked out the door pane nearest the handle. Glancing around, I waited for an alarm or a call from a neighbor. I could feel the sweat under my arms, but I ignored my anxiety. Slipping on one of the protective gloves that sat next to the barbecue, I reached my hand through the broken pane. The glove gave me just enough finger control to twist the lock in the handle of the door. I turned the handle and—presto—I was inside the house.

Burglary isn't as hard as its cracked up to be.

Fontana was neat. There were no scattered papers, no empty beer cans, no dirty socks on the floor. Everything was in its place. The inside was as rustic looking as the outside of the house with a large stone fireplace at one end of the living room and large, worn, leather furniture. At one end of the room was a massive circular table made of oak with four oak chairs gathered around it. I hadn't turned on any lights and the house was dim but I thought I could make out a kitchen beyond the circular table. Off to the left, past the front door, was a hallway that I figured led to a bedroom or two, maybe an office.

The hallway was dark enough that I was forced to switch on a light. I could see a door at the end of the hallway. To the right were two more doors. The first one was open and I peeked my head inside to find a spare room with a neatly made bed. Nothing to spark my curiosity.

The second room was more interesting. I'd hoped for a computer or files that might tell me what Fontana had been doing over the last forty years to insure the cover-up of the Erskine and Umstead/Lopez murders.

Randy Fontana wasn't that modern of a man. There was no computer. The room contained a desk as well as a small guest twin bed that was a match to the one in the other bedroom. There was a nightstand and a small pine dresser with a mirror hanging on the wall behind it. I switched on the light and moved to the desk. Fontana didn't seem to have a typewriter either, but he had plenty of papers stacked in a wooden in-box and a pile of envelopes held down by a heavy paperweight in the shape of a reclining Collie dog. A handsome glass clock sat atop the desk, telling me that it was already 6:22 in the evening. A sense of urgency hit me as I realized that Fontana might arrive home at any time. I began going through the file drawers located in the desk. The first drawer contained nothing but bills and tax records. The other file drawer was locked. Did I want to break it open? Fontana would already know someone had broken into his house from the pane I'd broken in the French doors on the deck. I stood debating my options when I heard the crunch of gravel outside on the road. Switching off the bedroom light, I raced down the hallway to turn off the other light. I raised myself onto my toes and peeked out the oval paned window that was at the apex of the front door. I saw no car in the driveway. One of the other local residents must have driven by the front of the house.

Turning back toward the office-bedroom, I heard what sounded like a curtain rustling from the room at the end of the hall. I'd assumed that the room was a bathroom, since I hadn't seen one yet. I stood motionless, straining to listen. Then I heard the rustling sound again. This time it was definitely from inside the room. I moved to the end of the hallway and carefully opened the door, ready to swing on whoever was inside. It was a bathroom, but an empty one. Then I heard the rustling again. It was coming from behind the shower curtain. I brushed the curtain aside. What I saw, gave me goosebumps. Lying in the bathtub, duct tape across her mouth and around her ankles and wrists was Lucia. She had blood caked on her sleeve and she looked up at me with a half-conscious look of fear, which turned to relief when she recognized who I was.

I bent down and pulled the tape from her mouth.

"Professor Routledge!" she murmured. "How did you find me?"

"Never mind how I found you," I said. "We've got to get out of here before Fontana gets back." I unwrapped her wrists and looked at her sleeve. She'd bled profusely but most of the blood had dried. I pulled the tape from around her ankles and helped her stand up. She leaned against me for support. I helped her out of the bathtub and held her for a moment. Her right arm hung limply at her side and I thought she might collapse at any moment. Her shirt was ripped and her breasts were exposed. She glanced down, then looked up at me, embarrassed, reaching her good arm over to hold her blouse closed.

I could feel her body trembling.

"Steady," I said. "You're safe now. Tell me what happened."

"I followed you to Elmore's house," Lucia began, trying to walk on her own.

I nodded for her to keep talking but kept my arm around her waist as we started back down the hallway.

"I snuck past the guard at the gate," she continued, "and I found Elmore's house. I thought you were inside so I went up to the front door and rang the bell. That bastard Fontana came to the door. He had a gun and made me go inside. Elmore was dead on the patio. Fontana had stabbed him. The pig took the knife that was all bloody and made me hold onto it so it would have my fingerprints. I tried to fight him, but he stabbed me in the arm. Then he stole a bunch of things and put them in a bag and forced me into his car. He put the tape around me and drove me here."

We'd reached the living room. I thought about searching the house for Elmore's stolen things but that would take too long and Lucia needed to get to a hospital. She'd lost a lot of blood and she was dehydrated. Besides, if Lucia and I got caught with Elmore's property in our possession no one would believe we hadn't stolen it ourselves. I wished Jim Stapleton would arrive. He was our only chance to prove that Fontana was behind the killings and Lucia's disappearance. At this point, our best bet was to get away from the house as fast as possible and try to contact Stapleton.

I helped Lucia across the deck and lifted her to the ground. We edged along the side of the house. The dusk had descended and I could barely see my way without keeping one hand against the side of the house and using the other to support Lucia, who was getting weaker by the minute. When we rounded the front of the house, a figure emerged from the shadows and stepped in front of us, the snub-nosed gun he was holding aimed at my belt buckle. I felt my skin go cold. Lucia stiffened. It was Randy Fontana. He didn't seem surprised to see either of us.

"Oh, there you are, " I said. "We were just checking to see if you were around back."

"Get inside the house," Fontana's voice was cold. His car wasn't in the driveway, and I realized he must have seen the light and driven by, then walked back to the house in order to catch his intruder in the act.

He walked us into the house and directed us to sit on the sofa in the living room, seating himself in one of the other chairs, while keeping his body turned to face us. He had on the same worn sport coat and open necked sport-shirt that he'd been wearing the first day I'd seen him on the movie set.

"I should have known I'd have to get rid of both of you," he said.

Lucia was leaning heavily against me. She was losing consciousness. She needed medical attention badly.

"No need to bother," I said. "We were just leaving anyway." I began to help Lucia up.

"Sit down," he growled.

I looked around the room. There didn't seem to be any obvious way out other than the way I'd come in or through the front door. Fontana was watching my every move.

"Can I get Lucia a drink?" I asked. "How about if I bring you something, Detective? I could run out."

"Shut up and stay put. You won't need anything at all in a little while. Not where you two are going."

"Heavens to Betsy, Detective. First Ramon Chavez, then Julio Cordoza, John Elmore, and now us? You're going to become famous as a serial killer. We ought to get his autograph, Lucia. Detective Fontana will probably end up on *Sixty Minutes* or *20/20* someday, or at the very least on *Americas Most Wanted*."

Fontana rested the fat little pistol on the arm of the chair, still keeping it pointed at me.

"You talk too much, Professor. You irritate me. So does your sexy little friend here. We're going up the Canyon as soon as it gets darker, and you're both going to have an accident...a fatal fall off of a cliff. People will think that you were hiding out after killing Elmore." His smile was cruel.

I smiled back. "You'd better go to plan B, Detective. I had a nice little chat with the duncecap boys over at the General Store before I came here. They'll tell the cops that I was asking about you. Besides that, I've already told Detective Stapleton I was coming here. It's not going to be as simple as you think." I started to stand. "You might as well hand over the gun. I'll tell them to go easy on you."

He pointed the gun at my chest. "For the last time, Professor, sit down! I might have to kill you just to shut you up."

I sat back down and reflected on how cold-blooded killers often lacked a sense of humor.

"What did Stapleton say?" he asked.

I'd never reached Jim Stapleton but Fontana didn't know that. "Stapleton put a warrant out for you. He's on his way here." I hoped there was at least a grain of truth to what I was saying. It depended upon whether Kim had reached Jim or not. On the assumption that she had, I wanted to stall Fontana as long as possible. Since he was planning to kill us, I wanted to stall him as long as possible—period.

Fontana gave a little "harumph," which may have been a laugh or a cough. With his free hand he pulled a pack of cigarettes from his jacket pocket and stuck one in his mouth. He replaced the pack and, still using his free hand, dug around in his pants pocket until he came up with a lighter. He lit the cigarette then took a long drag and blew the smoke out in a thin stream. Too bad the lethal effects of tobacco aren't more immediate.

"I was with Stapleton right before I came here," Fontana said. "He didn't mention arresting me."

"He probably decided to wait and let me trap you at your house."

"You sure crack wise for a man that's about to die."

"How about Elmore, did he crack wise before you stabbed him?" I asked.

"Elmore might still be alive if you hadn't gotten him fired up about Lopez."

"So you had to kill him?"

"That's right. I drove over to his house and we started talking. When I found out you'd snuck in there a couple of hours earlier, I knew I could kill Elmore and you'd take the rap for it. Then your nosy little friend here showed up and things got even better. I could pin it on both of you."

"What about Cordoza?" I asked, trying to keep him talking. "I saw you with Jim Stapleton at the murder scene. How did you manage to find Cordoza and kill him before Lucia and I got there."

Before he could answer, I heard a creak from the deck. Fontana's head spun around. Jim Stapleton was standing outside the French doors, his gun in his hand.

"Oh shit!" Fontana raised his own gun in what looked to me more like a wave of greeting than an attempt to aim. The next thing I knew, Fontana's chest was blown open by a blast from Stapleton's gun.

"Damn you!" Fontana gasped as he slid down to the floor, seemingly gallons of blood pumping in angry red spurts from his chest. His gun hand twitched around the handle of his weapon but he was beyond making any coordinated movement. His whole body began to convulse, splashing blood across the rug and onto the chair from which he'd just fallen. Finally he stopped moving. Lucia and I sat immobile on the couch, staring at the figure at our feet. Stapleton opened the door and walked across the room, his gun still pointing at Fontana's inert body. He leaned down and felt the man's neck for a pulse.

"He's dead," Stapleton said matter-of-factly. "Are you two all right?"

NINETEEN

"Anh, you didn't tell me you might be killed."

"It seemed wiser to leave that part out," I said to Kim. She was sitting next to me on our patio. The evening air was cool and the sky was clear, revealing millions of pinpoints of starlight. A sliver of moon hung low over the roofs of the stately houses on the tip of Balboa Peninsula across the bay. It was beyond midnight and the usual parade of walkers, cyclists, and joggers that passed by on the promenade in front of our house had disappeared for the night. The only sounds were the tinkling of halyards against masts and the soft lapping of waves against hulls. Across from us, a pair of ducks waded at the beach's edge, then launched themselves into the dark water and scooted a few feet away from shore, making tiny circles and nudging each other. I was having my fourth glass of Georges III cabernet and trying to take the tension out of my nervous system after my close encounter with Randy Fontana's plans for shortening my future.

"If you hadn't gotten hold of Jim Stapleton, I'd have been in a lot bigger trouble, Em," I said. "Five more minutes might have been too late. Fontana was intent on killing Lucia and me."

Kim reached over and placed her hand on mine. I could feel the warmth of her soft skin.

"Is Lucia going to be all right?" she asked.

"The knife wound wasn't serious. She lost a lot of blood and hadn't had any food or water for about twenty hours, but the doctor at the hospital said she'd be fine after a little rest." I drank more wine and looked up at the stars, reflecting on how lucky I was. A lot of people had not been so lucky. "I don't know why Fontana had to kill those people," I said.

"What do you mean, Anh?"

"Why take such risks to cover up something he did forty years ago? Nobody's interested anymore, except maybe writers like Elmore, and no one is going to reopen the case now. He should have just let things blow over. What a shame." I poured myself the last few drops of cabernet.

"In Vietnam we say, 'the hand of a thief may line the pockets of a rich man'."

I nodded in a knowing way. "I've said that a few times myself, Em." I hadn't a clue as to what she was talking about.

"Fontana may have been carrying out orders from someone else, Anh. Suppose Erskine's killer is still around. Suppose he's someone so powerful that the truth would ruin him—so powerful that he can stop a Sheriff's investigation."

"Maybe it was the Mafia, Em. Arturo Cordoza said it was men from Las Vegas who killed Erskine. The Mafia could threaten Fontana into doing their killing for them, especially if he'd cooperated with them in the past and they had something on him."

"Mafia in Orange County? Ged ouda heah," she said in a perfect *Mean Streets* DeNiro. Or was it James Caan from *Mickey Blue Eyes*?

"They're still in Las Vegas, Em. That's not very far away."

We were both quiet. The sounds of the night — the water and the boat sounds — punctuated our conversation, causing us both to ponder what we were saying.

"It doesn't make sense," I said.

"The Mafia committed too many murders in the last forty years to worry about somebody finding out about just one of them, "Kim replied.

"It has to be someone who has everything to lose. Someone..."

"...here in Orange County," she finished for me.

"Right."

"But who?"

We sat, contemplating the question. There was little sound other than one of the ducks shaking his or her wings and the clink of lines against a mast. Across the bay near the peninsula's point, an occasional light shone in a window. Further north most of the area around the pier was still well lit. The tiny four-car ferry from our island to the peninsula had shut down for the night and the only boats in the bay were those safely moored in front of their owners' mansions.

"Do you still talk to Janet Erskine Jones?" Kim asked.

I thought she was changing the subject, then I understood where she was going. "She's on the Chandler Board, but I haven't had a private conversation with her for years. Do you think she'd know something about this?"

"She might know who profited from her uncle's death."

"I doubt she was very involved in business back then, but it's worth a try."

"I think you should talk to her, Anh," Kim said.

It was a good idea. I drained my glass of wine and listened to the sounds of the night. "You ready for bed?"

"Uh huh," Kim said, scooting her chair back. "I'll get you a couple of aspirins and a glass of water."

It was wonderful having a wife who thought of everything.

The first thing I did the next morning was call Lucia to see how she was doing. Or at least the first thing after my third cup of strong black coffee and two more aspirins. Kim managed to make me eat some toast and cereal, just to preserve the lining of my stomach. Then she headed off to work. She was conducting an audit of one of the new businesses that had moved into Santa Ana to take advantage of the low rents, tax breaks, and ample labor supply offered in the State's Enterprise Zone. I felt guilty for keeping her up so late, but she'd risen well before me to take her usual five-mile run, so I guess she was ready for her busy day.

Lucia had recovered enough to be back to her hotheaded self. The fact that Randy Fontana was an ex-detective was all that she needed to set her off on a tirade about cops and Latinos. I reminded her that Jim Stapleton was also a detective and he'd killed Fontana and saved our lives.

"If your friend Stapleton had done his job earlier, our lives wouldn't have been in danger," Lucia said over the phone. Her voice was cold, then it softened. "I owe you very much, Professor Routledge. You were the one who really saved my life."

I felt like saying, "aw shucks," and maybe scuffing my foot on the floor like a shy adolescent. Instead I changed the subject. "You and your mother can feel free to take the settlement from the movie company now," I said.

"I think my mother will feel worse, finding out that Ramon was murdered. An accident was outside of anyone's control...an act of God. My mother can accept God's will but she'll have a hard time accepting such evil."

"I'm truly sorry," I said.

"Arturo Cordoza was the one who was right about all this." Lucia said.

"Are you going to talk to the Cordozas?" I asked.

"I'll probably talk to Arturo today...and John, too. Why?"

"It's possible that Fontana was working for someone else--the person who killed Winthrop Erskine back in '59. Arturo had some ideas about who that might be. I'd like you to jog his memory about who the Las Vegas people were that he was talking about."

There was a moment of silence on the other end of the line. "You mean we're not done with this, Professor Routledge?" I could hear the eagerness in her voice.

"*I'm* not done but *you* are, Lucia. Fontana admitted killing your brother. That's what you wanted to find out."

"I won't be done with this until you are, Professor. Remember, they were going to kill me, too."

I could feel my shoulders beginning to tense. I debated arguing with Lucia, but I knew it would be useless. I ended the conversation feeling uneasy. Lucia was my student and I didn't want to drag her into anything more. On the other hand, if she wanted to pursue the trail of her brother's killer, who was I to stop her?

The next call was a more difficult one. Janet Erskine Jones and I had ended our romance five years earlier and we only saw each other sporadically at social events such as the faculty fundraiser. I hadn't had a private conversation with Janet since he'd called me and told me about the opening on the Chandler faculty. Now I wanted to pry into what might be a sensitive situation for her, since it involved the death of her uncle.

Difficult or not, I made the call. She agreed to meet me, but not on the campus.

When I crossed the narrow bridge from Balboa Island to the mainland, I could see the first few splatters of rain on my windshield. Southern California needed the rain, but the sun-baked streets became like sheets of ice after a spring shower. I pulled over and raised the canvas roof on my roadster, then got back in the car and turned onto the Coast Highway, pointing myself southward toward San Clemente. The shower settled into a steady light drizzle that kept me running my defrosters to avoid fogging the windows of my antique car while I looked ahead at a bleak gray sky. The horizon to my west was brighter, which meant the morning rain was only a temporary blot on the standard fare of blue skies and bright sun that are Southern California.

I slowed as I passed Blue Bay, remembering John Elmore. A brisk breeze, accompanying the rain, was riffling the stand of pines on the land I'd crossed to get into Blue Bay Estates. I sped up and wound down the hill into the heart of Laguna Beach. A few hardy souls were out on the town beach, walking in shorts and rain jackets. Along the sidewalks, tourists in shorts and Hawaiian shirts carried umbrellas or hurried to duck into the next antique shop or gallery before getting soaked. The rain hadn't thinned the traffic and I crawled through the town center. By the time I passed the Ritz Carlton at Laguna Niguel, I was back up to speed.

The rain continued through Dana Point and past San Juan Capistrano and was still coming down in light gusty showers as I downshifted and headed down the hill and into the parking lot at San Clemente Cove. The bright horizon must have been an illusion because a light mist was rolling in from the sea. The end of the San Clemente Pier was visible but it had a surreal, fuzzy quality when viewed from the distance of the shore. Despite the weather, a small line of surfers stood on the beach, shoulders hunched against the rain, their boards wedged into the sand like a line of primitive totems along the edge of the sea. I could make out three or four intrepid surfers sitting on their boards farther out among the tossing waves. It was a good surf day for the hardy.

I crossed over to the little row of shops and cafes that lined the main street of the cove across from the Amtrak stop and the pier. Sitting at a table, straight as an arrow, with a steaming cup of coffee in front of her was Janet. She was wearing a bright yellow rain slicker, with the hood pulled over her head, but the proud, almost fierce way in which she stuck her face out into the rain, left no doubt that the figure at the table was Janet Erskine Jones. I zipped up my own blue nylon windbreaker and scooted in across from her.

Janet smiled and patted the seat next to her. "Come over here. You're missing the view. The sea is wonderful and mysterious in the rain."

I did as she asked. She didn't look at me, but kept gazing out to sea. There was no one else on the tiny veranda of the cafe. It was the most exposed seat along the street. No one would recognize one of Orange County's most famous people, since she was cloaked in anonymity inside her slicker. But she was outside, immersed in the rawness of the elements and that was what Janet liked.

I looked at her profile, the front of her face visible in outline beyond the edges of her yellow plastic rain hood. The contours of her face were soft and rounded, but her chin was strong. She'd been a beauty when she was younger and the lines were still there. I'd fallen for her looks as well as her personality when she and I had dated, and she'd been in her late fifties then. She'd aged more than I had in the last five years, as older people often did.

"How is your marriage?" she asked, turning her face to look at me. "Your wife is beautiful."

Her eyes crinkled in a friendly smile. Her eyes had always been large and pale—haunting when she was preoccupied as she had been when she was gazing at the ocean a moment ago, and piercing when she was looking right at you. As usual she wore little or no makeup. Her skin was still young, although I could see more wrinkles than before and she had numerous unconcealed age spots on her forehead and cheeks. She was smiling in the same half-smile that I remembered as being so sexual when we'd dated. She smiled now with fond interest.

"I always choose beautiful women," I said. "Kim and I are very happy. She's a sweet, intelligent, funny person. You and she should be friends." I looked over at her but she didn't say anything. "And your marriage?" I asked.

"My husband spends most of his time in Maryland. We have a house in the country outside of Bethesda and he needs to be near Washington. He still lobbies now and then. It's ideal. I spend nearly all of my time here." Her smile broadened and she gave me a sly wink. "He and I are more appealing to each other in small doses."

The rain was coming down harder and angry raindrops splattered her coffee. I could feel my head getting soaked and drops were starting to roll off of my nose and eyebrows. I held out my hand and watched the raindrops bounce off of my open palm. "They don't make roofs in San Clemente?"

Janet shook her head and smiled, then stood and picked up her coffee cup. "You academics can't stand even a little bit of nature."

We moved back to one of the tables under the roof. The front of the cafe was open and we still had a view but it was warmer and we had a chance of staying dry. Janet threw back the hood on her coat. She'd cut her hair in a mannish bob. Maybe it had been that way when I'd seen her at the Board meeting but I hadn't noticed. It robbed her features of some of their softness, giving her more of the look that writers sometimes described as "handsome." She peeled off the slicker, revealing a turquoise wool turtleneck and a pair of black riding pants. When she stood to shed her coat I couldn't help but notice that her figure was still as slim and girlish as ever. I took off my windbreaker and slung it over the back of one of the chairs from an adjacent table. We were the only ones in the cafe except the barman. He came around the bar and freshened Janet's coffee and I ordered a Bloody Mary. I needed something to cut through the gloomy weather and the thickness left over from last night's bottle of wine.

Janet shook her head at my order and smiled. "Some things don't change."

"I need to ask you about something from the past," I began, testing the water. I didn't know how sensitive Janet might be about her uncle's death. It had been forty years ago, but if I remembered correctly, her own father had died earlier and Winthrop Erskine had been her closest relative.

"Our past or my past?" she asked.

"Yours...your family's."

She said nothing and looked at me with her piercing gaze. The barman interrupted us by bringing me my Bloody Mary. I waited until he had distanced himself from us behind the bar.

"Your Uncle Winthrop. He died forty-four years ago. Suicide according to the papers."

She continued to look at me intently.

"What happened with the Erskine Company after your uncle died? Who took it over?"

She searched my face with her gaze as if trying to divine where I was going with my questions. "Winthrop's wife and my mother and I took over the company. We put Willard Starkley, who had been Uncle Winthrop's second in command in charge. After a couple of years, we fired Starkley and ran the company ourselves until we could get a buyer. That's when we sold it to the group that owns it now."

"You fired Starkley? Why?"

Janet looked down at her cup of coffee. She reached for her purse on the floor and fumbled with the metal clasp for a moment, then pulled out a pack of Virginia Slim's. With her thumb, she pushed open the top of the box then pulled out a cigarette. Turning around toward the barman, she caught his attention and held up the cigarette pack questioningly. He looked around at the empty cafe and gave a shrug. When she lit her cigarette she inhaled deeply then turned her head to blow the smoke away from me. "These are for emergencies," she said with a self-conscious smile. I hadn't been aware that she smoked at all.

"I was only nineteen years old when Uncle Winthrop died. He and Dora had been like another set of parents to me, especially after my father died. They took mother and me under their wing..." She took a long drag on her cigarette and a sip of coffee, then cocked her head to the side, as if her mind was moving among the figures from her past. She gave a shake of her head. "Sorry. You wanted to know about Willard Starkley."

"I want to know about your Uncle, too."

"First Willard," she said, recovering her self-possession. "Willard was the natural one to take over the company when Uncle Winthrop died. Willard had been running most of the business end of things for years anyway. But my mother and I wanted someone to oversee our interests. Even though we trusted Starkley, we hired an auditor. After about two years, we found that there was a lot of unaccounted for money—hundreds of thousands of dollars. When we confronted Starkley, he resigned."

"What happened to the money?"

She shook her head. "I don't know. We found out where it came from but not what Starkley did with it."

"Where did it come from?"

"He sold several properties that were peripheral to the main land holdings—industrial buildings that had been acquired as investments. He had records of the sales and receipt of the proceeds, but the money disappeared."

"He pocketed it?"

She nodded again and sipped her coffee before answering. "That's what we assumed."

"Did you prosecute him?"

She shook her head. "It would have brought too much negative attention to the company. The family members were planning to sell by then, and we didn't want a scandal to bring down the price or hold up any future sales."

"So Starkley got away with it."

"You might say so," she said with a bitter laugh. "What do you mean?"

"Willard died less than a year later. While driving to Nevada, he and his wife had an accident. They were both killed." She stopped and crushed out her cigarette on the corner of her saucer. "His estate had almost nothing in it. Certainly not enough to contain the stolen money. Everyone knew he had a gambling problem. He must have lost it all in Vegas."

I looked at Janet and tried to judge how ready she was to talk about her uncle's death.

"I'd like to ask you about your uncle's suicide," I said.

She fastened her gaze on me. "You mean his murder." I was surprised by her answer.

"Why do you think so?"

"My uncle wouldn't take his own life."

"I read about his death in the old newspapers. The article said he was depressed. It hinted that maybe he was ill."

"He had high blood pressure and he was taking medication that depressed him. He wouldn't have shot himself to stop the depression; he could have just stopped taking his pills." She looked out into the rain that was now coming down steadily. The end of the pier was no longer visible. "He was supposed to have shot himself three times." She shivered and took a drink of her coffee. "I don't believe it. I didn't believe it then."

"But the Sheriff's department ruled it a suicide."

She had a disgusted look on her face as she shook her head. "My mother and I tried to get them to look into it, but they were in a rush to close things up. No one would listen to us."

"What about his wife—your aunt?"

Her look became sad. "She was too devastated. She felt so guilty, that he might have killed himself, that she was completely immobilized. She never really recovered. Five years later she died herself...of cancer. She'd just been waiting to die."

I signaled the barman to refill Janet's coffee and bring me another Bloody Mary. I could feel the first one beginning to work. A young couple came into view on the street in front of the cafe. They were soaked. He was tall and skinny and in his mid-twenties, and she was short and dark. He held what looked like a handful of papers under his shirt to shield it from the rain. They both smiled broad smiles at the two of us. Janet just looked past them. I smiled back, but not enough to encourage them. They ordered two coffees from the bartender and moved to a back table where I could see that they'd pulled out the papers and begun looking at them. The papers appeared to be real estate flyers.

I lowered my voice. "If you thought your uncle was murdered, you must have had some theories about who did it."

She glanced at the two in the back of the cafe, dismissed them, and then gave me a quizzical half-smile. "You haven't told me why you're interested in this."

"There have been four murders recently that I think may be connected to your uncle's death."

She looked frightened then became angry. "How can that be? My uncle was killed more than forty years ago." She reached down toward her purse on the floor beside her chair, then hesitated and clasped her hands together in front of her on the table. "Do you mean Mr. Elmore and that student's brother?"

"That was two of them. Two people were killed making the movie, another young man was murdered because he knew why Lucia Chavez'

Pink Carnation

brother was killed, then John Elmore was killed when he tried to look further into things. Maybe Brian Thornberg's death was part of it."

She looked at me as if I'd just spoken in a foreign language. Finally she shook her head as if to clear it. "Who killed all those people?"

"A retired Sheriff's detective named Randy Fontana. He was the cop in charge of the investigation of your uncle's death and of the so-called 'Pink Carnation murders' a week later."

She repeated Fontana's name to herself as if trying to place it. "You mean there was a connection between those two teenagers' murder and my uncle's?"

"The Mexican boy apparently worked for your uncle and was at the house the day of the murder. He saw whoever did it. Fontana never reported the boy as a witness and then he or someone else killed him to keep him quiet."

"Oh my God," she said, "all these years and I was right. Poor Aunt Dora." She reached for her purse and this time pulled out the pack of Virginia Slims. She put one in her mouth and lit it. The barman cleared his throat conspicuously. I looked up and he nodded in the direction of the couple sitting in the back. Janet ignored him.

"Fontana is dead. He admitted the killings before he died and the Sheriff's department is trying to put all the pieces together. I'm trying to find out why Fontana covered up your Uncle's murder in the first place—who paid him off then and probably paid him off for these more recent killings."

"You mean you think the same person who killed Uncle Winthrop is behind these other deaths?" The look of amazement had not left her face. The story sounded amazing to me when I heard myself tell it.

"I think so. I don't think Fontana would have done all this on his own. That's why I want to know who killed your uncle."

"You think it was Willard Starkley?" she asked. Her look was skeptical. '

'Not if he died a year later. Whoever killed your uncle is still very alive and trying to protect his interests, whatever those may be."

"Who?" She asked. She was doing her best to blow the smoke toward the open door and the street but I could see the barman glaring at us. If he'd known who she was, he'd have offered to light her cigarette for her. As it was, her imperious dismissal of his objections intimidated him enough to keep him scowling at a distance.

"What if Starkley didn't steal the company's money," I said.

She raised her eyebrows in question.

"Suppose that he sold property to someone but took no money for it," I continued. "Just filled out the paperwork- the receipts and so forth."

She blinked her eyes in confusion. "Why would he do that?"

"Because he owed someone money," I said. As I talked, my hunch was becoming clearer in my own mind. "Someone from Las Vegas." I felt like slapping the table and shouting Eureka! "Willard Starkley had gambling debts. The only way he could pay them off was to either steal the money or give them something just as good as money — Orange County real estate. But to do that, he had to be the one in charge of the company, so he had your uncle killed. Probably by the people he owed the money to."

"Willard wouldn't kill my uncle. He might steal if he was desperate, but he wouldn't kill Uncle Winthrop." She looked at me with conviction. "I really believe that."

"Maybe he wasn't in on it," I said. "Maybe whoever he owed money to did it on his own, knowing that Starkley would be put in charge and then he could put the squeeze on him."

She tilted her head to the side and raised her eyebrows then began to nod her head. "It makes sense. Willard's gambling was a liability. We all knew that. "She paused and looked toward the ocean. "I guess we never imagined how much of a liability it was."

We both stared out at the gray sea and sky. The rain had stopped and a brisk cool breeze was blowing the clouds up the coast. It would still be raining on Balboa Island. Coastal weather was changeable enough that the sun could poke through the scattering clouds at any moment. When that happened, the cove would begin to fill with people. It was nearly noon and the small cafes along the street were popular lunch spots.

"I need to find out who Starkley sold property to. How do I lay my hands on those old sales records?"

Janet dragged her attention away from the ocean. She looked at me with a weak smile. For one of the first times since I'd known her, she looked old. "All those records are still in storage at the old company offices. The site used to be the headquarters for all the farming operations. It's right next to Uncle Winthrop's house."

"The house is still there? Where your uncle died?"

She shook her head. "It burned down a few years later. But the property is still intact. There was talk of rebuilding the house as an historic site." She stopped and inhaled sharply, then looked out at the ocean. "My family lived there for generations. I spent much of my childhood at that house."

"You don't have a key to the old offices, do you?" I asked.

"My lawyers might. Unless they've changed the locks."

"Could you get me in?" I asked.

She held up her hands in protest. "I'm the last person they'll let into their buildings." Janet had been involved in years of litigation with the present owners of the Erskine Company because of her claim that they had underpaid her for an interest she had retained in the company

"How about seeing if you can get hold of that key?" I said.

She smiled at me conspiratorially. "OK," she said. She held eye contact for a moment, looking amused and sad at the same time. "Be careful, Phineas." The sun came out, flooding the street with light. Out over the ocean a rainbow appeared, arching through the disappearing mist. Janet sat without moving, her eyes closed. I reached over and put my hand on hers. She turned her hand over and held my fingers in hers. She kept her eyes closed and pressed her palm against mine, drawing in her breath then letting it out. After a moment she opened her eyes and turned to me, giving my hand a squeeze before letting it go. I looked at her face. She looked young again; full of fire and full of hope.

Twenty

By that afternoon, I had the key to the Erskine Company's former headquarters in my pocket. Janet had contacted her lawyers—probably never more than a phone call away from her—and they had retained a copy of the key, which she managed to cadge from them in one way or another. She dropped it by my office at the college—along with another wish for good luck and a warning to be discreet. If I got caught with the key on me, she could be in as much trouble as I would be. For her, that could mean millions of dollars. The Erskine Company would like nothing better than to recoup some of the money they'd had to pay her when she'd won her lawsuit against them.

I promised to swallow the key if I was discovered.

The original headquarters of the Erskine Ranch was tucked away in a grove of palm trees east of the center of the valley. It sat in the midst of what had once been acres of orange and walnut orchards and now was endless tracts of nearly identical homes, occupied by a preponderance of Asian families, mostly Japanese and Chinese. Almost miraculously, a small cluster of old buildings remained intact in the middle of the housing tracts. The buildings were surrounded by a high chain link fence, which was posted with private property signs. The front gate, however, was inexplicably wide open. I cruised past the property twice, trying to see if anyone was inside.

Passing through the front gate, with at least four "no trespassing" signs warning me that I was not welcome, I was surprised by how much of the old ranch headquarters remained. So far as I was aware, the site had not been active for about thirty-five years.

The office building that contained the records was off to the right. A battered pickup truck and a newer Ford Explorer sat outside the two-story building. Beyond the building were two rows of abandoned workers' houses, with three houses in each row and the rows separated by a wide two-lane street that used to be a main thoroughfare but now stopped abruptly at the fence that surrounded the property.

Beyond the intersection of the dead-end with the road on which I'd entered, were two massive barn-like structures. The wooden sides of each, with their peeling red paint, extended only halfway to the ground and I surmised that these were drying sheds of some type—either for walnuts or beans. Driving by, I could picture the workers hovering over the drying tables inside. I looked back down the street and imagined children playing in the yards of the workers' homes, laundry hanging on the lines, dogs lying on front porches.

The grounds of Winthrop Erskine's palatial estate, surrounded by a faded and cracked concrete wall, fronted the same street as the workers' houses. A tall black iron gate still guarded the entrance, preventing me from driving my car up the curving driveway, which was flanked by two rows of perfectly spaced gargantuan palm trees; each at least seventy feet tall. Beyond the wall were two lonesome rows of orange trees--the last remnants of the once massive orchards amidst which the compound had been set. Beyond the orange trees the land had been bulldozed to make ready for the expansion of a shopping center. The Erskine compound was an island of history amidst a sea of development.

I peered through the gate up the curving driveway. An overgrown foundation was visible in the distance at the end of the drive. Remnants of chimneys sat at either end of the foundation; each rising a few feet and ending in crumbling masonry that tumbled onto the ground, forming a pile of bricks and concrete at each end of the house.

Gazing at the ruins of the heart of what was once the most powerful empire in Orange County, I had a vision of family and guests coming and going, automobiles, starting with model T's in the twenties and ending with finned fifties behemoths, circling up the driveway to the front of the mansion. I kept coming back to that fateful Sunday afternoon; Winthrop Erskine and his wife in the house, alone except for Raul Lopez, secure in the center of a world Winthrop and his family had controlled for generations. Outside, the drying sheds would be quiet because it was Sunday. The business offices across the street at the foot of the property would be empty. In the workers' houses, families would be sitting down for afternoon meals, or outside playing with the kids and the dogs. The main street passing the Mansion would have little traffic, running through the middle of the orchards, not really connecting any major residential areas at the time.

Did the intruders come on foot, peering through the gate as I was now?

Or did they drive right up to the front door? Winthrop's wife didn't recall anyone coming to the house, which made it more likely that the killers had left their car in the orchard and come in on foot, scaling the wall, and descending on the house from across the lawn. And then what? A demand that Erskine pay off Starkley's debts? Or was it already too late for that?

Erskine had been shot twice in the abdomen with a shotgun. If he'd really shot himself, holding the gun in his own hand, it would have been difficult to survive even one such blast, much less two. On the other hand, I'd read enough about gangland killings to know that the first rule a killer followed was to aim for the body from a safe distance. Stop the victim from fighting or fleeing. Once that was accomplished, the coup de grace was delivered by a headshot. Winthrop Erskine died from a single shot from a .22 caliber pistol, held flush to his temple…execution style.

The coroner said Erskine delivered the final shot himself. What nobody mentioned was that Raul Lopez had seen men leaving—men from Las Vegas. I headed back to my car. Inside the ancient office building down the road—the silent witness to a grisly murder forty-four years ago—might be the key to who killed Winthrop Erskine. If I could manage to find it.

I drove back through the gate and parked on the side of the road at the beginning of the strip of orange trees, just before the entrance to a shopping center that was under construction. I walked back to the gate and casually entered. In front of me was another two-story building, identical to the one with the two vehicles parked in front of it, but this one looked deserted. I edged along the outside of the building. A wide expanse of gravel, overgrown with weeds poking through the surface, lay between me and the building to which I needed access.

Walking hurriedly, I crossed the gravel lot and flattened myself against the building, listening for voices. I heard nothing. Edging around to the back of the building, I found a back entrance. A square window with four small panes was built into the top of the door. Inside there was a long hallway but no one was visible. I tried the key that Janet had given me and, to my relief, it worked. I stuck in my head and listened.

A radio was playing Mexican music from down the hall and from the same direction, someone was speaking. The voice was muffled, but its rhythms were English. Another voice, sounding more Spanish, answered.

I eased the door shut behind me. To my right was a small room, about six by eight feet, which looked as if it had held supplies at one time. Beyond the supply room was a stairway leading up to the second floor. Slipping off my Bruno Magli's, I inched up the stairway, half of my attention on the sounds corning from below and half anticipating what I might meet from above.

When I reached the top of the staircase, I was faced with another hallway, much like the one below. The third door on the left was labeled real estate. The door was unlocked.

The room stretched about half the length of the building. An oak desk faced the door by which I'd entered and behind that desk were two others. To the right of the desks was a low wooden wall that stretched all the way across the room. A swinging door in the middle of the wall allowed access to the rows of file cabinets that took up the rest of the room.

Pushing open the swinging gate, I looked at the first row of file cabinets in front of me. They were labeled by dates. The first cabinet began with 1948 printed on a small card inserted in a metal slot on the top drawer and ended with 1952 written on the card on the bottom drawer. I kept moving to the right, down the row. As the number of drawers devoted to each year increased linearly with the advancing years, I realized I was witnessing the progression of the Erskine Company from farming to land development. 1959 had an entire cabinet devoted to it. I moved over to the next row. 1960 also took up an entire cabinet. I glanced down the row. After 1960 the space devoted to each year increased exponentially. 1961 and 1962 took up the rest of the row of file cabinets.

According to Janet, the sales I was looking for were commercial properties, rather than residential tracts, so I quickly thumbed through files until, in the bottom drawer, I found the commercial transactions, which were far fewer in number than the residential sales. The Erskine company retained possession of most of its commercial property and leased it out, but Janet had said that Willard Starkley had claimed to have sold one or two pieces of property with nothing to show for it, so this was where I should find the record of the sale. Within a few files, I hit paydirt.

The property was a warehouse on a large parcel of land that had been part of the Erskine Ranch but was now part of Santa Ana, bordering the edge of the Tustin lighter-than-air base. The piece of land merged imperceptibly into the upscale business park area on the eastern edge of higher priced Irvine. Today the property was worth millions. In 1960, Willard Starkley sold the buildings and land for just under $135,000. The buyer was a familiar name, Jess Wolf, the same Jess Wolf who sat on the Board of Trustees of Chandler University.

It took me less than five minutes to find Jess Wolfs second deal; another set of office and warehouse buildings on the border of Santa Ana and Tustin, which he got for the bargain price of $143,000. My hunch was that no money had actually changed hands. These deals represented what Starkley owed Las Vegas. He had some pretty heavy debts. Maybe enough debts to justify murder. But did I really think that Jess Wolf-the Jess Wolf who was one of the most influential businessmen in Orange County—was a killer? And what did Jess Wolf have to do with Las Vegas gambling?

I pulled the files on Wolf's two transactions and stuffed the two folders inside my shirt, wedging them under the top of my pants to keep them in place. I crept back toward the door and opened it. Listening for the sound of voices or footsteps, I opened the door wider to peer into the corridor. I could hear the sounds of music from downstairs.

I eased down the stairs and into the hallway on the main floor. The sound of Mexican music was all I could hear from the other end of the building. As my breathing eased, I edged out of the door and back onto the dirt behind the building, slipping on my loafers and taking a cautious look around the corner of the building. The Explorer was no longer sitting in front, but the pickup truck remained. I took a deep breath and sprinted across the gravel parking lot, ducking around the side of the unoccupied building that stood by the gate. I was feeling very sleuth-like and proud of myself when I rounded the side of the abandoned building and was met by a short heavy-set Mexican-American in a security guard's uniform.

"Just dropped in to make a phone call," I said, nodding in the direction of a telephone booth next to the building. I continued to sidle around him, edging closer and closer to the gate.

"That phone hasn't worked for years," he said, not returning my cheery smile.

"I'm glad you know that," I said. "I was planning to report it."

"This is private property." He pointed to the nearest no trespassing sign, which was fastened to the side of the building about two feet from my head.

"Why didn't I see that?"

"What were you doing back there?" he asked, looking behind me toward the side of the building.

I gave him my best sheepish grin. "I had to take a leak."

"You'll need to leave," he said.

I thanked him and hightailed it out of the gate and back to my car. I drove back to the university and went immediately to my office. My first call was to Jim Stapleton.

Stapleton was in a good mood. "You should have seen Mellons' face when I told him it was Fontana who killed Elmore and not you," he chuckled. "He looked as if he'd swallowed a horse. It killed him to close the case without being able to put the cuffs on you at least once."

"Don't close the case too fast," I said.

"Oh shit!" Stapleton responded. "Now what?"

"Do you know who Jess Wolf is?" I asked him.

There was silence on the other end of the phone, then a sigh. "Sure I do. Wolf's a big mucky-muck in the business community. What's any of this got to do with Wolf?"

"Wolf killed Winthrop Erskine back in 1959. Then he killed or had somebody kill Sally Umstead and Raul Lopez a week later because Lopez had seen Erskine's murderers. Fontana probably got paid off back then, and now, Wolf hired him again to cover both their tracks by killing Ramon Chavez and the others."

Stapleton groaned on the other end of the phone. "Tell me this is a joke — a bad joke."

"I'm not joking, Jim."

"Then you'd better forget everything you just told me. There's no way either of us can go after Jess Wolf. We might as well accuse Michael Eisner of the murders."

"Wolf's that big?" The fact that he was on the Chandler Board meant he was rich, but his business enterprises had always been so shadowy that, except for the few tidbits that Kim had told me, I knew next to nothing about him.

"I don't want to say that he has supervisors in his back pocket, but he comes damn close. You don't get elected in Santa Ana unless Jess Wolf supports you. The state Enterprise Zone is practically drawn around Wolf's properties."

"Then he's very well connected, politically," I said.

"And untouchable," Stapleton added, an edge to his voice.

"Even for murder?"

"Dammit! Wake up and smell the coffee, Phineas. Wolf keeps the politicians well fed, he doesn't do anything obvious. His businesses are legal. If he commits any crimes, they're white collar ones — at least so far as we know."

"Hiring Randy Fontana to bump off anybody who had an inkling that Wolf was connected to the Pink Carnation murders and the bogus suicide of Winthrop Erskine is hardly white collar crime. You're not going to tell me that somebody who does that keeps his hands clean the rest of the time."

"I'm not telling you anything except we've got nothing on Wolf and never have. I can tell you that nobody from our department is going to go after Wolf."

"Including you?" I asked.

"Geez, Phineas. Don't ask me to stick my neck out on this. I haven't got the clout to win on this one. It'll be my neck not Jess Wolf's."

"It's a murder."

"And we got the killer. Let's quit while we're ahead."

"This is bullshit," I said. Then I hung up on him and glumly reflected on how frightened being middle aged and a bureaucrat can make a person — even someone as strong as Jim Stapleton.

I picked the phone back up and called President Stonehill's office. His secretary, Winnie Hanlon, answered in her rich, southern African-American drawl. I didn't bother to ask for Stonehill. "Tell your boss that Professor Routledge is demanding a face to face meeting with him and the Board to deal with my reinstatement on the faculty."

"No need to get so uppity, Professor," Winnie drawled. She and I were actually good friends. I was one of the few faculty who knew that her opinion of her pompous employer was the same as mine. "I typed up the letter this morning, informing you of your reinstatement," she said.

I modified my tone. "Tell King Stonehill that I reject his letter. I've been so insulted by this ordeal that I demand a face to face meeting with all the Board members."

"You sure know how to cause a problem, Professor Routledge," she said, her amusement barely concealed. "I'll relay the message to his highness."

I thanked her and started to hang up, then remembered one more thing. "Have you got resume's or biographies on the Board Members?" I asked.

"You are a problem, Professor," Winnie said, the good humor still in her voice. "We have to submit a detailed biography to WASC—the Western Association of Schools and Colleges—for accreditation purposes. They have to be sure that the Board is representative of the community and that there's no conflict of interest. It's public record, if you want a copy."

"Can you fax it to me at home?"

"Aren't you in your office?"

"I've rejected my reinstatement, remember. Better fax it to my house."

"It'll be waiting for you when you get there," she said.

"You're a gem, Winnie. Someday you'll be rewarded for your years of servitude under a cruel master."

"And I'll be free at last, Lord, free at last."

I hung up and left the campus. The Lakers had eliminated the Sonics and tonight they opened at Staples Center against Rasheed Wallace and the Blazers. If I could go at least one day without witnessing or being accused of committing a murder, I might be able to watch a playoff game. Once I confronted Jess Wolf at the Board meeting, it would be a different story.

Pink Carnation

Twenty-One

"Your work preceded you," Kim said, handing me a welcome home glass of wine and a stack of papers hot off the fax machine. She gave me a warm Vietnamese kiss on my cheek.

I took a sip of the new Chateauneuf du Pape Bordeaux that Kim had found for me and savored the soft, full flavor. I held up the handful of faxed papers and explained to Kim that I was checking out Jess Wolf's background. Not that he was going to list "Mafia" as a former employer, but maybe I'd see something that told me if I was on the right track.

Kim came back from the kitchen carrying a black lacquered tray of wheat crackers covered with melted sharp cheese.

"For the game," she explained, setting the tray on the coffee table and sitting down next to me on the couch. She had already changed from her work clothes into a pair of very short cutoff jeans—the kind with a designer patch on the back pocket—and a sleeveless pink cotton pullover. I noticed she'd also shed her bra underneath the top. She looked more delicious than the tray of snacks.

With reluctance, I sat down on the couch and started perusing the resumes. When I found Wolf's, I put the others down on the couch and took another sip of wine before I began reading.

"Wolf was born in 1930, Em. That makes him 73 years old this year. He was born in Patterson, New Jersey. That ought to be enough to convict him of being Mafia."

Kim raised an eyebrow, signaling a degree of skepticism regarding my perspicacity.

"There's more," I said. "He started his real estate venture in 1960. That was the year the Erskine Company sold him his first property in Orange County. So he wasn't in business around here before then." I flipped to the second page of the document. "All this lists as his activities before that date is being property manager for a number of companies; Tedescho in New Jersey and—bingo! Malvecchio in Las Vegas and Reno.

Here it is, Em, he was in Las Vegas from 1954 until 1960, managing property for this Malvecchio Company."

"But Janet told you that Starkley owed gambling debts. Why would he owe gambling debts to a property manager, one from Las Vegas?"

"You can buy someone's debts. Wolf might have found out that Starkley was the top executive of one of the largest real estate developers in California and he had a whopping gambling debt he couldn't pay. Wolf saw a chance to get into the real estate business the easy way, especially since he had been a property manager and already knew the business. The only thing that would have stood in his way was that Starkley couldn't deal any of the Erskine Company property as long as Winthrop Erskine was alive. My guess is that Wolf decided to eliminate that problem himself."

Kim picked up one of the crackers and began chewing thoughtfully. "So Wolf had Erskine killed then forced Starkley to trade him the property for his debts."

"And instantly he's in the Southern California real estate business. If we could see his business records, we'd probably find a lot of properties he bought for practically nothing. Maybe even some that suffered mysterious acts of destruction before they were sold."

Kim held up her wrist and pointed to her watch. "Five minutes until game time, Anh. We'll have dinner at the half." She rose from the couch and picked up my empty wineglass and headed for the kitchen. "More?" she asked. I nodded.

Kim returned from the kitchen with a fresh glass of Bordeaux. She switched on the television and snuggled next to me on the couch. I watched the Lakers miss a long outside shot and then lag behind Portland getting back up court. The Blazers got an easy lay-up and it was four-zip. This could prove to be a long night. Sports were supposed to be a mirror of real-life conflicts. At least that's what the pundits said. I watched the basketball game for some clue to my real life problems. Short of hiring Shaquille O'Neal as a bodyguard, I couldn't see anything that would help me.

"In Vietnam we have a saying, Anh." Kim said, her eyes still on the game. "The hungriest wolf leaves the largest pile of bones."

"Aha!" I said, with an air of profundity. "What does that mean?"

"A man as greedy as Jess Wolf will leave evidence of his greed. You just need to know where to look."

I turned away from the game. The Lakers were already down by eleven points. "Where?" I asked.

"What about the records of some of his acquisitions? You said that after he got a foothold in Orange County he probably intimidated other property and business owners to sell below market value. What if you could prove that?"

"How?"

She looked at me with a beatific smile. "I'll find out for you, Anh."'

I picked up the remote control and turned the sound off on the television. "What are you talking about?"

"MX Motorcycles. I'm doing their books. They're an Enterprise Zone company and they're required to have an external audit to qualify for their tax incentives."

"Wolf owns MX Motorcycles?"

"He owns their building. As an external auditor, I have to look at Wolf's books to be sure the lease payments claimed by MX match those recorded by Wolf."

"How is that going to help me, Em?"

She smiled the beatific smile again. "Wolf stores the records for all of his properties at his corporate offices in Santa Ana. That's where I have to go to check out MX Motorcycles. When I'm there, it's just a matter of me looking in the wrong files."

Four or five people had already been killed poking around in Jess Wolf's business. I didn't want Kim to put herself in danger.

"Don't they watch you when you're going through their books?" I asked. She shook her head. "They don't pay me much attention at all. They're used to outside auditors looking things up for their Enterprise Zone customers. It's part of the deal."

The idea of Kim putting herself at risk prompted a swarm of butterflies to take off in the pit of my stomach. Kim might be able to provide the only evidence that would prompt the authorities to look into Jess Wolf's business dealings, but Wolf was a far too dangerous man to allow my wife to involve herself.

"It's not worth it, Em. I doubt that Wolf lists any of his Mafioso tactics in his business files. Besides, I'm going to have a meeting with the Chandler Board tomorrow and I'll get to go head to head with Jess Wolf. After that we'll decide if we need to go any further."

"It can't hurt for me to take a peek." She looked up at me with doe eyes.

"Let's peek at the game. I don't want you taking any unnecessary risks."

I switched the sound back on, as much to put an end to our conversation as anything. Kim's suggestion continued to make me nervous. The more we talked, the more she might decide to do something even against my advice.

We turned back to the game. The first quarter was ending and the Lakers had only cut their deficit to nine points. Nothing was going to be easy.

TWENTY-TWO

At eight-o'clock in the morning, I got a call from Winnie Hanlon telling me that the Board had agreed to meet with me today at three p.m. Kim had already left for work and I was sitting out on the porch watching the boat traffic and enjoying the feeling of the warm morning sun through the cool, crisp ocean air. A mega-cup of Diedrich's Kona blend coffee steamed next to me on the table. I peeled an orange and thought about how to deal with Jess Wolf.

After ten minutes of getting nowhere with my thoughts, the telephone rang again. This time it was Lucia Chavez. She wanted to talk to me. I told her to meet me in an hour at my office at Chandler. It was time to start making my presence on campus known.

When I got to my office, Lucia Chavez was pacing in front of my door. She made a half-hearted attempt to replace her out-of-sorts frown with an insincere smile when I asked her how she was recovering from her ordeal, but it didn't work well. She began talking while I was still removing the key from my office door.

"Arturo Cordoza agrees that Fontana worked for somebody," she said, her old belligerence back in her voice. "He says that Fontana wouldn't have killed Ramon and Julio on his own."

I asked her in, which wasn't necessary because she already was, and offered her a cup of coffee. I was stalling to give myself time to think. Lucia Chavez could be a loose cannon and I didn't know if I wanted to let her in on what I knew about Jess Wolf.

"Does Arturo have any idea who Fontana worked for?" I asked.

I stopped fiddling with the little Braun coffee maker long enough to wait for her answer. If Arturo Cordoza had evidence that Fontana worked for Jess Wolf, my problem might be solved.

Now that she knew I was listening to her, Lucia calmed down. She stopped pacing and sat in one of my leather armchairs in front of the window.

"Listen to this," she said. "Arturo says that those people who he calls "Las Vegas people" are still operating in Orange County. They buy some of the goods that the Nitas steal. They may also supply some of the drugs—not on the street, that's the Nitas again—but at the top; they make the deals directly with the importers and then pass the stuff on to middle-men and distributors, who take it to the street dealers."

The coffee was finally dripping into the little four-cup pot and I sat down across from Lucia. "You mean the Las Vegas people make the deals at the top level?"

She frowned and nodded at the same time. "Arturo says they don't deal with the street gangs directly. They stay in the background but everybody knows about them and nobody crosses them. Anyone who has, has wound up dead. Arturo is pretty sure it's the same people who moved into the county back in the sixties. The same ones who killed Lopez."

I wasn't sure whether to believe this or not. It might just be a paranoiac figment of Arturo's imagination. "What makes Arturo think so?" The Braun had quieted down and the aroma of the rich Kenyan blend prompted me to get up and pour a cup.

Lucia dismissed my offer of coffee with an impatient grimace.

"They used to be more visible, back in the days when Arturo was running the Nitas," she said. "He had to deal with a few of them back then."

She'd caught my attention.

"You mean he had face to face contact?" I asked. "Does he remember any names? Does he know who ran the whole show?"

"Just that they moved in from Las Vegas, that's all."

"Do you think he'd remember a face if I showed him a picture?"

She gave me an eager look. "Do you have a face to show him?"

"Maybe."

"Then you know who hired Fontana?" Her dark eyes flashed with excitement.

I hesitated. "I've got an idea who it might be. Ask Arturo about him but I don't want you doing anything else."

"Who is it, Professor?"

"A man named Jess Wolf. He's on the Chandler Board of Trustees. I'm going to talk to them today and see if I can force him into admitting something."

"He's on Chandler's Board?" She said incredulously.

I held out a cautionary hand. "Don't go too fast. I think it's Wolf, but I need evidence and the police don't want to give me any help."

"I don't want to be an 'I told you so,' Professor…" she interrupted.

This wasn't the time to get back into a debate about police integrity with Lucia. "You can ask Arturo about him—and John Cordoza, too, for that matter. Maybe even the other brother, the flashy one, whatever his name is."

"Jorge," She volunteered. "I haven't talked to him yet, but I'll ask all of them about Wolf. Have you got a picture of him?"

I got up and pulled a five-year-old copy of the school yearbook from my shelf. It was one I'd saved because it was the first one that listed me as a regular full-time faculty-complete with picture. I flipped to the page with the photos of the Board members and tapped my index finger on Wolf's picture. He was a lot older than when Arturo would have known him, but maybe his cosmetic surgery had preserved his looks. Lucia stared at Wolf's picture as if she were looking at a specimen from the Reptile House at the Los Angeles Zoo.

"What are you going to say to Wolf at the Board meeting?" she said, looking up at me.

"I don't know. I have to figure that out before this afternoon."

"Then I'd better talk to the Cordozas today." She rose to go.

I wished her luck and she wished me the same.

Kim had been right about the hungriest wolf. It sounded like Jess Wolf hadn't been content sticking to white-collar crime. If he was the Las Vegas connection that Arturo Cordoza was talking about, then Wolf was into some of the more traditional pursuits of organized crime: fencing stolen property, drugs, and probably a lot more. Only these days he did it from a distance. He and his people stayed safely in the background while the less fortunate minority gangs did the dirty work and took the heat. It was a pattern that I'd read about in some of the bigger cities where the Mafia had retreated to the wings and let the African-American, Mexican-American, and sometimes even the Asian gangs take center stage. The gangs ran the streets, fought the turf wars, and got all the publicity — not to mention the arrests — while the old-line Mafioso reeled in the profits by supplying the drugs and providing buyers for the stolen goods that the gangs spent their time acquiring.

    I didn't know that anything like the Mafia operated in Orange County. True, the orange groves-turned-mega-suburb south of Los Angeles wasn't entirely the sun-drenched land of milk and honey that the rest of the country envisioned when they read that Orange County was voted the "best place to live in America" by People magazine. You found that out when you finally scraped together enough money to take that long-awaited trip to Disneyland that you'd always promised the kids. You got off the plane expecting palm trees and ocean, surfer dudes in woodies and blondes riding in the back of pink Mustang convertibles. The ocean and the beaches were visible from the airplane window as you landed and you could almost see them from John Wayne Airport. But when you pulled the rental car out of the airport parking lot and headed inland, you realized that you were driving through neighborhoods that made the wife so nervous that she told the kids to "lock the doors."

    Not only that, but you couldn't really get anywhere trying to follow the map that the rental car agency gave you because all the major thoroughfares were closed for major construction.

    The infrastructure of central Orange County was crumbling under the weight of a population load it was never meant to support. If you happened to scan the real estate section of the newspaper, you were appalled by the housing prices and left to wonder how all the obviously poor Mexican-American and Vietnamese families you saw around you afforded any place to live. You'd have to be a resident to know that they lived three or four families to a household, which sometimes consisted of a one-bedroom apartment.

Central Orange County was an area ripe for organized crime. It's just that I'd thought that the organized crime mobs were the indigenous ones, composed of local Latinos, Vietnamese, Koreans, Chinese; all representatives of newly acculturated minority groups. The county didn't have enough African- Americans to support any kind of organization, criminal or legitimate. There were a few cliques of East county bikers and Huntington Beach skinheads—white boys who passed their idle hours beating up minorities and chose crime because they were too stupid and lazy to make a living any other way—but Mafia? Next door to Disneyland? Who would have thunk it?

Evidently not the Orange County Sheriff's Department nor any of the other law enforcement agencies in the county. Jim Stapleton didn't have a clue with regard to Jess Wolf. As far as the Assistant Chief of Detectives was concerned, Wolf was a high profile businessman who was savvy at courting political favors. Wolf was hardly someone for the Sheriff's Department to spend time on when they had to worry about all that street crime and the gangs who perpetrated it.

It seemed miraculous that no gang member had ever leaked the word that there was someone else out there- someone bringing in the dope and buying up the goods. Someone for whom the deterioration of the central core of the county and the city of Santa Ana in particular, brought all sorts of benefits: low real estate prices, which were anathema if you wanted to sell, but a boon if you were into acquisitions. A disenfranchised, uneducated, linguistically alienated, and underemployed population who would reach out for drugs and turn to crime to afford them was just what organized crime needed to thrive. And to top it all off, state and federal programs like the Enterprise Zone that turned abandoned warehouses and office buildings into veritable gold mines—all for the price of a few political payoffs—could make a slum lord rich.

If Jess Wolf was Arturo Cordoza's Las Vegas presence in Orange County, then Wolf had parleyed Willard Starkley's gambling debts into a sizeable cache of illegally gotten profits—all stemming from the misfortunes of central Orange County.

All this was so much fantasy on my part unless I could get evidence against Wolf that would tie him to something illegal. If I could stick him with something big enough and serious enough, I might be able to expose his whole operation.

The phone rang and it was Jim Stapleton.

"Glad to see you're back at work,' Stapleton said. He sounded genuinely happy for me.

"Until this afternoon, anyway," I said. "I'm meeting with the Board around three and I'm planning on telling Jess Wolf that I know he was behind the killings that Fontana committed."

"You're a pain in the ass, you know that? A bull-headed pain in the ass." He stopped for a moment, struggling with his anger. "Do you know why I called?" he asked, sounding as though he was making an effort to force the friendliness into his voice.

"I guess it wasn't to tell me that you've decided I'm right about Jess Wolf."

"You got that right," he said. His tone was brusque. "I wanted to invite you and Kim to dinner tonight. Karen's taken the kids to her parents for the weekend and I'm batching it. I thought I might buy you both steaks at The Arches and we'd sit in the lounge and watch the Lakers."

The Arches on the Coast Highway in Newport Beach was one of our favorite haunts, especially the lounge on game nights. "You're on," I said. Kim would enjoy it and it would give me another crack at trying to convince Jim that he was wrong about Jess Wolf.

I hung up and tried reaching Kim at work. She didn't answer her cell phone or her page, but I left a message for her to meet me at The Arches after work. Then I poured myself another cup of Kenyan coffee and started thinking about what I was going to do at the meeting in the afternoon.

By the time three o'clock rolled around, I'd formulated a plan. At least it was an approximation of a plan. I called Kim's cell phone again, but she still wasn't answering. I tried her office and her secretary said she'd gone out to audit MX Motorcycles and wouldn't be back in the office, but she'd taken her cell with her. I gave Margie, her secretary, the message to tell Kim, if she called in, to meet me at The Arches at six-o'clock.

When I reached the administration building, Winnie Hanlon greeted me with the news that two of the Board members had arrived, and the rest were on their way. President Stonehill would be in in a moment, and I could go ahead and take a place at the table. I was the only item of business on the agenda.

Michael Umstead and Dr. Simon Flowers, the eye surgeon, were seated the Boardroom table. Since he was President of the Board, Umstead sat at the head of the table and Flowers sat one chair away. Flowers smiled a sort of half-smile, evidently not knowing whether this meeting was to welcome me back on the faculty or kick me out permanently. His expression could go either way.

Umstead gave me a curt unsmiling nod. Umstead would orchestrate the meeting and I hoped he would give me enough time to say my piece. I sat down mid-way from the ends of the table and waited. Janet Erskine Jones arrived next, dressed in a long, gray, bolero skirt and wide, white linen long-sleeved blouse with a turned up collar. She wore highly polished riding boots. She looked fresh and stunning, and not only did I, but Umstead and Flowers both took second appreciative looks as she strode into the room.

"Hello, Michael, Simon." She smiled and nodded to the Board members. "Welcome back, Professor Routledge," she said to me, with a wider smile and a wink. I could always count on Janet.

President Stonehill came in with the other three members, two of whom had not been present when we met before, Jess Wolf being the third. Wolf gave me his usual stony look, and the other two didn't look at me. President Stonehill blessed us all with his sunny smile, his insincerity all but lighting up the room.

Stonehill introduced us. The two Board members I hadn't met were Ralph Norbert, a large, well-fed gladhander who looked like an Iowa farmer and was one of the largest car dealers in the county, and Rafael Herrera, a diminutive Mexican-American who owned a chain of cantina-style restaurants that covered Southern California from LA to San Diego. Herrera was active in the community and his restaurants were the sites of many of the university fundraising events. Herrera and Janet had teamed up to develop the minority scholarship program at Chandler.

"First of all, we'd like to welcome Dr. Routledge back to his teaching duties here at Chandler," Stonehill began, still smiling as though we'd all gotten together just to celebrate my return. "It's a relief that this unfortunate problem has been cleared up and Dr. Routledge, as I understand it, was not only innocent of any wrongdoing, but instrumental in helping the Sheriff's department catch the actual perpetrator." He neglected to mention that this very Board had jumped on the bandwagon and practically declared me guilty right along with the Sheriff's Department. All was to be forgiven and forgotten.

I cleared my throat and adjusted my position in my chair. All eyes focused on me. President Stonehill's face still had a sappy smile plastered on it, but his eyes belied his confidence.

"One of you is going to need a good lawyer," I said, returning Stonehill's sick smile.

Stonehill's face froze. He made a futile attempt to keep smiling, but ended up looking as if he'd eaten something rotten. "I hope that's not why you asked for this meeting," he stammered. "We only did what we thought was necessary."

I looked around the table. Michael Umstead looked at me with an impassive gaze. Dr. Simon Flowers' eyes darted from me to Stonehill and back again, hoping to obtain some sign of reassurance from the university president. I could imagine him thinking he'd done thousands of eye surgeries, half of them unnecessary, and avoided any malpractice claims only to get sued for sitting on the board of Chandler University. Janet looked, amused and Hererra's face was a mask. Ralph Norbert, the car dealer, looked on the verge of a panic attack, and he hadn't even been present when the board had voted to suspend me. But then car dealers had a right to panic when anyone around them mentioned a lawsuit. Jess Wolf sat waiting, his eyes half closed under his heavy black eyebrows, as though he knew where I was heading.

"Ramon Chavez was the brother of one of our students," I began. "Two weeks ago he was killed in what was labeled an accident while making a movie about a murder that occurred forty-four years ago. His sister, Lucia is a Chandler student and when she came to me to ask for help because she thought her brother's death was not an accident, I agreed to do what I could to convince the Sheriff's Department to look into it. While helping her, I became a suspect myself in one of two killings that followed Ramon Chavez'. That's when this Board acted to suspend me from teaching." I punctuated my speech with an accusatory look at each of them.

"As it turned out, Ramon Chavez' death was not an accident," I continued, "and the same person who killed him, killed another young boy named Julio Cordoza and the author, John Elmore."

Wolf still appeared bored and President Stonehill looked impatient for me to get to my point. The others were listening with rapt attention.

"The killer was an ex-Sheriff's detective who investigated the original murders that were the subject of the movie in which Ramon Chavez was killed," I continued. "The ex-detective got himself killed before he could say what he was afraid Chavez and the others might find out about those old murders."

I looked directly at Wolf. "What he was afraid of was that someone would find out those murders were committed in order to cover up another murder; one that also happened forty-four years ago. It was a death that gained a lot of attention, but it was declared a suicide by the investigating detective, who was this same detective. The death of Winthrop Erskine forty-four years ago wasn't a suicide, though; it was a murder. The deaths of two youngsters a week later, one of them the sister of Mr. Umstead here, was an effort to silence a young Mexican-American who was a witness to Erskine's murder."

Both Janet Erskine Jones and Michael Umstead had edged forward in their seats. Umstead glanced at Janet and gave her a quick sympathetic smile. Until now, he hadn't known that their two tragedies had any connection with each other.

Jess Wolf glanced at his wristwatch. He looked over at Stonehill as if to say, "do we have to listen to anymore of this?" Instead, he addressed me. "Fascinating as they are, Professor Routledge, your theories about a couple of forty-four year old deaths are something you should be telling the Sheriff's Department, not us. I think we've heard enough."

"No we haven't," Umstead answered. He directed his cool gaze toward Wolf, then around the room at the others. "Two of us lost close relatives forty-four years ago. These are not just a couple of forty-four year old deaths to us. We're going to hear the rest of the Professor's story."

Wolf sighed and shook his head.

Janet Erskine Jones slapped the table with her hand and glared at Wolf. "We sure as hell are, Michael." She turned to me. "Go ahead Phineas, finish your story."

I looked over at Jess Wolf. He was scowling, but I had his attention. "It took me a while to figure out who would have profited from Winthrop Erskine's death. It wasn't Willard Starkley, the man who took over the reins of the company, even though Starkley committed theft and fraud almost as soon as he assumed the power to do so. The man who profited from Erskine's death was the man to whom Starkley owed several hundred thousand dollars in gambling debts—gambling debts he could only settle by pretending to sell parcels of Erskine Company land. In reality, Starkley gave away the land to settle the debts. It looked as if he had pocketed the profits from the sales himself, and he had to step down from the company in order to avoid being charged with theft. In fact, he never received a cent for the property. The man to whom he owed the money simply took it as collection for Starkley's debts." I paused to let the drama build. "The same man had killed Winthrop Erskine to allow Starkley to take over the company."

Jess Wolf continued to try to stare me down, but he could contain himself no longer. "This is all just so much fantasy, Professor. There's no way you could know what went on forty-four years ago." He was trying for an air of disdain but the anxiety was evident in his voice.

I stared back and smiled. "I didn't have to know what went on, Mr. Wolf. I just needed to find out who purchased business property from the Erskine Company after Winthrop Erskine's death—who bought property and pretended to pay Willard Starkley for it." I could feel my smile widening indecently. "I found the records of that purchase, Mr. Wolf. The records of your purchase of business property from Willard Starkley."

"You?" Janet said, aghast. She looked at Wolf with unbelieving eyes. "You killed my uncle?"

"Are you sure about this, Professor?" Michael Umstead asked in a low, serious tone.

I nodded.

Jess Wolf no longer looked anxious. He was gazing at me with a mixture of amusement and hatred. "You were absolutely right when you began this meeting saying that one of us was going to need a lawyer, Professor Routledge. You've just accused me of murder and fraud in front of five witnesses. I'm going to sue you for all you're worth." He looked around the room. "And because you've all let this go on, I'm going to sue each of you also, and the university."

President Stonehill came out of his state of shock and managed to squawk, "Wait a minute, Jess. You can't blame us!" With difficulty, he brought himself under control. "The professor has made reckless charges, Jess. None of us is taking his accusations seriously. Let's all cool down for a minute." Stonehill turned to me, furious. "This could be grounds for your permanent dismissal, Professor Routledge."

"Not if it's true," Janet interrupted him. "I admit that what the professor says sounds reckless, but it could also be true." She looked Wolf squarely in the eye. "I don't want Professor Routledge silenced until the authorities look into his accusations." She looked over at Michael Umstead for support.

Umstead nodded gravely. "I agree with Janet." He turned toward Jess Wolf. "If what the Professor says is true, then Jess is the last person we should listen to in this matter."

Wolf smiled, a cold thin smile. "And how have the authorities responded to your theories, Professor? Surely you told them before you broke the news to us."

"I'm still talking to them about it," I obfuscated.

Wolf rubbed his bony hands together like two dry sticks. "Still talking? You mean they haven't taken you seriously, don't you?"

I looked around the room. Janet was waiting for me to put Wolf in his place. Umstead's look had wilted into skepticism.

"I haven't told them the whole story yet." I said.

"Because the Sheriff's Department, unlike this group, has no time to listen to malicious theories about supposed murders from the past," Wolf said. He swung his dark gaze around the room. "I propose that you all take a lesson from actual criminal investigators and stop listening to this drivel. I also propose that Professor Routledge take his false accusations and fertile imagination out of this room. I have reservations about someone like him teaching at Chandler, but I'm willing to overlook his indiscretion if he'll just go back to the classroom and stop playing amateur detective."

"Yes, yes!" Stonehill slobbered, his relief removing any semblance of self-control. "That's very magnanimous of you, Jess. Now I submit that we adjourn this meeting and we all forget what we've heard in here. As for you Professor Routledge, consider yourself fortunate that Mr. Wolf is not going to sue you, and for God's sake, go back to teaching."

I gave Wolf a satisfied smile. He looked back at me with narrowed eyes. He knew that I had his number. If looks could kill, I'd never have made it out of the Boardroom alive. I gave him a small nod of acknowledgment. He and I both knew that there was only one way to silence me.

Twenty-Three

I scanned the parking lot of The Arches for Kim's car. The lot was starting to fill, as it always did on Friday night and I was surprised that Kim hadn't arrived before me. She loved The Arches almost as much as I did. The posh steakhouse had been a Coast Highway landmark since 1927. The restaurant had seen flappers, prohibition, rumrunners, movie stars, and political figures over the last three-quarters of a century. It preceded the prestigious Balboa Bay Club down the street by decades. The name had apparently derived from the nearby double- arched bridge that crossed the Pacific Coast Highway, bringing Newport Boulevard down to the old Lido Pier—the one that the Sternwood's chauffeur drove a car off of in *The Big Sleep*. The Arches' steaks were renowned locally but the real attraction was the local gossip, political wheeling and dealing, and the business that went on, hidden away in the deep leather booths of the restaurant and bar.

Jim Stapleton and I were semi-regulars, although our visits to The Arches' cocktail lounge had been replaced by dinners in the main restaurant since Kim and I got married. Not that the lounge had ever been a place to pick up a date. The small bar was home to a few locals who preferred to meet and socialize there. Men outnumbered the women four to one and the average age was around fifty. Jim and I were younger, but we enjoyed the talk of sports and boating, politics and just plain gossip, and the TV that was always tuned to the biggest game. Tonight there was no question about which game that was. The Lakers were leading the series for the Western Conference Championship one to nothing. Tonight was the second meeting with the Trailblazers in Staple Center before Shaq, Kobe, and company would have to travel north to Portland for a pair of games at the Rose Garden. The Blazers were almost unbeatable at home so this was a must win for the Lakers.

"Kim's not coming tonight?" Tony, the Italian manager and sometime Maitre'd asked. Like a lot of people, Tony had become attached to the

Pink Carnation

quiet beauty and open warmth of my wife. He didn't try to conceal his disappointment.

Tony pointed me to Jim, who was sitting in one of the small booths in the lounge where he had a clear view of the TV, which was attached to the wall, high up in one corner.

I was surprised by Kim's absence. I was nearly half an hour late, but she was always on time for everything. I told Tony to keep an eye out for her and I joined Jim at his booth. He already had a whiskey and soda and his eyes glued to the TV set.

"Where's Kim?" he asked when I scooted in across from him. "Late, I guess." I glanced up to see if the game had started.

Jim raised his eyebrows. "Well, you're just in time. The tip-off is in a few minutes."

"I told Kim six." I glanced at my watch. It was nearly six-thirty. "I couldn't get her all day, so I just left messages. I think I'll call home to be sure she's not waiting for me."

"What can I get you?" Jim asked.

I told him to order me a gin and tonic and I asked Tony if I could use the phone. He directed me to his office, which was down a short hallway behind the bar. I'd been in the office before so I wasn't as awed as I might have been by the scores of autographed photos of celebrities that covered the walls.

There was only one message. It was Jess Wolf's low monotone. "Your wife is my guest and she'd like you to join us."

I felt a cold ball of ice in the pit of my stomach. The blood was rushing in my ears so loud that I could barely hear the rest of the message.

Wolf ended by giving me an Anaheim Hills address. Despite my panic, I played the message a second time, while I scrambled for a pen and paper. I copied the address and saved the message on the machine.

"What in the hell happened to you?" Jim Stapleton asked, staring at my face. "Is Kim okay?"

"Jess Wolf has got her."

His jaw dropped. "Wolf...got her? What are you talking about?"

"I accused Wolf of murdering Winthrop Erskine today." I looked down at the table and thought about how naive I'd been. "I thought he'd come after me, not Kim."

Stapleton downed the rest of his whiskey and soda in one quick gulp. "Goddamit, Phineas, you don't know who you're messing with."

"Yes I do, I just didn't think he'd involve Kim." I thought about how he'd gotten her. She must have decided to investigate his company's records, despite what I'd told her about holding off. If Wolf had found her in the midst of his real estate records after what I told him that afternoon, he must have put two and two together and known she was snooping for evidence.

"You go home and wait for me," Stapleton said, leaning across the table. "I'm a cop and I can get her back for you."

I felt a rush of anger, even though I knew it wasn't Jim who should be the target; it was Wolf.

"The hell," I said. "Wolf wants me. If I send cops, he'll do something to Kim and I'll never see her again."

Jim started to say something, then stopped himself. He was grinding his teeth. "Shit!" He said. "The bastard! We're going together. He won't know I'm with you until we're already there."

"I don't want to risk Kim."

Jim's face showed his anger. "You already have, dammit!" His voice softened but his eyes remained steel-hard. "I'm not letting you walk in there by yourself, Phin. It's either me, or three carloads of deputies. Take your choice."

"Let's go," I said.

We took my car and drove up Newport Boulevard. The bay lay behind us, and, as we went inland, the street merged into the Costa Mesa Freeway heading east. I was traveling at ninety miles per hour in the carpool lane. I could barely focus on the road ahead of me. Inside my head I felt like there was a tornado spinning out of control.

Pink Carnation

"How did Kim get involved in this?" Jim Stapleton asked, snapping me back to reality. He was wedged in next to me in my MGA as I sped past the exits to downtown Santa Ana.

"It's my fault," I answered, feeling as though I should kick myself for even considering Kim's offer to look for evidence against Jess Wolf. "Kim was doing an audit on a company that leased from Wolf, and she said she could get into Wolf's records. I told her to hold off, but she apparently didn't. Wolf must have found her going through his records and tied her to me."

Stapleton smacked his fist against the inside of the car door. "Your vendetta against Wolf is stupid. You know that don't you?"

At that moment, I couldn't argue. I reflected on why I'd been so hell-bent on pursuing Wolf at any cost. I drove silently.

We were almost to the merge onto the Riverside Freeway. Anaheim Hills would be coming up soon, perched among the foothills that stretched upward from the bottom of the Santa Ana river valley.

"I happen to know from some of my sources that Wolf has been involved in criminal activities in Orange County since the sixties," I finally said. "He didn't just kill Erskine and take a few acres of land, he started a whole criminal operation that involves drugs, stolen property, intimidation and murder."

"Who told you these things?" Stapleton asked.

I glanced over at him but he was looking out the window. His face, from the side looked frozen. "The Cordoza's. They told Lucia Chavez."

Jim was silent. The Anaheim Hills were a dark mass off to the right, with pinpoints of light scattered across their face where streetlights and homes shown through the cover of trees.

"I'm looking for Montclair Road," I told Jim.

Jim stirred. "The Cordoza's don't know shit," he said, looking up at the hills. "They've been claiming there's mob activity in Orange County for years. They're trying to take the heat off the Santa Nitas and the rest of the Mexican gangs. Don't you think we'd know if Wolf was running a mob operation right under our noses?"

I looked over at him again. He was looking at me and I stared back. "Yes, I'd think you would," I said.

He turned away, hunkering down in his seat and gazing out the window. "Montclair's coming up on the right," he said.

"Have you been here before?"

"I've been through this area a few times."

A street light shone on the sign that said Montclair Drive. The street was a narrow two-lane road that went for about a hundred yards along the bottom of a hill, then took an abrupt turn and headed steeply upward. I saw no houses at first, then I noticed gates and driveways along the unlit winding street. Behind them were distant lights from houses flickering through the trees.

I kept climbing, pushing the little 1500 cc engine in third gear, slowing as I passed each driveway to read the mailboxes, and then downshifting to get back up to speed. Jim was hunched forward, trying to see the names and numbers. Neither of us said anything. My mouth was dry and my palms were so sweaty, I could barely grip the steering wheel. Every time I thought about Kim being held prisoner down one of these driveways, my whole body became weak, my arms leaden. I tried to keep my mind off thoughts of what might happen to her.

As we climbed the hill, the trees grew closer to the narrow, twisting road, providing a canopy of leaves that filtered out the light from the early evening sky and making identification of the house numbers even more difficult. At the occasional breaks in the trees, we could catch glimpses of spectacular vistas stretching west toward the ocean behind us. It was a sea of lights, one city merging imperceptibly into another, with occasional clusters surrounding business centers, probably in Anaheim and Orange.

The road began to level off and I sensed we were nearing the top of the hill. To the left was a gated drive with a lone mailbox marked by a number and no name. It matched the address that Wolf had left on my answering machine.

"This is it," I told Jim.

Pink Carnation

"Pull over and let me out," he said, his voice flat and emotionless. "You go in alone and I'll go in on foot. I don't want Wolf to know you brought me with you."

"Are you armed?" I asked.

A smile flickered across his face. He patted his left side. I pulled over across from the driveway and he got out of the car. "You go first," he said, nodding toward the gate.

I turned across the road and pulled up to the gate. A camera swung around to scan my car. There was a flash of movement behind me. Jim was following me in, crouching close enough behind the tiny car to avoid being seen by the camera.

The gate slid open. It was two interlocking gates that slid apart in either direction. Ahead of me the paved driveway was well lit with waist high lamposts every twenty yards or so. I pulled through the gate and caught a glimpse of Jim leaving the protective cover of my car and heading off into the bushes. I moved ahead with caution.

The first things I saw were the cities below, visible as flickering points of light through the thinning trees. Turning a corner in the driveway, I was overwhelmed by the sudden appearance of the panorama of lights in the distance below. The house sat back from the driveway, at the end of a flat expanse where it clung precariously close to the edge of the hillside. A stark, white, modern affair, the size of a small office building, it looked like a sharply-angled castle, with an outside walkway running it's length at the level of a second floor and two, tall, square towers sticking up above the flat roof, like sentries standing guard. The driveway continued past the house to another set of buildings that I took to be garages or work sheds, but a curving drive broke off from the main road and led between rows of small manicured bushes to a parking area in front of the house. I wound down the drive and pulled into the parking area, next to a long, white Mercedes.

The trees ended at the border of the lot on which the massive house was perched and I wasn't sure how Jim was going to make it from the forest to the house without being seen. Before I had much time to worry about that, the door opened and a medium height, cadaverously thin man with dark, slicked back hair and a long, narrow nose looked me over with bright, eager eyes. He was dressed in a black suit and tie and I had the distinct impression that I'd arrived at a mortuary for a fitting. He held out a long thin hand and pointed at me with a bony index finger, then motioned toward the house. When I reached the door, he held up his skinny hand and I halted. He raised his long dark lashes to look up at me.

"Please raise your arms, Professor Routledge," he said.

His voice was surprisingly soft and soothing. Perhaps he *had* been a funeral director.

He didn't measure me, but instead patted me down and asked me to follow him inside. The house's entry led to a sunken living room that had an unobstructed view of the spectacular scene below. The picture window in the front of the house was ablaze with lights from the cities of south LA and north Orange counties. The view was like looking at a dark carpet, dotted with white Christmas lights that stretched as far as the eye could see. My guide pointed down a white, tiled hallway that ran around the edge of the sunken room and disappeared off to the right through an open doorway. I marched ahead, with my escort behind me. His tread was so soft that I glanced backward to be sure he hadn't slipped away. If l decided to do anything rash, I'd have to watch my back with this character gliding around the house.

Through the doorway was another room with a similarly smashing view, though this room wasn't sunken. It was a smaller sitting room, with modern metal and leather furniture, all black and chrome, distributed about in artistic fashion. As I entered the room, a high-backed leather chair swiveled around and the master of the house rose to greet me.

"So good of you to come, Professor Routledge," Wolf said, striding toward me and extending his hand. He was dressed in an open-necked shirt and a pair of slacks with loafers. A tuft of white hair showed at his neckline. The skin around his neck looked wrinkled and old. He eyed me like a boxer watching his opponent, ready to parry the first sign of a punch.

I kept my hand at my side. "Where's my wife?"

"I'm okay," I heard Kim say, as she rose from the chair next to Wolf's. I brushed past the old man and put my arms around her.

For the first time since I'd received Wolf's message, I felt my muscles relax. I held Kim tight and didn't want to let her go.

"Are you all right?" I asked.

She nodded, and then dropped her eyes. "I'm sorry Anh. You told me to wait, but I wanted to help you."

I turned in anger toward Wolf, who was still standing in the middle of the room, a half-smile on his face.

"What the hell do you think you're doing, bringing my wife up here?" I took a step toward him.

Bela Lugosi in the black mortician's outfit moved between us with the speed of a cat. He held out one hand and the other slipped inside his jacket. It was all I could do to stop myself from reaching out and grabbing him by his skinny neck and launching him through the plate glass picture window. I didn't give much of a damn what he had under his coat.

"Easy, Professor," Wolf growled in his low voice. "Ronald is very protective of me. He is a polite man, but he is ruthless when he thinks I'm in danger."

"Well, you're in danger all right," I said, calming myself and looking past "Ronald" into Wolfs eyes. "I knew you were a murderer, a thief, and a dope dealer. Now you've added kidnapping. We'll see how well Ronald can protect your ass from being fried by the state."

Anger flashed in the old man's dark eyes, but then he just shook his head. "Such talk from an academic. You and your wife are my guests, Professor. I hardly kidnapped your lovely wife. She seemed to be quite interested in my business records. One of my employees found her going through my real estate files. That's a criminal intrusion, of course; but since you are employed by the university on whose Board I sit, I thought that I would invite her to my house and have you join her so you might explain what she was doing."

I looked over at Kim. She gazed calmly at me. I turned back to Wolf. "She made a simple mistake and was looking through the wrong files." I reached over and took Kim's hand. "Now that we've cleared that up, I think we'll leave." I tugged on Kim's hand and began to head for the door.

Ronald moved in front of it, one hand still inside his coat. He was starting to get on my nerves.

"Tell your anorexic Jeeves to get out of my way before I step on him."

"No need to be in such a hurry, Professor," Wolf said. "I think that you and I should talk." He moved toward a set of white, shiny, lacquered cabinets built into the wall. He pressed a button that was located where the cabinet's handle should have been and the doors slid back, revealing a wet bar, complete with a half-size refrigerator and as many varieties of liquor as a well-stocked cocktail lounge.

"Perhaps you'd like a drink," he said without turning toward us. "Mrs. Routledge?"

I looked over at Ronald, who was no longer standing in the middle of the doorway, but had moved over a few feet. He stood relaxed, his long thin hands dangling loose at his sides, a blank expression on his face, as if killing us if we tried to leave was the last thing on his mind. Kim declined a drink and I did the same. Wolf began pouring himself a glass of scotch over ice.

"You found out a great deal about me, Professor. I'd like to know who your sources were." He raised his glass toward Kim and me, the Parkinsonian tremor in his hand rocking the ice back and forth in his glass. "To your wife's health."

"I bet you stole that scotch," I said.

"Now, now, Professor, you're getting petty," Wolf said, sipping on his drink and moving over to gaze out the window at the lights below. "The Chavez girl got you involved, but she knew nothing—unless her brother told her. Anyway, she'll be dealt with more successfully this time. But someone else must have given you information about Erskine and Starkley and those so-called Pink Carnation deaths." He turned back around and narrowed his eyes. "Am I right?"

If I said anything, Janet could be put in danger—or Arturo Cordoza. "What makes you think I needed help? It wasn't difficult tracking you down. You're a cheap hood, Mr. Wolf, not a mental giant. You've left a trail a mile wide. When I tell the authorities, they'll see it as clearly as I did."

Wolf smiled, one side of his mouth curling upward. "For a professor, you're not very smart. If there's an official in this county who doesn't know who and what I am, and can't be paid to ignore it, then I haven't met that official."

He was right. It had been too easy for me to find out what I'd found out for someone in law enforcement to not have figured out that Wolf was the kingpin behind organized crime in the county.

"There are some honest cops in this county and they'll be very happy to know about the evidence I have against you," I said.

"You never cease to amaze me with your naiveté," Wolf smiled back. "Your belief in honest cops is anachronistic, to say the least."

This would have been a good time for Jim Stapleton to burst into the room, flashing his badge, but nobody was at the doorway but Ronald. I glanced over at Kim and tried to look confident.

"You leave me no choice, Professor," Wolf said, draining his glass. He looked at his henchman at the door. "Ronald take Mrs. Routledge down in the basement and shoot her. Perhaps that will loosen the professor's tongue about his sources of information."

Without emotion, Ronald started to move toward us from the doorway. I stepped in front of Kim. With speed that I hadn't imagined, Ronald's right hand was inside his coat and then out again, an ugly looking gun in his bony fist.

I stood my ground between Ronald and Kim. If he shot me that would end Wolf's chance of pumping information out of me. If he didn't use his gun, Ronald was too small and skinny to be a match for me. The little creep glanced with uncertainty toward his boss.

Wolf shook his head, and then waved Ronald off. The old man's lips curled in a cruel smiled.

"Charlie, Vance!" he called. My heart sunk. I should have realized Wolf would have had other flunkies in the house besides Ronald.

Sure enough, two beefy thugs appeared in the doorway. I recognized them as the two men who attacked me on my boat. Neither of them looked very bright, but I doubted that Wolf had called them in to debate me. They both had on open sport shirts, crisply pressed slacks, and short, neatly combed hair. Despite their spiffy appearance, they still looked like thugs. Maybe it was because each of them wore a holstered gun under his right arm. They lumbered into the room and gave their boss an inquiring look.

"Move our guest out of the way so Ronald can take the man's wife downstairs," Wolf said.

Despite being outnumbered, I wasn't going to let Ronald take Kim without a fight. I'd beaten these two before and I could do it again. I took a swing at the first of the two goons who approached me. My punch caught him squarely on the chin. He went down like a sack of potatoes. Before I could get set to throw a second punch at his partner, the big baboon connected with a short chop to the side of my head that knocked me back on my heels. I was rocked, but I managed to retain my balance enough to swing a leg up at the oncoming Neanderthal and catch him solidly in the groin, staggering him backward. By this time his partner was back on his feet.

I set myself for another straight-arm jab at his face, when I caught a flash of something metal out of the corner of my eye. Ronald cold-cocked me with his gun, the butt of it coming down flush against the side of my head. I fell forward, almost to my knees, then managed to catch myself and turn to face Ronald. But by then the two gorillas were at my side, pinning my arms and jerking me from in front of Kim. I struggled, but they were each at least as strong as I was and I couldn't move.

Pink Carnation

Ronald glided past me and snaked a skinny hand out around Kim's arm. She followed him toward the door without a struggle. I fought against a feeling of despair. I still had the hope that Kim would be able to overpower Ronald when they were alone. Kim was in good shape and I knew she had courage of steel. After all, she'd escaped the Viet Cong. Ronald looked as if he was good with a gun, but that was probably the extent of it.

As Ronald and Kim passed me on their way out of the room, I made one last attempt to lunge at Ronald, but the two henchmen held me with vise-like grips.

Wolf smiled over at me. "I'm impressed, Professor, but you continually prove that you don't know who you're dealing with."

A shot rang out, sounding as if it came from the next room. My heart stopped. I looked at Wolf. He looked panicked.

"Vance, Charlie!" he shouted.

They both let go of my arms and reached for their guns. Charlie was too late. Jim Stapleton appeared in the doorway, crouched waist high, his gun held in his two outstretched hands. He fired and Charlie staggered backwards and bounced off the wall behind me. Jim swung his gun around, but Vance had more time than Charlie to get his gun out. His shot, deafening next to my ear, hit Jim in the shoulder and spun him sprawling back out into the hallway, his gun clattering off the wall. Vance aimed again as Jim winced in pain and looked up at him in defiance.

"Stop!" Wolf shouted. "Get his gun," he told Vance. The thug crossed the room and stepped into the hallway. Jim sat on the floor, one leg bent underneath him. He was holding his shoulder and swaying. Vance pushed him over with his foot and Jim gasped in pain as his shoulder hit the floor. Vance reached down and picked up the gun.

"Is Ronald out there?" Wolf asked.

"He's here, but he's not moving," Vance answered in a dull voice.

"What about the Asian lady?"

I could see Vance looking down the hallway. "She's gone," he said.

My shoulders sagged. I breathed a sigh of relief.

I looked down at Charlie. He wasn't moving. Stapleton had killed two of them and managed to set Kim free. I looked over at Jim. His face was contorted in pain. He'd struggled back to a sitting position. While Vance handed the gun to Jess Wolf, I crossed the room and knelt down beside Jim.

"Thanks, bro," I said. "How bad is it?"

"I'll manage," he said. "I told Kim to get as far away as possible."

I nodded and hoisted him up. Wolf and Vance gave me threatening looks, but I didn't care. I half-dragged and half-supported Jim into the room, then guided him to one of the high-backed chairs.

Wolf hissed at Vance to go find Kim, then turned to Jim. "When push comes to shove, you turn back into a cop, Lieutenant?"

Jim just stared at him. Then he looked over at me and dropped his gaze. "That creepy asshole Ronald was going to kill the woman. These people are my friends," Jim muttered.

"You're a dead man, Stapleton." Wolf said, looking down at Jim with disgust.

"Fuck you!" Jim answered.

Hold on a minute," I said, my apprehension rising. "You two know each other?"

Jim didn't meet my eyes.

Wolf began laughing. "Routledge, I should keep you around just for laughs." He looked down at Jim Stapleton, who was holding his shoulder and looking at the floor. "The detective here has been on my payroll for over ten years. Who do you think helped Fontana knock off the Cordoza kid? Who fixed things with the coroner after Thornberg's so-called heart attack?" Wolf began nodding his head. "Now I get it, Stapleton. I couldn't figure out why you killed Fontana, rather than the Professor when you found them together. That story that Fontana might blow your cover never made any sense. I see that you had divided loyalties. How very cozy."

"You work for Wolf?" I asked, incredulous.

Wolf watched me with an amused look on his face.

Jim still didn't look at me. "Half the department does," he said. "It was that way when I got there. I just went along with procedure. We don't work for him, we just close our eyes to some of his operations."

"And cast the blame on the Mexican gangs," Wolf added. "Orange County the easiest place in the world to do what I do. Not only does most of the county not care what goes on in poor cities like Santa Ana, but they've already made up their minds that the bad guys are Mexican-Americans and their gangs. Why should the Sheriff's department rock the boat? No one would believe them if they said there was someone like me running things. They get lots of money to fight gangs, the crime never hits the privileged classes down south, a few cops in critical positions get big bonuses from me and everyone's happy."

"How far up does this go?" I asked, addressing Jim rather than Wolf.

"The Sheriff has no idea," Jim said, weakly. "He's too new and we only tell him what we want him to hear."

"I suppose you've had to pay a few supervisors over the years," I said to Wolf, "and mayors and councilmen; how about the DA?"

Wolf had stopped laughing. He stared at me coldly. He looked as if he was tired of giving me a lesson in civics.

"I pay who I have to. It only takes one or two people in the right positions to get me what I want." He took two steps toward Jim and thrust the gun up under his nose. "Now let's get down to business. Your friend the professor has found out way too much about me, and I want to know how he did it. I can't shoot his wife until Vance finds her, but I can do the next best thing and that's to shoot you if he doesn't tell me."

"Let him shoot," Jim said, turning his head away from Wolfs gun and finally looking me in the eye. "Don't tell the bastard a goddamn thing, bro." He looked back at Wolf, who was still pointing the gun down at him. "Your days are numbered you son-of-a-bitch. Go ahead and shoot me."

"Very well, " Wolf said. He pulled the gun back then pointed it down at Jim's leg. He fired and the knee of Jim's pant leg was torn away, revealing a bloody mass of cartilage and flesh where his knee had been.

Jim screamed and grabbed his knee. He doubled over in pain. "Bastard!" he yelled.

Wolf looked over at me. "He has another knee. Are you ready to tell me who your sources were?"

From a distance, there was the sound of a shot. I felt my skin go cold. I'd almost convinced myself that Kim had gotten away. Vance must have caught up with her. In a minute there were two more shots. "I guess Vance found your wife," Wolf said. "I still have time to blow out the detective's other knee before Vance comes back. Shall I go for the other leg or do you want to talk to me?"

"I wouldn't do anything if I were you, Mr. Wolf." The voice from the hallway was heavily accented and vaguely familiar. Wolf looked up, startled. So did I. Four men with guns pointed at Jess Wolf stood in the doorway. One of them was John Cordoza.

"Who the hell are you?" Wolf asked. He still was holding his gun but it wasn't pointed at anything but the wall.

"I'm Julio Cordoza's father and these are some of my friends." Cordoza edged into the room and three more hard looking Mexican-Americans followed: one of them was Jorge Cordoza, still dressed like a car salesman. All of the Mexicans' guns were trained on Wolf.

"And I'm Ramon Chavez' sister," Lucia said, appearing in the doorway. In the next moment, Kim appeared at her side. I breathed a sigh of relief and I could hear Jim do the same next to me, in spite of his pain.

"What do you want?" Wolf asked, no fear, only anger in his eyes." What are you doing in my house?"

"We're killing people," John Cordoza answered. "We killed one of your men outside and we killed the one who was chasing Mrs. Routledge. Now we are going to kill you."

Pink Carnation

For the first time, Wolf looked panicked. He was still holding his gun but he was careful not to point it at anyone. "Wait a minute," he said. "I can pay you. I can make all of you rich."

"You killed my brother," Lucia said." Her eyes were filled with hatred. "And my son," Cordoza said.

"I didn't do it." Wolf protested." The police did it. Detective Fontana and Detective Stapleton here. They killed your relatives, not me."

"You ordered it," Lucia said.

"You can't prove that," Wolf said, sticking his chin out belligerently." If you think I did that, then turn me over to the police and let a court decide." He looked at their unwavering eyes. "You can't take the law into your own hands!" he whined. "You have no authority!"

John Cordoza stared at him with disgust then smiled sardonically. "Authority? We don't need no steenking authority," he said and fired three rapid shots into Wolf's body. The force of the blasts knocked Wolf backward against the huge plate glass window. The window gave and with a look of utter disbelief still on his face, Jess Wolf hurtled backward through the glass. I watched in shock as Wolf's body disappeared over the edge of the window. I walked over and peered through the broken shards that clung to the window frame. In the dim shadows forty feet below, I could just make out Jess Wolf's body splayed out on a large flat rock. l turned around and looked at Cordoza. He was shaking his head.

"I wish he had asked to see our badges," he said, a small smile creeping onto his face. He turned and pointed his gun at Jim Stapleton.

"Don't," I said.

"He killed my son."

"He saved my life—and my wife's."

Cordoza looked at me and then down at Jim. The detective was still clutching his shattered kneecap. A large dark bloodstain covered his right shoulder. He looked up at Cordoza calmly.

"Did you kill Julio?" Cordoza asked him.

"I didn't kill him, but I didn't stop the man who did it." Cordoza aimed his gun at Jim's face. Stapleton didn't flinch.

"He's your only official witness that all of tonight's killing was self defense," I said. "Wolf still has lots of friends in important places, including in the Sheriff's Department. He can tell them about Wolf...and he can clear you of his death."

Cordoza kept his gun pointed at Jim's face but turned his head toward me. "He will lie. He will say we killed Wolf for no reason."

"No he won't. There's no turning back for him now. He's got to come clean about all of this and arrest the others who are involved." I looked down at Jim. "I'm right aren't I?"

"It's time to clean house," he said. "I can get immunity if I expose the whole thing—within the department and without."

"And we won't be prosecuted for tonight?" Cordoza asked, lowering his gun.

"When I get done, you'll be heroes," Jim said, sizing up Cordoza's reaction. Stapleton was bloody and in pain, but I could see he was still the old Jim, wheeling and dealing.

"Maybe we let you live," Cordoza said. He looked over at Lucia Chavez. "What do you think, Lucia?"

The fire of hatred still burned in the young Latina's eyes. She looked at Stapleton. Then she turned to me.

I nodded.

"Okay, we let him live," she said.

I breathed a sigh of relief and for the first time, looked over at Kim. She winked at me. I smiled back.

"You'd better make a phone call, Detective," I said to Jim. "You need some medical attention and you're going to have a lot of explaining to do." Kim moved over to help Jim. She had had experience in Vietnam tending wounds and she would be able to make him more comfortable until the paramedics arrived. As she passed me, she stopped and whispered in my ear.

"In Vietnam, Anh, we say that evil cannot stand up against a just heart."

Pink Carnation

"Evil lost tonight, Em." I looked down at Jim Stapleton. "And maybe we were able to rescue a just heart."

She smiled at me and moved over to tend Jim's wounds.

Maybe, I thought. We'd have to wait and see.

Made in the USA
Middletown, DE
23 September 2025